Wash Her Guilt Away

A Quill Gordon Mystery

Michael Wallace

ISBN: 978-0-9903871-0-7

Also by Michael Wallace

Fiction
The McHenry Inheritance (Quill Gordon mystery)

Non-Fiction
The Borina Family of Watsonville (California history)

In the spirit of John Dickson Carr

For Nick, in fond remembrance
of our hours fishing

NOTICE TO THE READER: This book contains several descriptive and detailed passages about fly fishing. They are there for the benefit of those who fish, those who enjoy the outdoors, and those who might want to learn more about this pastime. These passages are not germane to the solution of the mystery, and readers who fall into none of the categories above may feel free to skip past them, if so inclined, without missing out on a vital clue.

Song

When lovely woman stoops to folly,
    And finds too late that men betray,
What charm can sooth her melancholy,
    What art can wash her guilt away?

The only art her guilt to cover,
    To hide her shame from every eye,
To give repentance to her lover,
    And wring his bosom — is to die.

Oliver Goldsmith, 1730-1774

Visitor on a Snowy Night

"Oh. It's you."

"Who did you think it was?"

"I didn't think it was anybody. After what happened tonight, I wasn't exactly expecting company."

A long silence ensued.

"Can I come in?"

"You're already in," she said, "but close the door, will you. It's freezing." She moved to the nightstand by the bed, picked up a pack of cigarettes, and lit one as she looked out the window at the falling snow.

"Jesus," she said as she exhaled. "I left Syracuse to get away from this, and now I get it in California in fricking May. Where's the justice?"

"This is a non-smoking room, you know."

"So what are you going to do about it — tell the owner? Anyway, we can afford to pay the penalty."

There was no response to this, so she looked out the window again and shook her head.

"Snow," she said. "I can't believe it."

"I don't think it's snowing just to annoy you."

"God, you sound just like my father." A pause. "And there's a reason he and I haven't been speaking for five years."

Another awkward silence. The visitor, wearing a heavy parka, slipped a gloved hand underneath it and felt to make sure the bungee cord was there.

"Aren't you going to ask why I came here?"

"You probably want something from me." Another deep drag on the cigarette. "Everybody seems to want something from me."

"Not much, really. Just a little restraint."

"As in?"

"Tomorrow's the last day here, right?"

"I'm counting the hours."

"Then don't stir up any more dirt than you already have."

"Who, *moi?*" she said. "Whatever are you talking about?"

"You know damn well what I'm talking about. You said way too much tonight."

1

"What if some of it was true?"

"That doesn't matter. It's bound to make people suspicious."

"So now we're cutting to the chase. You just want me to help save your sorry ass."

"I just want you to act decently for the first time in a week. Go quietly tomorrow and don't make things any worse than they already are. That's all I'm asking, and it's not much."

She took her final puff from the cigarette and looked for an ashtray, but of course there wasn't one, so she carried it to the toilet, threw it in and flushed, then came back to the main room.

"Save your ass, save everybody else's ass. Just go quietly like a good little girl. Actually, that gives me an idea. Maybe I should walk into the dining room tomorrow morning when everybody's having breakfast and say, 'Excuse me, ladies and gentlemen. I have an announcement to make.' They'll all be expecting me to apologize, only instead I'll tell everything I know. Maybe even make up a story or two to cause a little more trouble. Wouldn't that be a hoot?"

She laughed almost hysterically, and the laugh decided it for the visitor. The bungee cord was out from under the parka and around her neck before she had finished, turning the last laugh into a choking, panicked snort. Taken by surprise, she never had a chance and flailed ineffectually for a minute or two before she stopped breathing and went limp. Two minutes later, the visitor let the cord and the body drop to the floor.

It was a mistake. The visitor realized that and immediately regretted it, but now the only thing that mattered was not getting caught. With any luck the body wouldn't be discovered until morning, but there would be a full-scale investigation. Something had to be done to misdirect the sheriff's detectives when they eventually came. The visitor walked around the room slowly, thinking, for several minutes. The idea came out of nowhere.

"Yes," the visitor thought. "With any kind of a break, it could work. And what have I got to lose at this point?"

Outside, the snow was still falling.

Sunday May 7, 1995

1

A THICK BLANKET of lead-gray clouds covered Paradise Valley as Quill Gordon and Peter Delaney drove down from the pass. The tall grass of spring, blown about by a biting wind from the northeast, undulated at the side of the road, and the wind also bent the branches and tops of the occasional trees. Gordon, at the wheel of his Cherokee, looked methodically around as he drove, checking to see if anything had changed since his last visit three years ago. Peter, seeing it for the first time, focused on the pervasive gloom, which felt as though it might be permanent. Finally he broke the silence.

" 'When the hounds of spring are on winter's traces ...' " he said. "Actually, it looks as if the hounds of spring are still in the doghouse. Where it's warm. Was that Shelley or Keats — the hounds of spring?"

"Swinburne," Gordon said absently.

"Vile weather in any event. It feels like it's going to snow."

Gordon shook his head. "We're just over thirty-five hundred feet. It doesn't snow much here in the winter, never mind May."

"If you say so. Are we getting close to lunch?"

"Only a couple more miles to town."

"So what's the plan when we get there? I'm sure you have one."

"Stop for gas at the Chevron station, which should get us through the rest of the week, then lunch at Rose Malone's. It's where everybody goes."

"Any particular reason it has to be the Chevron station?"

"A little unfinished business, actually," Gordon said. "Last time I was here, a kid just out of high school was pumping gas and fixing flats. He was thinking of taking law enforcement classes at the community college."

"So you want to see if he's still at the gas station?"

"Actually, I'm hoping he's not. He asked me what I thought, and I said he should take the classes."

A moment later they reached the sign that said they were entering Eden Mills, population 900. The road dipped slightly into a depression through which Eden River flowed. A hundred yards wide, with only a hint of current, the river normally had a glassy, surface, bright with the reflection of the sky. Today the inky-dark surface was rippled and choppy in the brisk wind. They drove over the river on a bridge that stood just a few feet above it, then up a brief ascent to the town proper.

At the top of the rise Gordon began to turn into the Chevron station, but instead pulled off to the side of the road. The skeleton of the station was still there — the pumps, the service bay, and the small building that used to house the cash register and restrooms — but weeds grew in its pavement, out-of-order signs hung on the pumps, and three of the windows were broken.

They sat in the car, staring at the ruin.

"I hope your kid went off to school," Peter finally said. He shook his head. "You know a town's got a tough economy when it can't support a Chevron station."

"Let's eat instead," Gordon said. "Rose's is just a half-mile up the road."

At the far edge of town, on the right side of the state highway, Rose Malone's sat at one side of a large parking area, while Jake's mini-mart and gas station (two pumps) was on the opposite side, its interior lights suggesting a warm haven from the gloom and cold outside.

The restaurant was boarded up.

"Now *this* I can't believe," Gordon said. "Last time I had breakfast here, the place was packed."

"Looks like we're back to getting gas," Peter said. "Quick — before Jake's goes out of business."

Gordon drove up to the pump and jumped out. Wearing the jeans and flannel shirt he had put on that morning before leaving the hazy sunshine of San Francisco, he was instantly chilled by the wind and damp. He put the nozzle in the gas tank, started the flow, and walked purposefully toward the entrance to the mini-mart. Throwing on a parka, Peter followed him.

There were no customers in the store, only a clerk at the register, a man in his forties with a sallow complexion, wearing jeans and a hoodie, watching an NBA playoff game on a black and white TV perched on the wall behind him. Gordon brought a bottle of water and a Snickers bar to the counter and set them down. The clerk rang up the sale manually — no scanner.

"Two dollars and 19 cents, please."

Gordon handed him a five and, trying to sound nonchalant, said, "You heard from Rose lately?"

The clerk set the bill next to the register and looked at Gordon more carefully. Then at Peter.

"Creditors?" he asked.

"No," said Gordon. "No. Just — I used to eat there when I came up to go fishing and I was wondering what happened to her. To the café."

The clerk nodded and took Gordon's change from the register, handing it to him across the counter.

"You're not the only one asking," he said. "Been the talk of the town so to speak. All anybody knows is she closed up early Wednesday night before Thanksgiving and didn't open for breakfast on Friday morning. Some of the regulars waited outside for an hour, and it was cold that morning." He gestured outside with a jerk of his head. "A lot colder than this."

"Not possible," muttered Peter under his breath.

"Her house was locked up, and the furniture was all there, but the mortgage was five months delinquent. I've had people come in from Cascade Electric, the State Board of Equalization, several restaurant supply companies and the IRS, all looking for a piece of her. So when a stranger comes in and asks, I naturally expect the worst."

"Thanks," said Gordon, scooping up the candy bar and water. As he and Peter reached the door, the clerk said:

"Good luck with your fishing. I hear they were biting last week."

Back at the car, Gordon removed the nozzle, replaced it on the pump and jumped inside. He was shivering after less than a minute outdoors.

"What now, boss?" asked Peter. "I didn't see much along the road."

"There's actually a Main Street that runs off the highway back at the Chevron station. Where it used to be. Let's check it out."

Once on Main Street, theirs was the only moving car on the road, so Gordon drove slowly. Nearly every building could have stood a coat of paint; wind-blown trash scudded across the road in front of them; and most of the businesses were closed. An exception was the Eden Mills Hotel and Grill two blocks in, which had a neon "Open" sign in the window. Gordon stopped in front of it, still in the middle of the road.

"What do you think?" asked Peter.

"I tried it a few years ago, and it was kind of dodgy."

"How about the Mexican place a block back?"

"It's new. I don't know anything about it."

"There were a few pickup trucks in front. My father always said that was a good sign."

"Sure. Why not?"

Gordon executed a U-turn in the deserted street, and instead of eating at Rose Malone's as planned, they had lunch at Casa Rosita.

2

INSIDE THE RESTAURANT, it was bright, warm and cheerful. Ten formica tables, their perimeters sealed with serrated metal bands, were well spaced within two small rooms. They were set with white paper placemats, topped with generic, well-worn flatware. A pretty girl of about 14, presumably the owners' daughter, seated Gordon and Peter at an empty table and returned promptly with a basket of chips and a bowl of salsa. Gordon was pleased to note that the chips were warm.

As they studied the menu (a laminated, double-sided sheet of 8.5x11-inch paper), Gordon cast a glance at his companion. Nothing was going as planned on this trip, and that included Peter being part of it. Peter Delaney was a surgeon in San Francisco, in his early forties and several years older than Gordon. A former basketball player at Cal, Gordon, at six feet, four inches, was trim and fit, with a clean-cut, angular face that women tended to regard as more sympathetic than handsome. Peter, just under six feet tall, had brown hair that was beginning to thin in front, a full beard, showing some salt amid its pepper, a slightly florid face with a beaked nose, the beginning of a good paunch and a bit of a slouch.

Just over a year ago, Gordon had been diagnosed with a hernia and was referred to Peter for a routine surgery. ("Best hands in the city," Gordon's doctor had said.) Gordon had by that point quit his job as a stockbroker in San Francisco, having made enough money from his own investments to live comfortably. That included fishing whenever he liked, and as opening day was only a few weeks away, Gordon asked Dr. Delaney how long it would be before he could fish. It turned out that Peter had taken up fly fishing two years earlier and become passionate about it. By the time of Gordon's last follow-up visit, they had decided to go on a long fishing weekend in July. They hit it off well and took another weekend trip in early October.

When the Eden River trip was booked in February, Sam Akers, Gordon's longtime friend, was going to accompany him. But in the middle of April, Sam's mother-in-law fell down the front steps of her house and broke her hip. Under the circumstances, Sam didn't feel he should take a week off. Gordon waited three days before calling Peter, figuring a busy physician wasn't likely to be able to get free on such short notice. To his surprise, the invitation was warmly received.

"Everybody is telling me I've been even more of a miserable bastard than usual, and that I should take some time off," Peter said. "That includes my partners, who'll probably be willing to cover for me." And so it was arranged.

The girl returned to take their order. Peter had the lunch combination with cheese enchilada, beef tamale, rice, beans and a beer. Gordon had the combination with chicken taco, chile relleno and a 7-Up. Peter leaned back in his chair after they ordered and stretched his arms.

"So," he said. "You were telling me earlier that there's a story behind this place we're staying. Now would be a good time to hear it."

"Quite a story," Gordon said, shoveling a chip and salsa into his mouth. The waitress returned with a perspiring bottle of beer for Peter and Gordon's soft drink in a dappled plastic glass with a straw. Gordon took a sip and began.

"You've never heard of Harry's, I take it? Not too surprising considering what it's been like lately, but for almost 30 years after the War, Harry's Riverside Lodge was a legend in Northeast California."

"Was there actually someone named Harry?"

"Oh, yeah. Harry Ezekian. Born to be in the hospitality business."

"Armenian?" Gordon nodded.

"Originally from Fresno, then he worked at some restaurants in Stockton during the thirties and ended up in Sacramento just before the war, managing a joint where a lot of the politicians hung out. He was in his thirties and had a heart murmur of some sort, so they didn't draft him. In the next four years he got to know everybody who was anybody in Sacramento, plus quite a few heavy hitters from the Bay Area who had business in the capital. By the time the war was over, a lot of people who mattered knew Harry; he was about to get married; and he decided he was ready for his own place.

"He was looking for something in Sacramento when the Assemblyman from these parts gave him a tip. Seems one of the logging companies was selling some of its assets in Northern California, and they had an executive lodge and retreat on Eden River that nobody else wanted. Harry realized that with things getting back to normal, there'd be a market for a getaway destination. It was just a few hours from Sacramento, and the roads were getting better all the time, so he had the Assemblyman put in a word for him and bought the place for a song. It was a cash cow from the day it opened.

"At peak fishing season, you just about had to be the governor to get a room, and it was busy all year long. Even in the winter, a lot of the powerful men realized it was a discreet place for a romantic getaway if you didn't want to be widely seen with the lady. Story goes that the only employee Harry ever fired was a young waiter who came up to the table of State Senator Ralph Powell and addressed the much younger woman with him as Mrs. Powell. It was a sore spot with the senator because she wanted to be, and he had no intention of getting a divorce."

"Sounds like high times," Peter said.

"It was. And Harry was at the center of it all. Every night, he worked the dining room with a glass of Ancient Age in his hand. Same glass all night long, and he barely sipped from it. He charmed the women, told jokes and reminisced with the men. Asked everybody if their steak was cooked right, which of course it was. There was a big outdoor patio, and in the summer, he'd work that, too. I heard that north of Sacramento, it was one of the top ten restaurants in terms of alcohol tax paid. And people drank a lot more back then.

"If there was a wedding, anniversary or birthday party, Harry would stand a round and offer the first toast, and he always hit the right note with it. Like I said, a born host. And he came up with some great stunts. Some time in the early fifties, he got the idea of bringing in the local priest for a blessing of the fish the Friday night before the season opened. All the papers in Northern California did stories on it, and the crowds got so big — a lot of locals, too, by the way — it was almost impossible to make your way to the bar. Yeah, it was crazy."

Gordon paused and took a long drag on his soft drink. The waitress brought their lunches, along with a basket of warm corn tortillas. Famished from the long drive, they ate silently and appreciatively for several minutes.

"But all good things must end some day," Peter said, "and I take it that happened to Harry's."

Gordon nodded and picked up the story again. "By the late sixties, Harry's circle of contacts had shrunk, and he wasn't replacing them fast enough. Then in the early seventies, the new environmental laws hit the logging industry really hard and this area started to decline. That really hurt in the winter, when they have to rely more on locals to keep the restaurant reasonably busy. My dad brought me here one summer in the early seventies. It still seemed pretty lively, but even to my 12-year-old eyes, it was looking kind of retro. Still, Harry kept it going, and he'd made so much money by then he was probably okay if it just broke even. The bar and restaurant were his living room, and as long as he had them to go to every night, he was fine.

"Then in June of 1978, there was a wedding reception here. It was a beautiful day, and everyone was outside on the patio. Harry went out to offer a toast, like always, and they say he nailed it. They were still clapping when he took one sip of champagne and collapsed from a heart attack. Dead by the time he hit the floor. Would have been 69 in three weeks."

"Died with his boots on," Peter said. "That has a certain appeal."

"And then it came undone," Gordon said. "His wife, Sophie, couldn't bear to be at the place without Harry around, so she moved to Sacramento to be near their daughter. Harry's son, Bob, took the place over ..."

"And ran it into the ground," said Peter.

"Not entirely his fault. Like I said, the customers were getting older and the local economy was sinking fast. But Bob didn't have Harry's personality — who could have? And just before Harry died, Bob married a woman from the Bay Area and brought her up here. Ariel, if I remember right. She was a city girl at heart, or at least a suburban girl, and clearly something of a free spirit. She didn't take well to the isolation of Eden River, and with the economy sinking, it was getting more isolated. She began acting out in various ways, and after a while, the locals started talking. Some even said she was starting a coven of witches."

"You don't believe that, do you?" Peter said.

"Probably not, but the woods around here are vast and lonely. It's not so hard to understand how people could believe anything could happen in them. Anyway, the business and the marriage both deteriorated, and one day Ariel ran off with a lobbyist who'd been staying here. Just packed a suitcase and left without a word to anybody. But she left a note behind, and in it said something like, 'And for all the people who called me a witch, I put a curse on this place. There will be no love at Harry's' ..." Gordon paused and frowned. "I think there may have been a bit more to it, but it's probably not important.

"End of the story is this. Things got worse. Bob drank more. About a year after Ariel left, he took a small boat down the river at sunset, put a shotgun in his mouth and blew his head off. It was four years to the day after Harry dropped dead giving the toast."

Almost simultaneously, the waitress put the check on the table, and Peter grabbed it. "This is on me," he said. "The story was worth it." He took out a twenty-dollar bill and set it on top of the check. "Was Harry's just deserted after that?"

Gordon shook his head. "Thanks, Peter. No, it got sold. Several times, actually. There were about a half-dozen owners. A couple of them made it two summers, but nobody ever got through the second winter. I don't know if there was any love at Harry's, but there sure wasn't much business. I was there for a weekend five years ago and swore I'd never come back. Last time I came here I stayed in a motel."

"But you changed your mind."

"In December, a guy I know in city league basketball told me he'd been there in October and that Harry's was coming back under new owners and he liked it. It's always been Harry's, by the way; nobody even thought about changing the name. Then my friend Sam heard the same thing from someone he knows, and we decided to take a chance. If nothing else, there's some great fishing."

Peter handed the 20 and the check to the waitress, telling her to keep the change. She beamed at the generous tip and cleaned off their table. When she left, Gordon stood up.

"We'll see for ourselves soon enough," he said. "Let's go."

"I was just getting warm," said Peter, rising slowly. " 'There will be no love at Harry's,' " he quoted. "Too bad I never went there with my first wife. We would have fit right in."

CHECK-IN AT HARRY'S wasn't until four o'clock, so to pass time, Gordon drove Peter along the back roads of Paradise Valley. The heavy rains of the winter just ended had saturated the ground of the valley floor, carpeting it with lush green grass, the brightness of which stood out even in the dank of the persistent overcast. Every other field contained grazing cattle — plump, well fed and serene in the ignorance of their fate. The water table was so high that any slight indentation in the ground was likely to have become a miniature seasonal pond. The back roads along which they drove were just wide enough for two large pickup trucks to pass each other, with no shoulders or turnouts. Riotous spring vegetation grew right up to the edge of the pavement, as if straining to keep growing across to the other side of the road.

"Where's The Mountain?" Peter asked at one point.

"That way," Gordon said, gesturing slightly northwest. The Mountain, a volcano that geologists said might not be dormant, rose nearly 10,000 feet from the surrounding landscape and was one of Northern California's iconic features. "In good weather it'll look like it's right on top of us. You'll see when it clears up."

"*If* it clears up," Peter said.

"No worries. It's usually sunny and in the seventies this time of year. You'll see it for sure."

They drove over Eden River on one of the many narrow bridges that spanned it on its serpentine meanderings through the valley. Upstream of the bridge, a 14-foot boat holding two anglers was anchored in the middle of the river.

"Is that what we'll be fishing from?" Peter said.

"Pretty much. The Fisherman's Friend uses those aluminum boats with battery-powered motors. They help keep the speed down to five miles an hour, which is the limit on this river, and they don't leak fuel into the water."

"Is The Fisherman's Friend the place we stopped on the way up?"

Gordon nodded. "They have the best fly selection of any tackle shop, and offer the best guide service around.

We'll be going out tomorrow with Johnny Bauer, their number one man."

"Won't the water be muddy from the heavy runoff this time of year?"

"Not at all. Eden River doesn't get much runoff. It's a spring creek, really. All the snow that falls on The Mountain during the winter — a lot of it goes underground, then comes to the surface somewhere else. A little ways upstream from Harry's there's a wall of porous lava about 30 feet high. That underground water comes out there, and that's where the river starts. It's an even flow all year round, and the water temperature is always between 52 and 54 degrees."

"Perfect for trout."

"Exactly. If they're not biting, we'll have to come up with another excuse, because it won't be the heavy runoff."

At 3:30 they were on a road at the edge of the valley, where the meadows filled with cattle were giving way to increasingly forested land. The scenery was broken up by occasional residences, ranging from mobile homes to houses of recent vintage running 3,000 to 5,000 square feet. It was easy to tell which dwellings were occupied at the moment by the smoke coming from their chimneys.

A couple of miles into the forest, a well painted, professionally made sign announced, "Harry's ¼ mile ahead." Enhancing the lettering were images of The Mountain, snow-covered, and a jumping rainbow trout. Gordon turned right on to the next road, paved not too long ago, but hardly wide enough for two cars. They drove a few hundred yards through the woods, then emerged at a slight rise overlooking a large cleared area fronting on Eden River.

It was a beautiful, secluded spot. A full acre of manicured lawn, beginning at about 500 feet of riverfront, rose up a gentle slope to the main lodge. By all rights, the building should have been too big for its surroundings, but perhaps because it was made of logs from the forest in which it stood, it managed not to overwhelm. Gordon and Peter drove down the slope to a parking area near the river and a pier. Looking up at the lodge, they could see the main entrance, framed by a massive wooden arch decorated with a dozen sets of antlers. To the right of the main entrance was a large dining room, with the outer wall made entirely of glass, giving diners a fine view of the river. Along the right side of the lodge and part of the front by the dining room was an L-shaped deck for outdoor meals in better weather. To the left of the front door was the Fireside Lounge, with its own bar and tables where, in more electronically challenged times, people could play board games. Smoke rose from the chimney as Gordon parked the Cherokee, but the wind, which hadn't let up at all, blew the smoke sideways as soon as it escaped. On the second story of the lodge, the building was marked by a row of individual windows from some of the 20 guest rooms in the main building.

"I think we're going to like this place," said Peter, after taking it all in. "It's kind of like coming out of the mist into Brigadoon."

"We have one of the cabins," Gordon said, gesturing down to the river. A foot and a half above water level and extending 50 feet back from the river bank stood a shelf of flat land. Five cabins, built of blond pine wood that looked freshly varnished, had been built on the shelf, with a path in front of them leading to the lodge and to a crosshatched wooden fence at the far edge of the property, 30 feet beyond the last cabin. Downstream, close to the parking area, a pier jutted out 20 feet into the river, whipped into small whitecaps by the wind. A kayak and three aluminum boats, like the one they had seen earlier, were beached and anchored at the edge of the river next to the pier.

"Let's go down to the river first," Gordon said. "We're still a bit early."

Outside the car, the only sound was the whistling of the wind and the rustling of the trees. It seemed that, absent the wind, the silence would have been absolute. Gordon and Peter walked down the road to the pier, their feet crunching on the gravel, adding to the windsong. They walked onto the pier, which was rolling slightly from the wind-induced waves, and went out to the end, a ten-foot by ten-foot square of synthetic material. The cold wind stung their cheeks and made their eyes water.

From the trees behind them, three crows flew forth simultaneously, their cawing momentarily overlaying the wind noise. They flew toward the river, then turned left as they reached it and flew over the bank, heading upstream to the forest beyond.

"I hope that's not an omen," Peter said.

"What do you mean?"

"Three crows. Three black birds. There has to be some sort of superstition associated with that."

Abruptly, the wind stopped. The surface of the river quickly became smooth and placid. Looking at it, Gordon and Peter could see the leaves and pine needles on the surface moving ever-so-slowly from left to right with the gentle current. Gordon turned to his left, wiping the tears from his eyes, and looked back toward the bank and the cabins beyond. He grabbed Peter by the arm.

"Look!"

"What?"

"Just off the pier. Mayflies. They're hatching, even on a day like this."

A half dozen insects, pale tan in color with white wings flapping valiantly, were flying out over the water, moving slowly and erratically as if they couldn't believe they were no longer fighting the stiff wind. They began to fly farther over the water, dipping lower over it as they moved out over the middle of the river. The men watched raptly.

"Hardly fair, is it?" Peter said at last.

"Meaning?"

"The life cycle of a mayfly is one day, right? It hatches, mates and dies in 24 hours. These poor bastards only get one day in their whole lives, and it has to be a crummy one like this."

They watched the insects flutter over the water. In the silence, a door could be heard opening and closing. Peter kept watching the insects intently, but Gordon looked up toward the cabins in the distance. From the farthest cabin, at least a hundred yards away, a man emerged — at least, Gordon assumed it was a man. It was a figure dressed in dark clothing and a dark cap. The man, if such he was, walked from the front door of the cabin to the path leading to the lodge and turned left, facing them.

15

Then he seemed to notice the two men on the pier and stopped. He turned around and walked the other direction, going through the opening in the fence and disappearing into the forest beyond.

A loud splash, resonating like a thunderclap in the silence, came from the river. Gordon turned to see a widening ripple about 20 feet out from the pier, where a couple of the mayflies were hovering.

"Poor devil," Peter said. "Didn't even get his full day and ended up as dinner for a fish. 'Nature red in tooth and claw.' Was that Wordsworth?"

"Tennyson," Gordon said.

The wind started up again. They heard it moan through the treetops for several seconds before they felt its cold breath lash their exposed bodies at the end of the pier, going straight through their heavy pants and jackets as if they had been dressed for the tropics. Gordon looked back toward the cabins, but saw no sign of the dark-clad figure.

"I think we've had quite enough fresh air," said Peter. "Let's go to the lodge."

4

STEPPING THROUGH the front door of the lodge, they were greeted by a blast of warmth that contrasted sharply with the outdoor chill. A small reception counter stood before them, slightly off to the left; to its right was a hallway leading back into the rest of the building. To their immediate left was the Fireside Lounge, where a fire was burning down in the fireplace, which was framed with river rock and had an opening six feet wide and five feet high. Gordon stepped up to the reception desk, found a call bell with a button on top, and tapped it briskly with the palm of his hand. Its ping was unnaturally loud in the empty space.

The last of the bell tone was fading away when a young woman came through the hallway entry to the front desk. She was in her early twenties, five-eight, full figured without being plump, and walking with an affected swagger that seemed more practiced than natural. Her shoulder-length blond hair was cut, no doubt by a local stylist, in a way that seemed not quite right for her, yet didn't unduly diminish her overall projection of attractiveness. Three small earrings formed a metal cascade on her left ear. Her blue eyes were complemented by mascara daubed on a touch too heavily, but the apricot lipstick framing her smiling mouth was just right. Her tight-fitting knock-off designer jeans worked for her, and the unbuttoned, dark green short-sleeved top she wore was cut just low enough to show the beginning of some cleavage. Above her left breast was a small tattoo of a rose, which came down to the fabric line and seemed to be establishing roots underneath the blouse.

"Welcome to Harry's," she said. "My name's April. Are you gentlemen staying with us tonight?" Gordon nodded. "You must be Mr. Gordon."

"Are we the only ones?" asked Peter.

"No, but the other party coming in tonight is named Sakamoto. You'll meet them at dinner tonight. All the guests at Harry's get to know each other pretty fast. Now if we could just get a credit card, we can get you checked right in." She ran the card and got Gordon's signature. "Your cabin's ready, but Don — that's the owner — likes to show guests to their rooms personally. He said he'd be back at four and it's ten to." She slipped from behind the counter and moved toward the lounge. "You can wait in here if you'd like."

"That's fine," Gordon said.

"In fact, since you're staying for a week, the first drink's on us." She moved behind a well-stocked bar, set at a 45-degree angle to the walls. "What can I get you?"

"How about a scotch on the rocks?" said Peter.

"No problem. Johnnie Walker Black OK? It's on us, so you might as well."

"You make me feel right at home," said Peter, nodding and bowing slightly in her direction.

"How about you," she said, looking at Gordon.

"Could I just get a cup of coffee, if it's not too much trouble?"

"No problem. We just started a pot in the kitchen and it should be ready in a few minutes." She filled a small glass with shaved ice, poured the whisky to the top, and handed it across the bar to Peter. "Enjoy. I'll be right back with the coffee."

"OK if I put another log or two on the fire?" Gordon asked.

"Oh, yeah. I guess I should have done that. Be my guest."

They moved to the fireplace and took the two prime chairs, which faced each other, flanking a sofa in front of the flickering blaze. The chairs were covered with red leather, faded, scuffed and worn, but still comfortable after years of use. Gordon took a pair of three-foot-long logs out of a box near the fireplace and put them on what was left of the fire, then jabbed them with a poker to create air space. The fire quickly came back to life, and they took a closer look at their surroundings.

Above the fireplace was a large, unimaginative painting, eight feet long by six feet high, of The Mountain, rising above Paradise Valley, its snow-covered summit wreathed in light clouds, with deer and elk grazing in the green fields below and geese flying across the sky. A river ran beneath The Mountain, with a large trout, altogether out of scale, leaping from it. In the lower right hand corner it was signed, "Stoddard, 1954." Along the dark wood walls, in no particular pattern, were an eclectic mix of sporting prints and black-and-white photographs taken at Harry's decades earlier. A grand piano sat in the corner opposite the bar; two tables set up with chessboards were against the wall facing the river; and several chairs and two-seat couches filled out the room, with a few throw rugs covering the hardwood floor. It was a comfortable room, and the two men sat staring silently into the fire for a few moments.

"Peaceful," said Peter. "Just what I need after all the drama at work lately."

At that point the front door was thrown open, and a woman stomped, rather than walked, in.

"Where the hell *is* everybody?" she said in a loud, irritated voice. "I need a drink." She slammed the bell twice, and only then turned toward the lounge and saw Gordon and Peter. Immediately, she pulled herself together and walked toward them.

"I'm sorry," she said. "It's just that it's so cold, and I could use a little something to take the edge off. I'm Wendy."

As the men rose, she moved closer and into the light of the fire where they could see her more clearly. She was five-seven, with thick black hair, holding a slight wave, and dressed to make an impression in tan slacks, a demure light-pink blouse with the top button open, Manolo Blahnik heels, and a silver-chained pendant featuring a diamond-shaped cut of jade framed in silver, clearly by a jeweler who knew the business. Her features were well formed, with a Roman nose that suited her face, a sensuous mouth and deep brown eyes that conveyed a sense of hardness rather than welcome.

"Quill Gordon," he said, "and my friend Peter Delaney."

"Ooh, you're tall. Six-five, maybe, and athletic, too. I'll bet you played basketball."

"Six-four," Gordon said reticently, "and, yeah, a little."

"Come on, Gordon," Peter said. "It was more than a little. You were all-conference at Cal."

"Really," said Wendy, drawing the word out and putting just too much emphasis on it. "You must be pretty good."

"Second team," Gordon said. "That doesn't take you any further than college."

"So what do you do now?"

"I guess you could say I manage investments. Peter's a surgeon."

"How nice. So are you here for a while?"

April returned at that point with Gordon's coffee in a cup and saucer on a tray. Seeing Wendy from behind she made a face, then quickly wiped it off and stepped up to the group.

"Here's your coffee, Mr. Gordon," she said in a friendly, natural tone. Turning to Wendy, she immediately became more formal. "Hello, Mrs. Van Holland. Is there anything I can get you?"

"Mmm, well, maybe a little something from the bar," said Wendy, as if the thought had just occurred to her.

"A splash of Hennessey would be nice on this freezing day."

April moved behind the bar, and Peter invited Wendy to join the two men by the fire. She had just sat down on the sofa when April returned with the cognac. Wendy took the glass, swirled it gently in her right hand, raised it to her lips, then said:

"Oh my goodness. Did you make it a double?"

"I'm sorry," said April with no sincerity at all. "I thought that was your usual."

"Well, I suppose on a cold day like this, it wouldn't hurt. Thank you."

"Should I charge that to your room?"

"Sure." April turned away, and Wendy said, "Actually, I'll pay cash."

"That'll be nine dollars, please."

Wendy opened her clutch purse of chocolate-colored leather and took out a ten.

"Keep the change."

"Much appreciated, I'm sure." Gordon, whose seat commanded the best view of the bar, noticed that April took the bill to the register, placed it in a drawer, took a dollar back, folded it into fourths, and deposited it in her bra.

"So how long have you been here?" asked Peter.

"Since last Wednesday." She took a sip of cognac, but made the sip last a while, draining about a third of the contents of the glass and savoring it in her mouth.

"Has the weather been like this all along?"

She swallowed slowly and exhaled deeply. "No, thank God. It was sunny and pretty nice up until yesterday morning, then it started getting grayer and colder. I don't like the cold."

"You fish?" Gordon asked.

"No, but my husband does. Oh, does he fish."

"He came to the right place."

"That's what everybody keeps saying. Not much to do if you don't fish, though."

She lifted the snifter to her lips and took some more, this time in a big gulp that drained another third of the glass. Having no answer to her last comment, Gordon and Peter nodded and looked into the fire. After a moment of awkward silence, she said:

"I don't like this cold. I grew up in the snow, and I'm over it. It feels like it's going to snow."

"Not too likely at this altitude and time of year," Gordon said, "but it *is* pretty raw outside." Another moment of silence. "How long are you here for?"

"Just till Wednesday, then we get to go back home."

"And where's home?"

"Hillsborough." Gordon and Peter exchanged knowing glances at the mention of one of San Francisco's most prestigious suburbs. "Not much to do there, either, but at least it's close to the city."

She downed the rest of her drink and set the snifter on a side table. Seeing the empty glass, April left the bar and came to the group.

"Everybody doing all right? Is there anything I can get anybody?" Then, turning to Wendy, "Would you like another double?" She delivered the line perfectly, managing to convey contempt while maintaining deniability. Wendy began to respond, then stopped herself.

"No, thank you. That one was more than enough." She stood and looked at the men. "Nice meeting you. I'm sure we'll get to know each other better. Everybody gets close at Harry's." Looking at April, "Isn't that right, June?"

April drew in her breath sharply, but choked off a reply.

"I'd better get back to the cabin and get ready for dinner. See you then." She walked to the lounge entrance, then turned and waved. It was a gesture she had clearly practiced. "Ciao."

No sooner had she gone out the front door than April muttered, under her breath, "Ciao," drawing out the end of the word. "You guys OK?" she said, shifting gears. "I just saw Don driving up, and he can take you to your cabin in a few minutes."

"We're fine," Gordon said.

"Hit the bell if you need anything. Once should be enough." She left the lounge and turned down the hallway past the front desk.

"Well," Peter said when they were alone again, "that Wendy is quite the personality, though I wouldn't say she's your type. Did you notice anything unusual about her?

"What do you mean?"

"She's apparently married, and she lives in a high-end town, but she wasn't wearing a ring. I wonder what the story is there?"

"Also, she changed her mind about putting her drink on the tab, which makes me think she doesn't want her husband to know about it."

"Good point. You know, Gordon, if the other guests are half as interesting as Wendy, we could have ourselves a jolly little time here."

5

MOMENTS LATER the front door opened, and the owner came in. Don Potter was 45 years old, of medium height and build, wearing jeans, running shoes, a red and gold flannel shirt, and a down vest. He had a round face with regular, friendly features, a neatly trimmed goatee, and a short-cut head of dull brown hair, just beginning to recede. He saw Gordon and Peter in the lounge and advanced with an extended hand.

"You must be the Gordon party," he said. "I'm Don. Welcome to Harry's."

"Good to be back," said Gordon, shaking the extended hand.

"So you've been here before. I was going to ask. Amazing how many people remember Harry's from the old days."

"It was quite a joint."

"Will be again, if I have anything to say about it. The last two owners tried to cut corners, and you can't do that if you want to be a destination resort. Sharon and I are committed to making everything first rate. Still some work to do, but people see the difference already."

"I like what I've seen so far," said Peter. "And your lovely young bartender pours a good drink."

"April's a good kid. Life hasn't been easy for her, but working here has done her some good." He looked at Peter's glass. "Can I get you a refill?"

Peter considered the offer for a few seconds, then set the glass down on a table. "No thanks. Not now."

"Well, when you're ready for another drink, it'll be an honest one. Don't skimp, but charge a fair price, I say. Only way to do business." Turning to Gordon, he said, "I've been anxious to meet you. The first time I saw your name on the reservation, I said, 'Quill Gordon? Like the trout fly?' "

"I get that a lot," Gordon said.

"I bet you do. But you live up to your name. I hear from Johnny that you're a top-notch fisherman."

"We're going out with Johnny tomorrow. In fact, I've asked him to join us for dinner."

"If you're out with Johnny, you'll catch fish," Don said. "Or if you don't, it's on you. Nobody knows this river like he does." A pause, then looking at Gordon, "Another reason I noticed your name is that we just fixed up the five cabins by the river, and gave them names instead of numbers. Named 'em after trout flies. I was going to call Number Four Quill Gordon, but at the last minute I figured it was an East Coast fly, so we named the cabin Green Drake instead. And guess where you're staying?"

"The Green Drake, by any chance?" ventured Peter.

"You got it. If you're ready, I can take you there now."

"Sure," said Gordon, downing the last of his coffee, now cold. "Just out of curiosity, what are the other ones named?"

Don stepped to a window and they followed him. Through it, they could see the five cabins by the river.

"They were numbered one to five before, with one the closest to the lodge and five the farthest away, almost to the property line. Following the numbers, the first one is Blue Wing Olive, then Golden Caddis, Rusty Spinner, Green Drake, and Pale Morning Dun."

"So Pale Morning Dun is occupied," Gordon said.

"The Van Hollands," said Don. "He owns an insurance agency near San Francisco, really nice guy. Wife's quite a bit younger. A real looker."

"We've had the pleasure," Peter said.

"Then you know what I mean. Anyway, One, Three and Five are queen bed cabins, usually for couples. Two and four are twin-bed cabins, usually for two men, but sometimes two women."

"You get women coming here to fish?" Peter said.

"More than you might think. Some of them are really into it. We have one here now who's mad about it. Mrs. Adderly, but she's here with her husband, so they're in number three on the other side of you. At least I think it's her husband. He has a different last name, and the reservation was made under Adderly."

"Probably best not to ask," murmured Peter.

"You got that right," Don said. "None of my business as long as they pay and don't break the furniture."

"Actually," Gordon said, "if she's who I think she is, they're married."

"Then we have two more people coming in any time now. A. Sakamoto and D. Evans. They'll be in Golden Caddis. And that's it until next weekend."

"So a small group," Gordon said.

"We were completely full opening day weekend," Don said. "And from Memorial Day to Labor Day, we're averaging 75 percent occupancy already, with some weekends sold out. But in the middle of the week before Memorial Day, it's still pretty slow. Nice, though. You'll get to know the other guests, maybe even make some new friends. And you'll have some elbow room when you're fishing."

"Is the weather always this bad?" asked Peter.

Don shook his head. "You get a few days like this in the late spring, but it doesn't last long. Mostly sunny and in the sixties and seventies is more like it. You ready to go to your cabin?"

Gordon and Peter looked at each other and nodded.

"Where are your bags?"

"In the car. The silver Cherokee."

"OK if I show you the cabin first then bring your bags right over?"

They nodded again and followed Don to the front desk, where he took two keys from the rack on the wall and started for the front door.

24

"So how did you end up owning Harry's?" Gordon asked as they stepped outside. The wind was still strong, and he almost had to bellow the question.

"Lucky, I guess. Been in hospitality almost 20 years. Mostly restaurants, but a little in hotels. Always wanted a place of my own. Three years ago, Sharon's mother died and left her a house in Marin County, all paid for. We sold it and decided to look for something to buy. Harry's was on the market, and when we saw it, I knew. It needed some work, but I saw what it could be, and it's almost there now."

"And your wife?" Peter said. "Did she love it, too?"

"She wasn't as sure as I was, but she's come around. Now that she's made some friends, she likes it here."

Gordon zipped his parka up to the neck and wished he had a scarf to protect him from the icy wind. Peter crossed his arms over his chest. They were both thoroughly cold by the time they had walked two minutes to the cabin.

"You'll be fine when you get inside," Don said. "When we remodeled these babies, we put in electric wall heaters. They'll keep you plenty warm."

He unlocked the front door and stepped in. The cabin was 15 feet wide and 30 feet deep, with hardwood floors and walls paneled in knotty pine. Just inside, to the left of the door, was a wood writing desk that appeared to date back to the previous century. Farther against the left wall were two windows, offering a view of the Van Holland cabin and the river beyond, with two twin beds offsetting the windows. Against the right wall were a couch for two and a comfortable-looking padded chair, with a standing reading lamp between them. At the back of the cabin the door to the bathroom was on the left and a closet opened on the right. To the right of the chair on the right wall was the wall heater. Don flipped a switch, then set a thermostat farther down the wall. Within a minute the heater coils were glowing red and beginning to take the edge off the damp cold that had chilled them when they came into the room.

"No TV?" asked Peter.

"The jury's still out on that," Don said. "Harry never had TVs in the rooms. Some people like that, some don't.

But it's like the old joke in the hospitality business. What do you call the hotel room with a broken TV set?"

"I give up," said Peter.

"The honeymoon suite."

Gordon and Peter chuckled politely.

"I'll go fetch your bags. If you need anything, I'll be back in ten minutes. Hope you enjoy your stay at Harry's."

After he left, Peter walked over to one of the beds, sat on it, and pressed down. "Should be comfortable," he said. "And now that the heater's kicking in, my outlook on life is definitely improving. Anyway, after that long drive, I need to clean up before dinner." He took a quarter out of his pocket. "Shall we toss to see who gets the first shower? In the honeymoon suite?"

6

GORDON HAD ARRANGED to meet Johnny, the guide, for dinner at eight, which allowed them to unpack and clean up in leisurely fashion. At about 7:15 they headed to the main lodge. The wind had all but stopped by then, but even though there was nearly an hour of daylight left, the heavy cloud cover created a sense of twilight and impending darkness.

"I guess we won't be sitting on the deck and watching the sunset tonight," Peter said.

In the Fireside Lounge, two men were sitting near the fire in the chairs Gordon and Peter had occupied earlier. One of them had pulled a small table in front of his chair, placed a box of trout flies on it, and was setting some of them on the table for further examination. His companion was ignoring the flies and focusing on the drink in his hand. The woman who had replaced April behind the bar was in her early forties, medium height, trim, with brown eyes and ginger-brown hair neatly pulled back in a ponytail that stuck through the back of a cap with Harry's logo on the front. Sensibly dressed in jeans, a blue blouse and a burgundy sweater, she put out an air of confident competence.

"Good to meet you," she said, looking first at Peter then at Gordon. "You must be Mr. Gordon; Don said you were tall. I'm Sharon Potter."

"My pleasure," said Gordon, shaking her hand. "My friend, Dr. Peter Delaney."

"What can I get for you?"

"I'll have a beer, please," said Gordon. "Do you have Sierra Nevada?"

"We certainly do," she said, taking out a bottle and pouring it into a tall glass. "And you?" looking at Peter.

"Double Johnnie Walker on the rocks."

"Decisive," she said, handing Gordon his beer. "I probably would have guessed you were a doctor, even if he hadn't told me." She poured Peter's drink and handed it to him. "You should meet Drew and Alan. They're here through Saturday, just like you."

As Sharon said that, the man looking into his drink sat up and turned to look toward the bar. His friend was contemplating the flies on the table as if they were a floral arrangement. Gordon and Peter walked over.

"Good to meet you," Gordon said, extending his hand to the trout fly man. "I'm Quill Gordon and this is my friend Peter Delaney. This your first time at Harry's?"

"Alan Sakamoto," the trout fly man said. He looked up briefly to shake their hands, then, apparently considering the conversation at an end, returned to the flies.

"Drew Evans," said the man with the drink, rising to shake hands. "And it is our first time here, though I gather this place has quite a reputation."

He was six feet tall, in his early thirties, with darkish blond hair combed from left to right, slightly over his forehead, gray eyes, a flushed face and a physique that was beginning to turn from slender to middle-aged solid. Alan looked to be a few inches shorter, with straight black hair, brown eyes, and an owlish face marked by a pair of aviator glasses.

"Where are you from?" asked Peter.

"Silicon Valley," Drew said. "We both work for Miracle Software in Sunnyvale. Alan heads up one of the main design teams, and I try to sell what they come up with. Neither of us could do the other one's job."

27

"I've certainly heard of it," Gordon said. "Has a good reputation, anyway."

"The stock's sure going like gangbusters."

Gordon nodded. "But that could change, you know."

"Don't tell me you're a financial adviser."

"No, but I was a stockbroker for quite a few years. Long enough to see them go up and down."

Alan looked up from his flies for the first time since the conversation began. "Did you say Quill Gordon? Like the fly?"

"Afraid so," said Gordon.

"East Coast fly," said George, shaking his head. "Won't work too well out here. Trying to figure out what we'll need tomorrow."

Having no answer, Gordon merely nodded. Sharon saved him.

"Johnny's boat just pulled up," she said. "He's with you tonight, right?"

"Yep. Put his drink on our tab."

Taking their leave of Drew and Alan, Gordon and Peter moved to a sofa facing two chairs over a coffee table, situated halfway between the bar and the fireplace. A minute later, Johnny came in the front door, removing a battered Stetson to reveal a crew-cut head of salt and pepper hair. He stood five-nine, with a wiry build and precise, fluid body movements. The fluidity was displayed as, in one continuous motion, he hung the hat on a peg behind the front desk and removed a fishing vest from his torso and hung it on the peg below the hat. He rubbed his hands together as he stepped into the lounge and Sharon set a drink on the bar.

"Jim Beam and water, as usual," she said.

"Well, thank you, Sharon. That's mighty kind of you. This'll help take the chill off. Yes, it will. Ah, Mr. Gordon." He walked over, and after introductions, they sat down.

"How was the fishing today?" asked Peter.

"Not bad this morning. Not bad at all," Johnny said, with a perfect middle American accent, but drawing out the words as if speaking with a brogue. "We caught several nice fish this morning, but when the wind came up early in the afternoon, it was tough. Very tough indeed." He took a generous sip of the bourbon and swirled it around in his mouth, closing his eyes to better concentrate on the taste. Finally he swallowed.

"I like to say there are 20 ways to catch a fish in Eden River," he continued, "and this afternoon we were down to numbers 18 and 19 before we finally caught a couple more. You can have good fishing when it's bitter cold, and you can have good fishing when it's pouring rain. But when that wind is howling like a banshee from hell, it's almost impossible." He took another sip. "I hope it dies down tomorrow."

"I have faith in you, Johnny," said Gordon. "Whatever the weather is, you'll give us a better chance than anyone else."

"You're too kind, sir. Now where are you staying here."

"Cabin four. The Green Drake, I think it's called now. Right between the Van Hollands and the Adderlys."

"Ah, the Van Hollands," Johnny said. Then, leaning forward and lowering his voice, "A most interesting couple. *Very* interesting. As you'll no doubt see for yourself when you meet them."

"Actually," said Peter, "we met her this afternoon."

"And I saw her husband coming out of his cabin," Gordon said, "but he walked off in the other direction and we didn't have a chance to meet."

Johnny raised his eyebrows and took a breath, as if starting to speak, but held it a few beats. "Well, now, that's very interesting," he said in the low voice, looking quickly around the room. "Very interesting, indeed. But I'm afraid that couldn't have been Mr. Van Holland you saw. No, not at all. You see, Mr. Van Holland was out with me on the river until 15 minutes ago."

7

AFTER THEY FINISHED THEIR DRINKS, Sharon led them into the dining room. Gordon stopped at the threshold, looking carefully at the couple seated at the corner table by the window. The woman was 34 years old, long-limbed, and had brown hair, well cut to her shoulder for a professional look. Her face had regular, appealing features, somewhat tightened by a sense of intensity, and even in this casual setting, she was casually but carefully dressed in gray slacks, a light blue blouse and a waist-length black leather jacket. The effect was that of someone who had just thrown on a couple of things pulled from a suitcase — but of course all bought at the finest stores. The man was a few years older, with lighter brown hair and a clean-shaven face that conveyed a sense of solidity. He was wearing rumpled chinos and a denim shirt that really had just been pulled from the suitcase. He looked well on his way to being called "distinguished" in another decade.

The woman looked up, saw Gordon in the entryway, and waved, flashing a smile that momentarily wiped the seriousness from her face. Gordon waved back and started for the table; after hesitating briefly, the others followed him.

"Gordon!" she said, rising from the table in a swift, graceful motion, and giving him a hug. She was six feet tall, but still a few inches shorter than he, and for a second they looked like a pair of well matched dancers. "Imagine you being here. It's great to see you again."

"This is a pleasant surprise," he replied. "You look great, Rachel." Turning to his friends, "Rachel Adderly."

"I know Johnny, of course," she said, shaking his hand. "We were on the river together Saturday."

"And you did very well, my dear," Johnny said.

"More the guide than the angler. Johnny's the best."

"And my friend, Dr. Peter Delaney," Gordon said.

She shook his hand as well. "You have quite a reputation, doctor. You did an emergency appendectomy on my brother and he spoke highly of you."

"My pleasure," said Peter. "Your name sounds vaguely familiar, but I can't place it."

"Rachel's on the Oakland City Council," Gordon said. "And there's some talk you might be running for the open Assembly seat next year."

"I didn't know that," said Sharon, "but politicians have always been welcome at Harry's."

"I'm glad to hear that; there aren't too many places we are. And if I end up in Sacramento, maybe I can come here more often." She turned to her companion. "Darling,

I'd like you to meet an old friend of mine, Quill Gordon. We both played basketball at Cal. My husband, Stuart Bingham."

As he stood to shake hands, it was clear that even without heels, Rachel was three inches taller.

"Good to meet you," Gordon said. "Rachel started for the women's team three years. One of the pioneers of Title Nine."

"It's served her well," her husband said. "I've never known anyone with such drive and energy."

"Stuart is the director of the Morgenstern Museum," Rachel said. "We met at a fund-raiser there for my first campaign."

"You have an excellent collection," Peter said. "I try to get out there at least once a year."

"Thank you. We put a lot of effort into keeping it fresh, while still showcasing the old favorites."

The conversation paused, and Gordon took the opportunity to get his party to its table, which was along the window, two down from Rachel and Stuart's. Between the dense clouds and the late hour, it was almost dark outside, but they could see the reflection of the lights from the lodge on the river surface.

"The special tonight is lamb stew," Sharon said, giving them their menus. "But the steaks are always good, and Eddie's chicken piccata has acquired quite a following."

Near the door where they had come in, a party of six — three couples in their late thirties and early forties — were sitting. Later in the evening, when cake was brought and everyone sang happy birthday while one of the women blushed, the nature of their occasion became clear. Sharon brought Drew and Alan to a table in the second row from the window, and April followed them, moving to Gordon's table. She took drink refill orders from Peter and Johnny, but Gordon decided to stay with his glass of water for the time being. She moved to Drew and Alan's table.

"What can I do for you guys?"

"I don't think you want to know," said Drew, attempting a raffish smile.

Without missing a beat, April said, "Maybe you should have another drink. It might make you witty."

Drew hesitated for a second then laughed, but the laugh seemed a bit forced. "I like a woman who talks tough. Reminds me of the lady I met at a bar once. Jeans were so tight it looked like she'd been poured into them. I asked her, 'Excuse me, miss, but how do you get into those jeans?' And you know what she said?"

" 'You could start by buying me a drink,' " April replied. "Hey, if you're not ready to order, I can come back in a couple of minutes."

He laughed again. "No, no. Can you get me a margarita with extra salt on the rim?"

"Sea dog margarita, coming right up. And for you, sir?" turning to Alan. He had opened his fly box and set several flies on the table, staring at them intently.

"Get him a Seven and Seven," Drew said. "He'll thank you when he finally sees it."

She left for the bar, with Drew watching her all the way out the door. Peter turned to Johnny.

"So can I ask you a question?" Johnny spread his hands as if to say go ahead. "You were saying in the lounge earlier that because of the wind you were down to your last couple of ways to catch a fish. Could you talk about that a bit?"

"Sure. You see, doctor, most of our fishing here is either with dry flies on the surface, when there's an insect hatch going, or drifting a nymph along the weed beds a few feet below the surface if the fish aren't rising. Those are the tried and true methods, they are. When the wind's really blowing and the water's disturbed, the fish tend to move to the bottom and stop feeding, so the usual approach doesn't work."

"What does?"

"Well, your friend Mr. Gordon here is an excellent fisherman. I'd be interested in hearing what he'd do in such a situation."

They looked at Gordon. Drew was watching and eavesdropping as well, and even Alan had looked away from his flies to follow the discussion.

"OK," Gordon said, leaning forward to respond. "If the fish are at the bottom and not really feeding, I'm thinking you need to do something to get their attention. You could try getting a weighted nymph down that deep, but you'd probably have to hit the fish on the nose before he went for it. So it might make more sense to put something in front of them that moves and looks like a bigger meal. I'd probably start with a Woolly Bugger, which can mimic a leech or a minnow, with a split shot a foot or two above it to get it down deep, then retrieve it in short little jerks, maybe six to nine inches at a time. That'd look like a good enough meal for a big fish to chase."

"And they did," said a deep, cultivated voice approaching the table. "Two of them, anyway, nice rainbows. What would you say, Johnny — 18 and 20 inches maybe?"

"Now, I don't know, sir," said Johnny, standing up. "I think that second one might have been closer to 21 inches."

"Did he say Woolly Bugger?" asked Alan.

"I heard 21 inches," said Drew.

"Charles Van Holland," said the man who had just walked up to the table with Wendy at his side. He was a bit under six feet tall, in his mid-50s, and looked fit and robust. His face, with its square jaw and patrician nose, had a good color, perhaps from being outside on the river all day, and he was the best-dressed man in the room, with crisply pressed gray slacks, black loafers, a button-down shirt that alternated quarter-inch stripes of white and navy, and a blazer with gold buttons and light blue handkerchief neatly flowering out of the breast pocket. Wendy was wearing an emerald-green knee-length dress of silky fabric with an off-white sweater thrown around her shoulders, but left open to provide a good look at the dropping V neckline of the dress, framing a string of pearls. Seeing her legs for the first time, Gordon noted that they were well shaped, and quickly forced himself to look back at Van Holland. Drew was looking at her so intently that he didn't even attempt to get off a line as April set down his drink.

After introductions all around, Van Holland turned back to Gordon and Peter. "I hear you're going out with

Johnny tomorrow. You should have a great day. He's the best."

"How was it today?" Peter said.

"Good in the morning. We had a hatch that ran for three hours and were catching fish on dries, then they were taking nymphs pretty well until the wind kicked up around two. Then nothing for about three hours until we tried the Woolly Buggers and caught those two really nice ones."

"Was this your first time out?" Gordon asked.

"Oh, no. I've been coming to Harry's off and on since I was 12. And this trip we got in Wednesday and went out with Johnny Thursday, Friday and today. Doing it again Tuesday."

"And we're out with Johnny Monday, Wednesday and Friday," Gordon said. "Johnny's a popular man."

"The best are the busiest. Right, Johnny?" The guide raised his glass to Van Holland and smiled.

"And does your lovely wife go with you?" asked Peter.

"She came out on Thursday, but it was too hot for her. I know, hard to believe if you got here today, but it was probably in the nineties on the river in the sun. She wasn't feeling well, so we brought her back mid-afternoon, then Johnny and I went out again. But Wendy says she can amuse herself here, though I'm not sure how."

Gordon had the best look at the two of them from his chair, and he could see that Wendy, standing slightly behind Charles and out of his line of sight, was casting furtive glances in Drew's direction. He was returning the favor more intently and unabashedly.

"Well, I hope you left a few for us," Gordon said.

"Now I wouldn't worry, Mr. Gordon," Johnny said. "There are so many fish in this river, what with it being catch-and-release, that you can hardly drop an anchor without hitting one. You and Mr. Delaney should do just fine. Just fine indeed."

Van Holland and Wendy moved on to Rachel and Stuart's table and began making small talk with them. When he judged that they were immersed in the conversation, Peter leaned forward to Johnny and said in a low voice:

"So what's it like, generally speaking, going out with a husband and wife, or a man and his girlfriend? What does that do to the dynamic in the boat?"

Johnny set his glass down on the table, looked around at the other tables in the room, and leaned forward. When he spoke, his voice was barely a whisper.

"As a general rule, sir, I don't gossip about the clients. No, I don't. Bad for business. But I'll have to tell you. Last Thursday, I earned my money. Yes, I did."

8

AFTER AN EXCELLENT DINNER, the three men let April talk them into trying dessert. When she left, Gordon, feeling full and sluggish from the meal, excused himself from the table to get a breath of fresh air. Walking past the corner table where Rachel and Stuart had been sitting, he unlatched the sliding glass door and stepped out onto the deck.

Night had descended completely. In the enveloping darkness, Gordon would not have been able to make out the river a short distance away, had it not been for the lights from the five cabins, reflected on the calm water. The air, even colder than before, had taken on an almost liquid quality, and when a breeze kicked up, it seemed to be wafting a fine spray onto his face. The breeze, which lasted less than a minute, went straight through his clothing, chilling the body underneath. He zipped his parka all the way up, pulled the hood over his head, and crossed his arms in front of his body in an attempt to keep warm. Holding that position, he focused, trance-like on the lights reflecting on the river and on the vapor of his breath as he exhaled.

Behind him, he heard the sound of the glass door sliding open again.

"A penny for your thoughts," said Sharon.

"The price is too high, but thanks. I'm in a food coma from that fine lamb stew of yours, and I'm afraid my mind is entirely empty."

She laughed. "I'm glad you liked the food, anyway. Do you mind if I sneak a quick smoke? This is the first time all night I've been able to get a little break."

"Go right ahead."

"Thanks." She lit up, inhaled deeply, then exhaled at the same time Gordon breathed out, her cigarette smoke and his breath both exuding a fog into the air.

"So it's been busy?" he asked.

"We had a good crowd this weekend. I have two more girls who come in and help on weekends, but today I figured I'd pick up the slack. Now the weekend before this, opening day, was really crazy."

"Usually is. I try to wait a week now before I start fishing."

"It was the weekend before this one, last Saturday and Sunday of April. Every room was booked, lodge and cabins, and there was a lot of restaurant trade. One of the waitresses was new, and I had to hold her hand, plus a lot of guests stayed through Sunday night and left Monday morning. I had a night out with the girls on Sunday and almost didn't make it."

"I guess it's good that business is humming."

"Can't complain. And the summer is shaping up nicely."

"That's what your husband was saying."

"Don's really happy here. This place means the world to him. I'm not sure I'll ever feel the same way about it myself, but I'm liking it a lot more. And there is something spiritual about this place."

"Maybe the Native Americans considered it sacred."

"Maybe. There's something about it, anyway."

"Has to be good for Harry's, I guess."

They stood silently for a moment, and with another drag, her cigarette burned past the halfway point.

"There's just one thing, though." Gordon nodded without saying a word, and Sharon continued, "I guess you've heard about the curse?"

"It's common knowledge."

"I don't know if it's because it's on my mind, but it does seem like there's been a lot of romantic sadness since we came here. With the guests, I mean."

"Like Mr. and Mrs. Jones — married, but not to each other?"

"That, and obviously married men bringing their mistresses here ..."

"Mistress. You don't hear that too much, any more."

"Would you rather I said whores? And some fooling around among the guests. Last summer, one of the maids didn't show up one day so I filled in. I went into Pale Morning Dun without knocking because I thought it was empty and found the lady in bed with her husband's best friend. Or so her husband thought."

"Part of the lodging business, I suppose."

"That's what Don always says. He's very matter of fact about it — says people will be people and there's no point in worrying or being disapproving. He's a good man himself, but it's almost as if he's cynical about marriage in principle. All that fooling around, and I don't know that it makes anyone any happier."

"Probably doesn't most of the time. I think we have a culture where it's easy to yield to temptation, but hard to enjoy it much. Puritan hangover."

"Puritan or not, a marriage is a marriage. The vows should be taken seriously."

"That's an experience I've yet to try, but when I do, I hope I'll feel that way."

"I think you will. Your friend, on the other hand, I'm not so sure about. But none of my business." She walked over to a standing ashtray and ground her cigarette butt into the sand. "Nice talking to you, Gordon, but I have to get back to work."

"And there seems to be a slice of apple pie waiting for me." He opened the door for her and followed her back into the restaurant. Dessert had just arrived. The crust of the apple pie was a golden caramel color and the whipped cream on top of it was clearly homemade. The coffee was black and steaming hot. The three men dug in and enjoyed their pie and coffee in silence. After Peter had drained the last of his coffee, he turned to the guide.

"So, Johnny, at what ungodly hour do we have to get up tomorrow?"

"You don't have to rise before the rooster, doctor. No need for that. The fish in this river are real gentlemen.

Almost keep banker's hours, they do. Don't start their breakfast until 8:30 or nine o'clock. If we cast off by eight, we should be fine."

"Want to join us for breakfast?" Gordon said. "Say seven o'clock."

"You could make it 7:15 if you like. Breakfast is a buffet, and we only need ten minutes afterward to get the boat ready."

"Seven fifteen it is." Gordon stood up and extended his hand. "We're looking forward to it."

9

BACK IN THE WARMTH of the cabin, Gordon was feeling drowsy, despite the coffee, and declined when Peter pulled a bottle of Courvoisier from his duffel bag and offered it. Peter poured three fingers for himself into a standard-issue eight-ounce motel glass as the men settled into their respective beds.

"It'll be nice to be on the water tomorrow," Gordon said. "It's been five and a half months since the last fishing trip."

"Longer for me. Are you sure it's not too cold for fishing? The trout might get frostbite on their noses if they came up for food."

Gordon shook his head. "Not at all. Ask Johnny tomorrow, and he'll tell you why."

"Can't you just tell me now?"

"You wouldn't believe me. Maybe coming from him, you'll buy it."

"Johnny seems like a character anyway. Is it customary to take the guide to dinner the night before?"

"Probably not."

"So why did you do it?"

"Helping out. It's a way of letting him stretch his paycheck."

"Really? From what I paid for my half of his fee, he's doing pretty well. Three-fifty a day, isn't it?"

"That's what the Fisherman's Friend charges, and they keep a big chunk of it. What's left over isn't bad money, at least for these parts, but you have to remember Johnny's only booked for probably a hundred days a year. The rest of the time, and all winter when it's off-season, he's doing odd jobs or working for minimum wage. No health benefits, no retirement plan. And it's a shame, too, because he knows more about Eden River than any Ph.D. does about international finance. It just isn't valued as much. So, yeah, I'll buy him dinner and breakfast."

"When you put it that way, it seems like the least we can do." Peter took another gulp of cognac, poured a splash more into his glass, and put the bottle, down a quarter, back in his bag.

"So let's gossip about the other guests. Are you getting the impression that our young Wendy has a bit of an itch that her husband isn't scratching?"

"I don't know, Peter. From what my married friends tell me, they don't always know what's going on inside their own marriage, so how could I say?"

"Nonetheless, it seemed to me that she was making goo-goo eyes at the half of the Silicon Valley tandem that can say more than three words at a time. And she gave you a good look when she walked into the bar this afternoon. You seeing anybody now, Gordon, or are you available?" Gordon hesitated before answering, and Peter jumped on the silence. "Aha! Has something been going on since I saw you last?"

"It's complicated."

"It always is with women."

"I've been out three times the past month with a woman named Jennifer."

"Age? Occupation?"

"Twenty eight, and a commercial real estate broker. Handles office space in the city. She's a real live wire, and we had a good first date. In fact, her personality is so bubbly it took me two more dates to figure out she's incapable of talking about anything but real estate. I was going to sort it out this week, but I don't think there's going to be a fourth date."

"Aw, don't give up now, Gordon. After the third date is when the perks start getting good."

"Maybe so, but you still have to have something to talk about."

Peter swallowed some cognac. "That might have been true before Cable TV, but I guess you know your own mind. And it sounds to me like in your own mind you're available."

"Not to a married woman."

"Really? You never struck me as being an exemplar of puritan morality. Should I start calling you Deacon?"

"It's not so much a question of morality as it is public health. You never know when the husband's packing heat."

"I'm not so sure about that, Gordon. I think you just don't want to admit to being a moral man in an immoral age."

"There's a long day ahead tomorrow," Gordon said after a pause, "and we have to get an early start. Let's call it a night."

"Just one more thing. You knew the other couple that's here. Rachel and Stuart?"

"Just her. From college."

"Where you both played basketball. So tell me, did you and she ever play a little Horse together," Gordon shot him a villainous look, "if you know what I mean, and I can see you do. But, hey, you don't do married women, and you answered my question without saying a thing."

"Party's over, Peter. Good night." Gordon turned off the lamp by his bed and rolled over to face the wall. Peter finished the drink and turned out his light. After a few minutes of silence he had the final word.

"It must have broken Rachel's heart when you split, Gordon. You're probably the only man she's ever had who's taller than she is."

Monday May 8

1

THE ALARM CLOCK was set for 6:15, and Gordon, as he often did, woke up five minutes beforehand. An occasional chirp of birdsong outside mingled with sporadic snores from Peter in the next bed, but otherwise it was still. And dark. Looking at the cabin window near his bed, Gordon could see only a slightly lighter shade of darkness on the other side of the blinds, even though sunrise had been at the top of the hour. He lay in bed, momentarily disoriented, then got up, moved to the window, and pulled the blind aside. A dense fog, dropping all the way to ground level, enveloped everything. He could see the Van Holland cabin 20 feet away and a small bit of river beyond that, then the mist obscured everything and seemed to hold all light at bay.

With his friend sound asleep, Gordon decided to shower first, and when he emerged from the bathroom, Peter was working himself into wakefulness.

"You didn't tell me we had to get up before dawn," he growled.

"Dawn was half an hour ago. Heavy fog outside, but maybe it'll burn off and we'll have a nice day. Don't be too long in the shower. I need a cup of coffee."

While Peter showered, Gordon methodically dressed for the day. He pulled on a pair of jeans, wondering if he should have brought long underwear, then put on a pair of light socks, covering them with a heavier pair of wool socks before putting on his hiking boots. For the upper part of his body, he donned a T-shirt, covered it with a flannel shirt, pulled a light sweater over the two, and topped it with a lightweight, waterproof parka. He turned down the heat in the room and figured that during the day he could shed clothing as needed once the sun came out and the temperature got warmer. Peter came out and gave his friend a quizzical look.

"Fishing the Yukon today?"

Gordon let it pass, and Peter dressed similarly, substituting a heavier parka for the sweater. When they stepped out the front door of the cabin, the lodge was visible only in hazy outline. It was still cold, and the mist imparted a chill clamminess that seeped through every breathing space of their clothing and worked through the layers to their skin. The thermometer by the front door of the lodge read 37 degrees Fahrenheit.

Johnny had stayed overnight at the lodge and met them as they came in. April seated them at a window table and began to pour coffee. When she got to Johnny's cup, he put his hand over it.

"In the water glass if you would, Miss April." She blinked and froze, so he picked up the water glass with his other hand and set it next to the coffee cup. "On a morning like this, I want to have the coffee in something I can put my hands around and warm them up." She did as he asked, pointed them to the buffet and told them to help themselves.

They sipped their coffee first, and a moment later, Rachel and Stuart came in.

"Where are you fishing today?" Gordon asked.

"Since you've got Johnny, Stuart's going to take me to the Big Hole River."

"You fish, too?" Peter asked him.

He shrugged, and Rachel answered, "He wants to go into Eden Mills and Muirfield and check out the craft shops. Right, darling?"

"Check out the local talent," Stuart said. "Maybe I'll find another Stoddard," referring to the painter who had done the landscape over the fireplace in the bar.

"Good luck," said Gordon as they moved on.

"Checking out the local talent," muttered Peter under his breath. "That should take about five minutes."

Johnny was cradling the water glass full of coffee with both hands. He took another sip and turned to Peter.

"So, doctor. Did Mr. Gordon tell you the story about why you can go fishing on Eden River today?"

"Never got to it," Gordon said. "Go ahead, Johnny. You tell it better."

"Well it goes like this. About 25 years ago, the whole river downstream from here was in private hands. More

42

cattle ranches and fewer private homes back then, and the cattlemen were jealous of the water. They put up barriers to keep people from floating downstream, so that part of the river never got fished."

"Where did Harry's guests fish?"

"Upstream to the source of the river is National Forest land, and they could always go to the Big Hole or Saddle Creek. But then, a lot of them really weren't here to fish. Or so I've been told. Anyway, a group of local sportsmen didn't like the situation, and an attorney from the Bay Area who wanted to buy a house here agreed with them. So they filed a lawsuit claiming that under the California Waterways Act, this was a navigable river and the owners had no right to put up barriers. The ranchers were furious and fought it to the bitter end. They won in local court, but when it was appealed, they lost every step along the way. In 1971 the California Supreme Court upheld the appeal, and they had to take down the barriers. And that's why we get to go where we're going today."

"But the land along the river is still private property?"

"Except for a public access easement a few miles downstream. We'll be in the boat all day because we'd be trespassing if we fished from the shore. So let's get some food and get to the boat."

They rose as one and moved to the buffet, loading their plates with eggs, sausage, bacon, potatoes, fruit and toast. While they were away, April came by and refilled their coffee cups, including Johnny's. He emptied the cup into his water glass without comment. Drew and Alan came in.

"A little overcast is good," Alan was saying. "If it's too hot and bright, the fish can sit on the bottom and sulk."

"You know more about that than I do," Drew replied. "I'm hoping it'll get a little warmer."

Don was following them through the door. "Weather forecast on the radio said it should clear up this afternoon. I think you gentlemen are in for a fine day of fishing."

"What do you say, Johnny?" Gordon asked.

"I'll tell you when I can see Cavalry Mountain." Peter gave a look of incomprehension. "That's a smaller peak, about fifty-five hundred feet, to the northwest. Our weather comes from that direction."

"You think the mist will lift?"

"Almost always does."

The Van Hollands arrived several minutes later. She was wearing a pair of snug designer jeans and an off-white pullover that was clingy enough to show the contours of her breasts to good effect. Drew was sitting facing the entrance, and as they walked past his table, he flashed Wendy a smile.

She was at just enough of an angle to her husband that he couldn't see her face. She returned Drew's smile.

"Take good care of Johnny today," Van Holland said. "Tomorrow's my last day with him, and I don't want him worn out."

"Don't worry. We'll keep him fresh," Gordon said. "What are you doing today?"

"Going out with one of the other guides."

"Bob Barnett?" asked Johnny. When Van Holland nodded, Johnny continued, "Good man. He'll put you over some fish. And I look forward to seeing you tomorrow."

"How about you, Mrs. Van Holland?" asked Peter.

"Oh, I'll just stay here and catch up on my reading, maybe go into town for a bit." She heaved a theatrical sigh. "It's so restful here."

The three men finished their breakfasts and opted for another cup of coffee before departing. As they were finishing, Wendy got up from her table and walked across the dining room to the entrance, then turned right into the hall leading to the restrooms. Gordon couldn't help following her with his eyes. The woman knew how to walk.

A couple of minutes later, Drew got up from his table and headed in the same direction. At the corner of the entrance and the hallway, he "accidentally" brushed against Wendy, who was on her way back. He said something Gordon couldn't hear, and she smiled and gave him a playful slap on the shoulder. Gordon quickly looked to see if her husband had observed the exchange, but Charles Van Holland was focused on his breakfast and hadn't seen a thing.

"Let's get moving, gentlemen," said Johnny. "The fish will be stirring shortly."

2

BY THE TIME they got to the pier, the mist had lifted enough that the other side of the river was barely visible. Johnny had tied up his boat, an aluminum 14-footer, at the end of the previous day. He got into the boat first, placed a mid-size ice chest at the back by the motor, and checked the two plastic seats where Gordon and Peter would be sitting. He had each man hand over his fly rod, which Johnny placed carefully along the inside edge of the boat so it was completely within. He took their gear bags and tucked them under an overhanging seat at the front of the boat, offsetting the weight of the ice chest. He worked precisely and economically, and the two anglers had little to do except hand over their gear and shiver on the pier, watching the vapor they created every time they exhaled.

On the way out of the lodge, Gordon had briefly ducked into the fireside lounge to take another look at the Stoddard painting over the fireplace. It still struck him as kitschy and ordinary, and he concluded Stuart had been joking about finding another.

"I don't think it's for sale, but you can always ask." He hadn't realized April was behind the bar, unloading glasses from the dishwasher.

"That's all right. I wasn't planning on bidding," he replied.

"So what did you think of that little scene a couple of minutes ago?"

"I'm sorry," he said.

"Yeah, I thought you saw it, too. You don't miss much. Our little trophy wife is getting more blatant every day."

"Maybe. Not my concern."

"You may not have a choice. Even her old man's going to notice pretty soon." Gordon did a quick mental calculation and realized he was nearly as close to age to the "old man" as he was to April. The thought did nothing for his mood.

"We had a situation last Labor Day weekend," she continued. "Guy left his wife unattended while he went fishing and another guest made a play for her. I think he succeeded. Anyway, the husband figured it out and they had a big shouting match." She tapped the edge of the bar. "Right here. One of them threw a sucker punch and gave the other guy a black eye."

"Which one got punched?"

"The husband."

"Ouch. That's adding insult to injury."

"He hasn't re-booked for this year," April said laconically. She wiped off the last glass and set it in place on the shelf. "You know what I don't understand?"

Gordon shrugged.

"Why did Wendy marry him? I mean, I can see where it might be fun for a while to have an older guy with a lot of money who takes you nice places and buys you nice things. At least it seems like it could. Nobody's ever asked. But *marrying* him? That's a lot of work."

"Well, my father always said that a man who marries for money earns it in the hardest way imaginable. Probably goes for a woman, too."

April hooted. "That's the truth."

"Your turn, Mr. Gordon," said Johnny, bringing him back to the pier. "Plant your foot right behind the chair, then come on in." Gordon did as he was told and was quickly seated in the boat. Johnny untied a rope from the pier and pushed the boat into the river before starting the motor. It came on with a purr, rather than a roar, and the boat slowly moved forward.

"Doesn't feel like you have much horsepower here," Peter said through chattering teeth.

"Don't want it. Don't need it. By county ordinance, the speed limit on this river is five miles an hour. I like to say this is such a beautiful river we should take our time on it. This is a battery-powered motor, non-polluting. Don't you worry, doctor. It'll get us to the fish soon enough, and it won't scare 'em off with a lot of noise, either."

"Anybody ever come out here with a really big motor?"

"We see the occasional jackass. I'm afraid we do. Usually a weekend visitor, though. We know each other out here, and any local who did that would be feeling mighty lonely before long."

They were moving downstream, leaving a barely noticeable wake. On the left side of the river was a large clump of cattails, with a group of red-winged blackbirds fluttering about them. The right bank sloped up from the river and had two residences perched on it, about 50 yards apart. One looked to be brand new, around 4,000 square feet, painted a light blue-gray, with a veranda running along its entire length facing the river. There was no sign of life. The other house looked to be about 25 years older and 2,500 square feet smaller. Its wooden exterior was stained and weathered, and an older man drinking a cup of coffee stood on the deck, wearing a heavy bathrobe and flannel pajama bottoms. He waved at them and Johnny waved back.

"Oscar Stern," he said. "Retired now but he used to be vice president at Tri-Valley Bank."

"Who owns the other house?" Gordon asked.

"Man named Summitt. Makes a lot of money in Silicon Valley, I'm told, but he's too busy to get up here much. Probably see him Memorial Day and Labor Day, then his family'll be here a week or two during the summer. Maybe he'll come up for a weekend."

"Seems like an awful lot of money to spend on a place you hardly use," Peter said.

"His money," shrugged Johnny. "We're seeing more and more of that — people building big, expensive houses and hardly ever coming to use 'em. I call these places the ghost homes of Eden River."

"Ghost houses, witches, curses," said Peter. "Pretty supernatural area you have up here."

"Well, doctor, we have a saying in these parts. What happens in the woods stays in the woods."

They cruised downriver in silence for five minutes, covering less than half a mile. The air was cold, bracing and pure, and after a winter spent mostly indoors in San Francisco, Gordon breathed it in deeply and

47

appreciatively, taking in the surroundings as well. Though the mist had lifted a bit, it was hard to see too far beyond the river. Still he was able to take in the passing panorama of green fields, farm buildings, grazing cattle and barbed-wire fences.

"Indian Hollow Bridge, gentlemen, prepare to duck," Johnny said. Gordon looked downstream and saw that they were approaching a bridge across the river. It stood only six feet above the surface of the water, supported by weathered pilings driven deep into the river bed. Between these were narrow gaps through which a boat of their size could pass, but the lowest part of the bridge dropped enough to make the clearance only three or four feet, with the boat a foot and a half above water level.

Having been on the river before, Gordon knew enough to get out of his chair and crouch as low in the boat as possible. He motioned for Peter to do the same, and Johnny cut the motor to its gentlest idling speed and crouched in front of it, keeping his head just above the edges of the boat. With his hand behind him, he guided the boat slowly through the opening to the open river on the other side. As they passed under the bridge, Gordon noticed that its bottom was just a foot above them.

"Ever lose a fisherman who didn't duck low enough?" Peter asked, as they emerged onto the open river.

"Not yet." Then, after a minute more, "We'll be going under several of these bridges today. Never heard of anybody hitting one, but a couple of years ago, one of the ghost house owners was coming back from town one night after maybe a bit too much to drink. Most of these bridges don't have railings, and he went right over the side. Nobody heard it, and his wife spotted the car the next morning. He drowned in six feet of water because it came in through an open window and he couldn't get out fast enough. Never heard it myself, but a couple of the other guides claim they've heard cries for help by that bridge after dark. I'll point it out if you'd like when we get there."

They floated downstream five minutes more, then came to a big bend. Rotting pilings near the shore hinted at the presence of a bridge or pier in the past, and Johnny gave them a wide berth. The river had widened slightly, and in its clear, pure water they could see an occasional trout, spooked by the boat, scurrying for cover in the weeds. The fish appeared to be 16 to 18 inches long and solid and muscular.

Johnny slowed the motor again and leaned forward, squinting downriver through his sunglasses. Gordon, too, began to look carefully at the water in front of them.

"Think there may be some fish here, Johnny?"

"Have been before."

Gordon sat up and pointed. "Over there by the right bank."

"I saw him, too. Lone wolf. We want a pod of fish so you and the doctor each have a shot at one." Half a minute later, "Here we go."

Fifty yards away they could see the still surface of the river periodically broken by rising fish feeding on insects on the water. When a fish took a bug on the surface, it did so with a gentle slurp, rather than a loud splash, leaving a small ripple that quickly disappeared. There appeared to be a half dozen fish feeding in a channel about six feet wide. Johnny maneuvered the boat into the channel, directly upstream from the fish and stopped the motor when he was 40 yards away. Gently and without a splash he lowered the anchor, a block of cement on a chain, into the water, and when it caught on the bottom the boat came to rest 60 to 75 feet above the fish.

"What size leader do you gentlemen have on?" Johnny said.

"Thirteen foot, 6X," Gordon said.

"Twelve foot, 5X" said Peter.

"Not the right one, doctor. You could get away with the length, but 5X is too heavy. In water this clear and slow the fish are likely to see it by your fly, and you won't get any business. Swing your rod tip over toward me and let me fix you up right."

Peter did as told. His rod and reel were fitted with a five-weight line in bright yellowish green, standard for western waters. The leader — clear, nearly invisible nylon monofilament — extended from the end of the line. When a fly fisherman casts, the rod whips the line forward to the area where the fish are. The leader, with artificial fly tied at its thinnest end, called the tippet, turns over at the end of a good cast, allowing a seemingly unattached fly to drift toward the fish. Johnny was letting Peter know that his tippet was likely not fine enough to escape detection by these fish in ultra-clear water with almost no current. Accordingly, he added four feet of thinner tippet, or leader end, to Peter's rig, then tested the knot with which he had done so. From Gordon's gear bag he removed two small, off-white flies, the bodies about the size of a sowbug, but with a single white spiky wing sticking up.

"Number 16 tan paradun. I see you brought the right stuff, Mr. Gordon."

"I learned from you, Johnny." He turned to Peter. "This is Johnny's preference for the Pale Morning Dun, the big morning hatch here."

"How do you know that's what they're feeding on now?" Peter said.

Johnny swiped his hand through the air, closed his fist, then held it out to Peter and unclenched it. In the palm of his hand sat a slightly dazed insect that bore a striking resemblance to the flies he had just taken from the bag. After a few seconds, the insect flew out over the river again.

"That's how," said Johnny.

As he tied the flies on, Gordon and Peter looked downstream at the rising fish. On most streams fish feeding on the surface can be nearly frenzied, rising aggressively and vigorously smacking the water to suck in the bugs on the surface. The Eden River trout, on the other hand, were almost nonchalant, rising slowly and sipping the bugs from the surface of the water. Their feeding had a steady rhythm; every few seconds one of the fish would rise to almost the same spot as before and take in another morsel.

"Aren't we a bit far away for a good cast?" Peter said.

"We are," Johnny said, "But you won't really be casting to them. Watch Mr. Gordon, doctor, and he'll show you how it's done."

Gordon stood up and lobbed the fly about 20 feet downstream and to his right. When it landed, he pulled his rod to the left to bring the fly more into a direct line with the fish downstream. He lowered the rod and the line went temporarily slack, the fly drifting naturally with the current, like the real insects on the water. He stripped additional line from his reel and fed the line through the tip of his rod with a series of rhythmic wrist jerks. The line being released was under no pressure from the rod and the fly kept going downstream with the slow current.

With Gordon feeding the line out steadily, the natural drift of his fly continued 30, 40, 50 feet downstream. It was headed directly for a spot where a fish had been repeatedly rising to feed. The fish rose and took an insect from the water ten feet ahead of the dry fly coming its way. Peter and Johnny leaned forward to get a better look; Gordon's fly was in line to be the next thing the trout rose to eat.

The fly was a foot from where the fish had been rising when it rose again. Gordon automatically raised his rod tip, jerking the fly back toward him.

"Took the bug just in front of you," Johnny said. "But you got a great drift. Keep fishing like that and you'll be catching some today."

"You try it, Peter," Gordon said. "Once you get the hang of it, you should be fine."

That proved to be easier said than done. Peter made seven casts in a row, all ending the same way. Before his fly could get downstream to the fish, he got behind on letting out line. The line that was already out tightened, and his fly began to careen on the placid, barely moving water in such an unnatural way that not even the dimmest of fish would mistake it for a real insect and try to eat it.

Surgeons are not generally known for patience and tolerance of error, and Peter was no exception to the rule. With each cast and drift gone bad, he became more agitated and frustrated. After he let the line get too tight, yet again, on the seventh cast, he let out a torrent of profanity, then said:

"Why are we doing this, anyway? Why don't we move closer to the fish and just cast to them like any other river?"

"The Eden isn't any other river," Johnny said calmly. "It's so clear and the current is so slow the fish can see more than almost anywhere else. If we were closer, they'd notice us, and any problem with a cast would put the whole lot of them down. Trust me. It's better this way."

Gordon stood up again.

"Let me talk you through it, Peter," he said. He cast again and began letting out line. "You just have to be regular. Strip the line. Shake it through the rod tip. Strip the line. Shake it through the tip. Like a metronome. Make sure the line is always slack, but that there's not too much slack so you can't tighten it when a fish comes to your fly. Watch the fly and the line, not the rod and reel. Strip. Shake. Strip. Shake. Easy does it."

Seventy feet downstream a trout rose to Gordon's fly. He raised his rod to set the hook, and the fish was on.

"I think you have a brown trout there," Johnny said.

"How can you tell?" Peter asked.

"Saw his nose when he took the fly."

Gordon's companions watched him play the fish for several minutes, finally getting it near the boat, where Johnny reached out and pulled it in with his hand.

"Brown trout. Seventeen inches," Johnny said. With a quick twist he removed the barbless hook from the lower lip of the fish and put it gently back in to the river. It shimmied away, taking cover in a nearby bed of weeds.

"All right," said Peter. "If that's the payoff, I can learn this. I mean, it's not brain surgery, right?"

3

FOR THE REST OF THE MORNING they drifted downstream, stopping to work on groups of fish until they had exhausted their chances and had to move on. Gordon had caught and released nine fish by morning's end, all of them 16 inches or larger. Peter showed gradual improvement. He reached a point where every third or fourth cast resulted in a good drift. On a couple of those drifts, a fish rose to his fly, but he wasn't able to tighten the line quickly enough to set the hook and get the fish on.

By eleven o'clock the ground fog had dissipated completely, but a layer of dingy gray clouds hovered about a thousand feet above the valley floor, thick enough that it was impossible to tell where the sun was. Van Holland and his guide had passed them at ten o'clock and had gone far enough downriver to be out of sight. For an hour, the only human being they saw was a farmhand working a tractor on shore. He recognized Johnny and waved.

The temperature had slowly and gradually risen into the mid-40s by the time Johnny dropped anchor in the middle of the river for lunch. On the left bank, a large barn and corral could be seen 150 feet back from the river, with a well kept ranch house about 30 years old in the background. On the right bank a large, empty field of rich, green grass was dotted with grazing cattle until it gave way to a pine forest several hundred yards from the river.

"I usually go downstream a half a mile to where there's a big tree overhanging the river and providing some shade," Johnny said. "But I don't think we need the shade today, and this is as pretty a place as any to stop for lunch."

From the cooler at his feet he got out soft drinks for everybody, and cold cuts, cheese and condiments for sandwiches. Chips and apples from a canvas bag next to the cooler finished out the meal. The cold, the exercise and the concentration had given them a good appetite, despite the large breakfast earlier, and they ate with a purpose.

Halfway through his sandwich, Gordon took a sip of 7-Up and turned to Johnny. "So what do you think about Harry's?" he asked. "Are the new owners going to make a go of it?"

Johnny carefully finished chewing the bite of sandwich in his mouth, considering his response from all angles, like a politician at a hostile press conference. "Well, now, it's hard to say," he said after swallowing. "Pretty hard. They seem to be getting more people than before, but then I don't see the books. And I'm sure you know, Mr. Gordon, that it's not the volume but the profit that matters."

"Fair enough," said Peter, "but you've probably seen several owners at Harry's over the years. You must be able to make some kind of comparison."

"All right, but you didn't hear it from me. Don's been willing to put some money into the place, which is more than a lot of the previous owners did. If what I hear is right, it's his wife's money, but I expect they both profit if it does well. And he's been more liberal than some of the other owners about certain types of recreational behavior, if you catch my drift."

"You mean ..." said Gordon.

"Last summer, there was a band here most weekends, and there was talk that one of the musicians was selling some of the guests a few chemical concoctions that our sheriff might frown upon. I never saw anything conclusive myself, but it seemed as though it could be happening. And I do know that Don told April that if she'd like to supplement her income by providing a bit of private entertainment for willing customers, he'd have no objection. Almost seemed to think it would be a selling point for Harry's in fact."

"Do you think she did it?" Gordon asked.

"Once again, I've seen nothing conclusive, but there have been," he paused and took a deep breath, "indications. Don thinks his wife doesn't know about it, but I believe he may be mistaken. Of course it could be me who's mistaken. Harry's is a bit like a river. You can't always see beneath the surface."

They finished their sandwiches in silence. As they were about to raise anchor and move on, Peter asked, "So, Johnny, do you think it's going to snow today?"

Johnny smiled. "It is a cold day, doctor. I grant you that. But we're at thirty-five hundred feet here. We don't get much snow in the winter — never mind May. But if you want to predict the weather, I can tell you something that the local TV station never seems to figure out." He turned and pointed to the distance, where a conical mountain rose above the valley floor, its summit smothered in smudgy gray clouds. "That's Cavalry Mountain over there. It's to the northwest, and 90 percent of the time our weather comes from the other side of it. Now those clouds behind it are getting darker ..."

"How can you tell?" Peter said.

"When you've seen as many clouds as I have over the years, you can tell the differences. If our weather's coming from there today, we might be seeing a little rain by three o'clock."

4

THE FIRST DROPS of rain fell at 2:54, quickly turning into a steady, soaking light shower. Within ten minutes, the men's jeans were drenched and water was rolling off the brims of their hats. In another ten minutes the rain water was beginning to find every minute gap between their jackets and their bodies, seeping into the undergarments beneath. With the onset of the rain, the temperature dropped slightly, adding to the overall level of discomfort. Only the absence of wind and the prospect of fish made their situation endurable.

"A good fisherman doesn't mind a little rain," Johnny said cheerfully, guiding the boat downstream and scanning the water with his professional eye. "The fish don't mind it, and sometimes it actually gets 'em hungry. No, sir. Give me rain over wind any day, as long as there's no lightning or thunder."

"Good God," Peter said. "I never thought of that. You'd be dead out here in a thunderstorm."

"Dangerous for sure," Johnny replied. "At the first flash of lightning or the first rumble of thunder, no matter how far away, I get off the river and into a protected area. Being in these aluminum boats with graphite rods is like wrapping a lightning rod around your body. Bad odds."

He cut the motor and dropped the anchor.

"Here," he said. "Let's do a little nymphing." They were at a point where the river narrowed and deepened, with a channel running down the middle between two dense beds of weeds. He set up their rods with a small fly that imitated an emerging nymph, a recently hatched mayfly, and put a bright cork indicator on the line above it. If a fish took the artificial fly below the surface, the floating indicator would move, showing that they had a bite. He adjusted the distance between the fly and the indicator carefully.

"You want it nine feet below the surface," Johnny said.

"How do you know it should be nine feet?" Peter said.

"Because that's where the fish are," he replied. "Take it easy, doctor. Like Fats Waller used to say, it's easy when you know how."

Peter caught a fish on his first cast, and Gordon on his second, proving Johnny right. They drifted downriver to two other spots, and at each one Johnny moved the indicator up or down the line to get the fly to the depth he wanted. Each time the fish took the fly where Johnny had them fishing. At 4:30, he suggested heading back upstream.

"We're about an hour and a half from Harry's now," he said. "If we're making good time, there are a couple of other places we can try on the way back."

As they moved slowly upriver, the clouds were darker and lower. The forward progress of the boat took their faces straight into the falling rain, the water rolling off their cheeks, chins and noses. On the positive side, the temperature had reached a comparatively toasty 50 degrees.

A half-mile from Harry's the rain stopped abruptly, an insect hatch broke out, and several fish began feeding on the surface. Chilled and tired as they were, the men leaned forward and checked out the action. Johnny focused on the left bank of the river.

"Tell you what," he said. "If you gentlemen don't mind, let's finish the day at the office." Gordon and Peter looked at each other. "There's a place here I call the office because there's almost always a nice fish working there. Not easy, though. Not at all. You up for giving it a try?"

They agreed, and Johnny pointed to where an almost sheer slope rose about 25 feet above the water at a slight bend of the river. Along the base of the cliff, there was a moderately fast current, unlike the glassy surface of the rest of Eden River. Johnny pulled even with the rise and dropped anchor about 60 feet away.

"I see it," Gordon said, pointing with his rod to a trout rising regularly a foot from shore, where the current was washing a steady chow line of insects to it.

"A very difficult cast, gentlemen," Johnny said. "You have to put the fly no more than three or four feet above that fish. That's as far as it'll drift naturally before the current grabs the line and starts to pull the fly out into the main part of the river. You also have to put it 12 to 18 inches from the cliff edge; any less, and you miss the current going to that fish. It's as fine a test of precision casting as you'll find on any river. Want to go first, doctor?"

Peter nodded and stood up in the boat to get the best possible leverage for his cast. He made several false casts, gradually letting out enough line to hit the spot he was trying for. With a deep breath, he finally made his cast. The line shot toward the cliff wall in a picture-perfect tight loop, but Peter had overestimated the distance. The fly and tippet drove directly into a shrub growing out of the vertical wall four feet above where the fish was feeding and immediately became hopelessly entangled. He let out a torrent of profanity.

"So tell me," Gordon said smiling, "is this what you say when you screw up a surgery?"

"I don't screw up surgery," Peter snapped. "That's easy compared to this."

"Frustrating to be sure," Johnny said, "but don't take it personally. It's part of the game — like going into the rough when you play golf."

Pulling on Peter's line, Johnny broke off the leader and fly. "Would you like to try, Mr. Gordon?"

Gordon nodded and stood to make his cast. He did everything Peter had done, but so smoothly there seemed to be almost no effort involved. He was spot-on. The fly landed a foot from the bank and two and a half feet above where the fish had been rising, and in a second the trout took it.

"I think you have another Brown," Johnny said, as Gordon worked the fish closer to the boat.

"Don't tell me," Peter said. "You saw his nose when he took the fly."

Several minutes later, Gordon had brought in a 20-inch Brown trout. Johnny scooped it out of the water with his bare hand, twisted the hook out of its upper lip with a confident snap of the wrist, and put the fish back in the river, where it swam back in the direction of the office. They realized it had started raining again.

"What say we call it a day, gentlemen?" Johnny said. "That was a mighty fine piece of fishing. You'll not make a better cast today. Perhaps not all year. That's the memory you want to take back to your cabin."

No one argued with that, and they motored back to Harry's.

5

BACK AT THE CABIN, they tossed a coin for first shower, and Gordon won. It made him feel much better, but the day in the rough weather had left a nagging inner chill that the hot water couldn't entirely soak away. After drying off, he put on khakis and a blue button-down shirt. Undressing for his own shower, Peter took notice.

"Pretty snappy for Harry's," he said. "Who are you dressing for — Wendy or Rachel?"

"I'm dressing for myself. Like I said, I leave married women alone."

"Doesn't mean they'll leave you alone. Remind me some time to tell you about some of the gunshot wounds I treated when I was working ER. None of the poor bastards would have had to come in if they'd had the sense not to hang around out of uniform, so to speak, until the husband came home."

"You'll have plenty of time to tell me this week. OK if I head over to the Fireside Lounge and meet you when you're ready?"

Peter shrugged assent, and Gordon put on a leather jacket and wool driving cap. He stepped outside into a darkening gloom. According to the almanac, an hour of daylight remained, but the thick clouds and rain had brought on premature nightfall. The rain had let up a bit, but the drizzle was steady enough that by the time he reached the front door of Harry's, half his trousers were wet spots, and raindrops that had hit his jacket were forming rivulets that ran down the front and back. The fire in the lounge, noticeably bigger than the day before, looked particularly inviting.

"What can I get you?" April asked from behind the bar.

"I'll wait for Peter, thanks." He walked to the fire and took off his jacket, looking for a place to hang it, but finding none.

"Just toss it on the couch," April said. "A little water won't hurt it."

He did, adding his cap to it, and stood with his back to the fire, as close as was comfortable, for a few minutes, then turned around and faced it. The heat and light of the fire were putting him into a trance-like state, and he was standing, motionless, looking down at the wisps of steam rising from his drying khakis when he was jerked back to the rest of the world by a voice almost at his ear.

"A penny for your thoughts, Gordon," said Wendy. As he turned to face her, she shouted across the room to April, "Hey, can you make me a Zombie?"

"I'm sorry," said April, with strained politeness. "I'm afraid I don't know that one."

"Hell!" Wendy muttered. "All right, make it a double vodka martini with two olives."

"Coming right up."

"Bitch," Wendy whispered to Gordon. "She could make it if she wanted to." Then, raising her voice to conversational level, "Sit down, Gordon, and tell me about the quest for Moby Trout today."

He joined her on the couch, taking care to sit as far away as possible. "I doubt it would be very interesting," he said. "Fishing's like golf. If you don't do it yourself, it's boring when other people talk about it."

"Tell me," she said. "Charles plays golf, too, and some of his friends definitely bore the living daylights out of even the other golfers. But I can already tell you're not boring. I want to hear somebody explain what it's like being out on a day like this. What do you get out of it that makes you keep coming back? All Charles ever says is 'Good day' or 'Bad day,' followed by 'caught blah-blah number of fish.' There has to be more to it than that."

Gordon was vaguely uncomfortable. On its face, her question was an innocent conversation starter, but she had a voice and a way of looking at a man that made the simplest remark seem sultry and weighted with a hidden invitation to wickedness.

"Your martini, ma'am," April said. "I recall you like it with Grey Goose."

"Thank you, I'm sure." The strained formality in both voices would have fooled no one.

Wendy took a gulp of her drink, leaving a faint imprint of cherry lipstick on the rim of the glass. "Tell me what it's all about," she said, putting extra breath into her voice so that she was almost exhaling the words. "I want to know, and I think you can tell me."

She crossed her legs and leaned forward in his direction, balancing the martini glass on her knee, and resting her left elbow on the back of the couch with her hand under her chin. Gordon realized that her eggplant-colored dress, of fine cut and fabric, was shorter and lower cut than he first thought. He tried to focus on his answer.

"It's complicated, but it really isn't," he said. "How can I put this? Maybe the best way is to say that a good day of fly fishing is as close as you can get to escaping completely from the rest of the world. You have to totally concentrate on it. You have to read the water, figure out where and how to cast, follow what the fly is doing on the water. When you're moving from one spot to another, or taking a break from fishing, you're completely in the moment, noticing the water, the mountains, the sky, the wind rustling through the trees. You can show up on a trout stream with a world of worries on your shoulders, and for eight hours, they're gone. It's like drugs, only without complications."

Wendy took her left hand out from under her chin and ran it through the hair on the side of her head as she tossed her head. "But what about a day like today, when it's cold and miserable?"

"You're still completely focused, concentrating on what you're doing, aware of now. It's like Woody Hayes used to say ..."

"Who's Woody Hayes?"

"Football coach. A bit before your time. He used to stand on the sidelines in games played in the Midwest in November, when it was in the twenties, wearing a short-sleeved white shirt with a tie. If his players complained about the cold, he'd tell them it was all in their heads, and the way he was dressed, they couldn't argue. But to get back to fishing, when you're concentrating on that, you don't think about the cold and the wind and the rain. It catches up to you when you stop, but when you're out there fishing, it's a minor distraction."

She took a languid sip of her martini. "I'm not sure I buy that," she purred, "but at least it makes some sense."

A brief silence ensued, and Gordon quickly glanced toward the entrance to the lounge. No relief was in sight, so he tried to pivot the conversation.

"How about you?" he said. "What brings you to Harry's, and did I detect a bit of East Coast in your voice?"

"Thanks for asking," she said. "Most men don't." Another sip of the drink took it below the halfway mark. "I'm here with Charles, obviously. He wanted to come, had been here years ago and had fond memories or something. I was promised cocktails on the deck on a warm spring night with a beautiful sunset." She gestured toward the dark windows. "You can see what I got instead."

"And the East Coast?"

"Right again. Upstate New York. Syracuse, if you have to know. Grew up in a conservative, Catholic family, went to the U, got bored and dropped out for a year and a half, kicked around in some jobs. Three years ago I parked my car on the street one night in February and went in to work the evening shift. When I came out a few hours later, two feet of snow had fallen and I couldn't find the car. I had to walk two miles home. That was it. As soon as the snow melted, and it took two fricking weeks, I packed a suitcase, threw it in the trunk of the car and started out for California. A friend who lived just outside San Francisco let me have her couch for a bit, and I found a help wanted ad for a receptionist at Charles's office. The rest, as they say, is history."

Gordon tried to think of a way to lead up to the obvious question, but everything he came up with lacked class, tact, sensitivity, or all three. Abhorring a silence, Wendy saved him the trouble.

"His wife didn't understand him," she said. "They used to have awful, screaming arguments over the phone. One day she called, and when I told her he wasn't in (and he really wasn't), she read me the riot act. When Charles found out about it, he took me out to lunch to make up for it. I guess that was our first date. The divorce was final the day before Thanksgiving last year. We got married the first Friday in December and honeymooned in Maui for two weeks. More to my liking than this."

"Maui's nice," Gordon said, trying to process the story. He was spared further reflection when the front door to the lodge opened, and Charles Van Holland came in. He looked at the two of them on the couch with an impassive face, and Gordon was overcome with a pang of guilt, as though he'd been caught naked in someone else's bedroom.

"There you are, darling," Wendy said, standing up. "Mr. Gordon was just telling me *all* about his day fishing. I hope you had a better day than he did." She turned slightly toward Gordon and winked at him with the eye that was out of her husband's view. Gordon rose as well.

"I probably owe your wife an apology," he said. "I tend to ramble when you get me going about fishing."

Van Holland cracked a slight smile and appeared to relax. "That's quite all right. So do I. She'll get used to it if she hasn't already."

Wendy crossed the room, threw her arms around her husband and gave him a kiss at the line where his jaw met his throat, making him squirm with pleasure.

"Are we going to have dinner now, darling? I'm famished."

"Sure," he said. "I'm pretty hungry, too." Then to Gordon, "See you in the dining room."

Gordon waved at them as they left, then sat down on the couch, leaned his head back, and stared at the ceiling. He was focusing on the texture of a massive crossbeam when April showed up at his side with a glass of red wine in her hand.

"On the house," she said, "to celebrate your narrow escape."

"Thank you," Gordon croaked.

"You shouldn't take her attention personally. No one does, except her husband."

She turned back to the bar, and seconds later the front door opened again as Peter came in. Gordon rose and headed to the bar to meet him.

"You took long enough," he said.

"I didn't exactly get warm right away," Peter said. A whiff of alcohol came from him, and Gordon realized he'd sneaked a drink before heading over to the lodge. Peter turned to April.

"I don't suppose there's any chance on earth you know how to make a Zombie?"

"Coming right up," she said.

6

THE MINUTE ALAN AND DREW came through the front door everyone in the building could hear them. Gordon and Peter, having met up with Johnny in the lounge, were about to go in for dinner when the door opened.

"Twenty two inches, Drew. I'm telling you that rainbow was 22 inches if it was one. Best fish of the day.

"You're hallucinating, Alan. I give it 18, max."

"You'd never pass for an eagle, my friend. I say 22."

"Of course if you hadn't let it slip out of your net, we could have taken a measurement and we wouldn't be having this argument."

"You don't want to be holding on to a fish too long, my friend. Now that net is 21 inches from handle to tip, and the fish was a bit longer than the net when I took him out and he squirmed out of my hands. Biggest fish of the day."

"Good fishing, today?" Peter asked unnecessarily.

"Pretty good," Drew said. "Maybe not as good as Alan thinks, but pretty good."

"You were on the Big Hole?" Gordon asked, and when Alan nodded, he continued, "Where were you fishing, and what did you catch him on?"

Alan needed no additional encouragement. "We walked down at the public access area by Holohan Road," he said. "Good pocket water. Nothing rising. Worked nymphs. Caught him on this #8 Golden Stone."

He reached into his shirt pocket and removed a fly, which he extended toward Gordon, Peter and Johnny in the palm of his hand. The men looked at it as if they had been shown photographs of a singularly ugly baby and asked for comment.

"That's a golden stonefly, all right," murmured Johnny. "A reliable standby on the Big Hole. Indeed it is. You chose your fly well."

"Just guessing now," Peter said, "but is that the exact fly you caught your fish with?"

"Sure is. Any time I catch a fish 20 inches or bigger — and this one was 22 no matter what some people (he glared at Drew) might say — I save the fly and have it framed and mounted on the wall in my home office. My goal in life is that when I die, there won't be a square inch of blank wall left in that den."

There was a moment of silence as that sank in, then Peter said, "It's a lucky man who knows what he wants in life."

"Guys, this is getting a bit weird," April said. "Anybody want to be seated for dinner?"

"Sure," said Drew. "Anything to get Mister 22 Inches off topic. You suppose you could throw your weight around and get us a window table?"

"As any gentleman can see, I don't have much weight to throw around. But since almost nobody's here, sit wherever you want."

Charles and Wendy were seated at the corner window table, with Wendy looking at the dining room entry and Charles with his back to them. Drew and Alan took the table next to the Van Hollands. As they got to the table, Drew looked over at Wendy and nodded his head. In response, she arched her eyebrows provocatively. Charles, looking down at his salad, saw nothing.

April, who had followed them to the table, asked, "Can I get you anything to drink?"

"Double Johnnie Walker Red, rocks for me. Usual, Alan?" He nodded.

"Double Red rocks, and a Seven and Seven," April said, making a note. "Be right back."

"Take your time, beautiful," said Drew, giving her what he no doubt considered a playful pat on the butt. Gordon saw a look flash across her face and vanish in an instant, and he remembered what Johnny had said earlier in the boat. He couldn't quite read the look — it had come and gone so fast. Was it annoyance, which she seemed to show Drew the night before, or might it have been a slight flash of pleasure at her sexuality being noticed by Drew. She was at an age, Gordon thought, where moods could shift faster than Paradise Valley weather.

"Anywhere you like," she said, as she passed Gordon's party on her way to the bar. "I'll be right back."

They moved in and took a table for four set back from the window, and placed between the Van Hollands and Alan and Drew's table. Wendy flashed a quick smile in Gordon's direction, and Charles looked up and turned around.

"How'd it go today?" he asked.

"Pretty good," Gordon said. "Could have asked for a little better weather, but the fish were feeding most of the day."

"Johnny take you to the office?"

Gordon looked at the guide, then back at Charles. "Yeah. Right at the end of the day."

"Either of you make the cast?"

"Gordon did," said Peter after a brief silence. "Came away with a nice Brown."

"Good for you. I could probably do it one time out of 20, but I haven't used up my 20 tries yet."

"You've got the technique, sir," said Johnny. "That you do. I'll bet you make that cast tomorrow."

"God!" snapped Wendy. "Do you use that line on everybody? Just tell them what they want to hear?"

"Wendy ..." Charles said.

Johnny's face had reddened more than his drink alone could account for, and he was gripping his glass tightly. He swallowed and took a deep breath before replying.

"Actually, no, ma'am. When I've been out with someone for half an hour, I know if they have a chance of making that cast. If they don't, well, I don't take them to the office. They'd just get angry at me, and that's a fact."

Before the ensuing silence became too awkward, Don came in from the kitchen and positioned himself between Gordon's table and Drew and Alan's.

"How are you gentlemen doing tonight?" Looking at Drew and Alan, "Can I get you something to drink?"

"Right here," said April, coming in behind him. She stopped next to Alan and set down his drink, then leaned across the table to give Drew his. Her top slid down enough to show all of the tattoo above her breast. Drew looked right at it.

"All right then," Don said. "We get fish in from San Francisco Mondays and Thursdays, so I have some really nice halibut tonight. We do it with a lemon caper sauce, rice and steamed vegetables. And our other special is chicken cacciatore over fettucine. Of course the steaks are good, as always. Sharon or I'll be back in a few minutes to take your order."

He moved over to the Van Holland table and stood by Charles.

"And your order should be up in just a couple of minutes. Can I get you another drink?"

"I think we're good," said Charles.

"Actually, I'd like another glass of wine for dinner," Wendy said.

Charles glared at her but said nothing. After a few seconds, Don said, "Very good, Mrs. Van Holland. I'll have April take care of that."

"Thank you," purred Wendy. "You're so good at taking care of your customers."

Don backed away from the table, then turned and walked briskly toward the bar, passing Sharon without a word as she entered the room. She turned and looked at him before moving on to the guests.

"You gentlemen ready to order, or do you need a few more minutes?" she said at Gordon's table. They ordered dinner, Gordon having the halibut, Johnny the chicken, and Peter a steak, medium rare.

"Thank you," Sharon said scooping up the menus. "Sorry you had such a miserable day today. It's supposed to clear up tomorrow."

"It wasn't that miserable," Gordon said. "We were catching fish, anyway."

"That helps, I guess. Feel free to stick around and thaw out in the lounge after dinner."

"I won't need much persuading," Peter said.

Rachel and Stuart came into the dining room, with April trailing them, holding Wendy's glass of wine.

"There she is!" Alan said. "My witness. You were just downstream when I caught that fish on the golden stone. Did it look like 22 inches to you?"

Rachel hesitated a second or two before replying. "I was too far away to get a size, but it was a really nice fish. It looked like it could have been anywhere from 18 to 24 inches."

"Always the politician," muttered Stuart.

"See! She said 24 inches."

"Alan," said Drew, "she said 18 to 24. She's letting us both be right."

Wendy took a swallow of her wine and set the glass down hard as April walked away.

"For God's sake," she said. "Why don't we just talk about religion or politics? There'd be less arguing." She shook her head. "Arguing about fish!"

Her observation temporarily brought all conversations to a standstill. It was after sunset and utterly dark outside, and through the picture windows and the illumination of the porch lights, everyone could see the rain coming steadily down.

7

"I DON'T KNOW how much more of this social stimulation I can take," Peter said, as they undressed for the night, back in their cabin. The rain had let up somewhat since dinner but was still coming down in a hard, steady drizzle.

"I thought we were here for the fishing," Gordon said.

"All-day showers, no extra charge. You really think it'll clear up tomorrow?"

"I don't know, Peter. The weathermen don't get it right half the time, so how should I know?"

"A little grumpy, aren't we? I think you're feeling the strain from being around the ex-girlfriend, who, if I'm not mistaken, still fancies you a bit."

"It's not Rachel who worries me. She'll do the right thing. Wendy, on the other hand, is an explosive device on a short fuse. I'm glad she's only going to be around one more night."

"April told me about the Dorothy Malone act she pulled before dinner. I'd have paid money to see how you handled that."

"Not as well as I should have, but as we say in basketball, no harm, no foul."

"At some of the ERs I've worked, the playground basketball rule was no autopsy, no foul." He pulled the bottle of cognac from his suitcase and poured three fingers. "Join me in a nightcap?"

Gordon waved him away, and Peter took a couple of contemplative sips.

"So what do you think, Gordon. April. Does she or doesn't she?"

"What — dye her hair?"

"You're being deliberately obtuse. Do you think she hooks?"

After a long pause, Gordon replied, "I hope not. I think she's a smart young woman."

"Agreed, but smart people make bad decisions. Take my second wife. A bad decision by both of us, but luckily we live in a highly civilized society, one that allows people to correct their mistakes, so we were able to complete the marriage and move on."

Peter took another sip.

"Want to know what I think about April?" Gordon threw up his hands in resignation. "I think she's a Voltaire hooker."

"You lost me there."

"Well Voltaire said, or maybe it was Pascal or David Hume … anyway, one of those enlightenment gentlemen said, 'Once, a philosopher. Twice, a pervert.' I think she tried it once, just to say she did. Being a philosopher, so to speak, but not a pervert. And if I'm right, and if there's a just and compassionate God, about which I have my doubts, I can't imagine He'd hold it against her. I mean, stuck out here at her age, what can she do?"

"Get married or move on."

"Here's to Paradise Valley, land of opportunity." He lifted his glass and finished it.

"Get some sleep and save your breath, Peter. Tomorrow, we're walking around, not sitting in a boat all day. And if they're wrong about the weather, we'll be doing it in the rain."

Tuesday May 9

1

"THEY" WERE WRONG about the weather. The sun rose unseen behind a thick canopy of dark clouds, and Gordon and Peter were awakened by a fierce squall, with gusts of wind that whistled around the cabin. It stopped raining before they left for breakfast, but halfway to the lodge another squall hit, leaving them drenched by the time they reached the front door.

Sharon escorted them to their seats and told them not to worry about dripping rain water on the floor. "On a day like this, we just keep the mop handy," she said. Rachel and Stuart were sitting at a window table, and the Van Hollands were at the next one, talking with their neighbors. Gordon and Peter sat at a third table that formed a triangle with the other two.

Sharon poured them each a cup of coffee.

"Where's April?" asked Peter.

"Off. This is her half-day today. She'll be back by five, though. Any questions about the buffet?"

They shook their heads.

"Where are you boys fishing today?"

"Hubbard Meadows," Gordon said.

"I'm afraid I don't know that one."

"It's part of a working cattle ranch, not too far from Pinewood."

"Quite a ways from here. Probably why I don't know it and why you asked for a box lunch today." Gordon nodded. "We're happy to do that for you."

She walked off, and as she did, Van Holland broke off his conversation with Stuart and Rachel, stood up and extended his hand to Gordon.

"I'm afraid I owe you an apology. Mrs. Adderly was telling me that you were quite the basketball player at Cal, and I didn't even recognize your name when we met on Sunday night."

"I told you he looked like a basketball player," said Wendy.

"I know, darling, but I thought you were just saying that because Mr. Gordon is tall." Then, to Gordon, "I gather you were all-conference. You must have been very good."

Gordon shrugged. "It was a long time ago. Not many people remember any more. I hardly do."

"I'm afraid I'm more of a football fan than a basketball fan," Van Holland said.

"You a Cal man?"

"Go, Bears!"

"I find it a bit hard to believe that you've forgotten it all, Gordon," Stuart said. "When a man gets to be really good at something, it usually becomes a part of him for the rest of his life."

"That's probably true, but it's not the main thing I do any more. I really don't think about it all that much."

"Coach Simmons," said Rachel, referring to Cal's women's basketball coach, "used to tell us you were one of the smartest players she'd ever seen. She had us watch the way you anticipated what was going to happen and got into the right position. She said we could learn a lot from you."

"Really. You never said anything about that at the time."

"But, darling, back then your ego didn't need any more inflating."

Stuart twitched noticeably at the "darling," and Wendy shot Rachel a look of understanding. Peter bit his lower lip and turned his head away from Gordon to look out the window. Van Holland soldiered on with the conversation.

"So did you mean by that," he said, looking at Rachel, "that if the other team had a player who was good at driving the baseline, Gordon would be assigned to stop him from doing it?"

"Well, actually," said Gordon, "you're not supposed to let anybody drive the baseline. The trick is knowing where you are, how fast the other guy is, and knowing what point you can beat him to so you can stop or slow down his drive."

"And how do you figure that out, when there's almost no time to react?"

"It's like Fats Waller says. It's easy when you know how." Rachel, Peter and Stuart laughed. Wendy frowned.

"Who's Fats Waller?" she asked.

"Jazz musician, my dear," her husband said. "Famous in his day, but probably not who you listen to."

"Hmm," said Peter. "Didn't he write *Ain't Misbehavin'*?"

Alan and Drew walked in, talking loudly at each other and ending the need for an answer.

"Look, Alan ," Drew said, "I like fishing as much as the next guy, but the whole idea is that it's supposed to be fun. Being soaking wet and freezing cold for eight hours isn't my idea of fun."

"You can't be serious," said Alan . "Don't you understand what this weather means?"

"Aside from frostbite?"

"No! No! No! It means we could have a Green Drake hatch."

Drew looked at him without saying a word.

"You've never fished a Green Drake hatch?" Drew shook his head. "Let me show you." Alan reached into his shirt pocket and pulled out a small plastic box filled with trout flies, taking from it a large dull green dry fly. "This is a Green Drake, and when they hatch, which is in the rain a lot, the fish go crazy. Pow! Pow! Pow! They're coming up to the surface and just *clobbering* those flies. It's some of the most exciting trout fishing there is."

"You're right about that," said Johnny, coming in. "Indeed you are. And I'm hoping Mr. Van Holland will be in a position to enjoy it later today. Are you about ready, sir, not that there's any hurry?"

"About five minutes, if that's OK."

"Green Drake, Drew " said Alan. "I told you so. Let's get some breakfast and hit the river."

"I'll give it half a day," said Drew as Alan walked toward the buffet. He lowered his voice and continued, "You gotta love Alan. I mean, if you took him into a stable full of shit, he'd just grab a shovel and start digging away, all the while going, 'Oh boy, oh boy! There has to be a pony in here somewhere.' " Everyone laughed, and he winked at Wendy. "See you later," as he followed Alan.

72

Van Holland turned to his wife. "I guess this weather probably isn't changing your mind about coming along with me today?"

"Oh, Charles, I'm sorry. If it was warmer and not raining, you know I would. But go on by yourself and have a good time. I want you to be happy."

"All right, darling." He stood up. "I love you." He leaned over to kiss her, and as he did, she pulled his head to her face and gave him a long, passionate kiss. He shook his head when it was over, mumbled, "See you tonight," and left.

Gordon and Peter made a beeline for the buffet, trying to get away from the scene. When they returned to their table a few minutes later, Rachel and Stuart had left, and Wendy was standing to leave and talking to Sharon.

"I'm really surprised about that," Sharon said. "Those heaters are nearly new. I'm sure it can be fixed pretty easily. Don will take a look right after breakfast."

"Thank you so much," Wendy said. She started to leave the dining room, then turned around to face Gordon, Peter, Alan and Drew."

"Ciao, guys," she said, blowing them all a kiss. "See you tonight," she paused briefly, "if not sooner."

Drew and Alan rose to go to the buffet, and when they were out of earshot, Peter leaned forward and said in a low voice, "Well, what's your take on that marathon kiss?"

"I don't have one," Gordon said. "I was trying not to look."

"Want to know what I think?" He checked to make sure the other men were still at the buffet. "Charles was flustered enough that I don't think that was standard fare for him. My guess is that it was a preview of coming attractions for Drew if he decides to quit fishing early today."

Drew and Alan were heading back to their table. Peter sat up straight, looked out the window, and said, in a slightly louder than normal voice:

"Yep, looks like it's going to be another cold, wet one today."

AFTER BREAKFAST, Gordon and Peter drove south from Harry's to the state highway and turned east. The road was mostly straight, and despite the bad weather, they made good time. In 30 miles they passed through three towns, all considerably smaller and more hardscrabble than Eden Mills. Most consisted of a gas station and general store (sometimes combined), a motel with one or two cars in the parking lot, and an auto salvage yard. Pershing, the largest town, had an elementary school that looked as if it would strain to hold 200 students. The towns clung to the ribbon of lightly traveled road as if it were a lifeline, though clearly an insufficient one.

Just past the third town, Gordon turned south on to County Road A17. For the first mile it skirted a large meadow filled with grazing cattle, then entered a long stretch of dense forest on both sides of the road. With the sun behind the clouds and no landmarks visible through the trees, it was hard to get a bearing. Peter broke the silence of the previous 15 minutes.

"So, the place we're going?"

"Hubbard Meadows. Named for the creek that runs through it, which in turn was named after a pioneer settler, Gregory Hubbard. Came east from Connecticut to get rich in the Gold Rush and pretty quickly came to realize he could do a lot better by raising cattle to feed the miners. The meadow is part of a ranch that's been in the family ever since."

"And how did we get invited?"

"We didn't. The Fisherman's Friend negotiated a deal to lease angling rights to the meadows, beginning this season. We're probably just about the first members of the public to fish here, well, since Hubbard acquired the land. Up to now, it's only been family and some of the cowhands fishing it for more than a hundred years. There's two and a half miles of spring creek full of wild brown, rainbow and brook trout."

"Now that it's open to the public, how many people are going to be there?"

"Not many. They only allow six rods per day, and on a weekday this early in the season, we may have it all to ourselves. Plenty of elbow room, even if we don't. Here. Grab those papers stapled together on the back seat and help me navigate."

Peter reached back and got the papers, put together by the outfitters, and flipped through them until he came to a map. It was a black and white photocopy of a USGS survey, with the path to the meadows marked with yellow highlighter.

"It looks like we make a left turn somewhere ahead, just before we get to a cemetery. I guess the cemetery's before the town, so we don't actually go into Pinewood."

"That's what it looked like to me."

"No matter. The cemetery's probably livelier than the town. Then it looks as if we take several different roads to the meadows. I don't suppose they're very good roads."

"Probably not."

They saw the cemetery a few minutes later, as the Cherokee came around a bend. Gordon slammed on the brakes and made a sharp left turn to get onto a dirt road, about a car and a half wide, that followed a chain-link fence marking the border of the burial ground. After a few hundred feet, they were past the cemetery, and the road began to rise, clinging to the side of a cliff on their right. It soon leveled off, leaving a drop of about a hundred feet on their left. Gordon slowed to 15 mph.

"The directions say to watch out for logging trucks," Peter said. "I guess that's so you can say one last prayer when you see one, 'cause there's no room for a logging truck and anything else on this road. Anyway, about a mile ahead, it looks like we take the left fork."

The road stopped skirting the cliff and began following what looked like a wide ridge top, heavily forested, with no clear view to either side. A few moments later, they saw the fork in the road. Just as they got to it, a logging truck, hauling eight enormous tree trunks behind it, roared out of the left fork at about 35 mph. Gordon was barely able to swerve on to the right fork and avoid it. The driver honked his horn at them.

Stopped in the middle of the road for a minute, they calmed down. Gordon shifted into reverse and backed slowly down to the fork and turned on to the left branch. They drove on alone, slowly, over a rough, muddy and rutted road, for another mile and a half, gradually descending. From time to time, they could see what looked like a meadow through the trees. At the bottom of the grade, they came to open meadow, with a road running off to the right, following the tree line.

"Says we turn right here," Peter said.

The road paralleled the edge of the meadow for about half a mile before reaching a padlocked fence with a cattle guard. Peter squinted at the directions.

"The key to the lock is supposed to be on the back side of the tree with the blue paint mark," he said.

"Right there," Gordon pointed to a tall pine just up the embankment on their right. Peter hopped out of the car and started toward the tree, but just before reaching it slipped on the muddy earth, landed on his chest and slid back down to the Cherokee. He unleashed a thirty-second burst of imaginative obscenity.

"I'm impressed," Gordon said. "Now get the key and unlock the gate." Treading more carefully, Peter did so, then replaced the key and snapped the lock shut after Gordon had driven through. A quarter mile ahead, they came to a turnout with a graveled-over parking area, empty save for a battered Chevy pickup of early 1980s vintage.

As they pulled in, a man climbed out of the pickup. He was in his fifties, wearing jeans, boots, and a checked flannel shirt under a heavy jacket. When he removed the Stetson he was wearing, he looked like an older, grayer version of John F. Kennedy.

"Bob Hubbard," he said extending his hand. "You must be the Gordon party."

"That's right. I'm Gordon, and this is my friend, Peter Delaney."

"Welcome to Hubbard Meadows," he said. "You're the first people to fish here since we signed the lease, so I wanted to be here to greet you."

Gordon surveyed the scene. The meadow was a half-mile wide and extended nearly two miles beyond the parking area, though it was fenced at some point in the distance. A stream about 20 feet wide ran through it in serpentine fashion, with a number of horseshoe bends. Downstream from them, a clump of cattails hugged the creek on the opposite bank, and a lone red winged blackbird flew over them, fighting the wind blowing against him. Aside from the wind and the slight tinkle of running water, there was no noise, and aside from the parking area, the two trucks, and the fence in the distance, there was no sign of human activity.

"Thank you," Gordon said. "That's very kind. This is a beautiful place."

"We like it."

"Can you tell us anything about the fishing?"

"Afraid not. Don't fish much myself. Too busy working." He looked out over the meadow and the stream. "A lot of 'em in there for a creek this small. You should do all right."

"We really appreciate your opening this place up."

Hubbard shrugged. "Business decision. We'll see how it goes. The meadow's still pretty wet from the winter. Deep mud some places. Muskrat holes, too. Probably no need to worry about rattlesnakes yet. Too cold and wet. Well, good luck to you." He shook their hands again and drove off in the truck.

"Let me guess," said Peter. "His nickname's Gabby."

"Nice of him to come all the way out here just to greet us, though. And since we're making history here today, Peter. Let's make the most of it."

The rain started to fall again, and Peter pulled his jacket tighter. "History doesn't keep you warm," he said.

3

BOB HUBBARD TOLD NO LIES about the wetness of the meadow. Traversing it was like walking across a large, slippery sponge. Gordon and Peter were grateful for their hip waders, which enabled them to navigate areas of ankle to knee-deep water. And that was in the meadow, not the creek. At Gordon's suggestion, they walked back in the direction from which they had driven in, looking to connect with the creek upstream, then work their way back down toward the parking area.

"After 20 minutes of slogging across sodden meadow, they came to a spot where the creek ran through a gap in a barbed-wire fence. Consulting the map provided by The Fisherman's Friend, Gordon declared that they must be at the edge of the Hubbard property and should begin working downstream. The grassy bank of the stream was a foot or two above the water, and they walked along it for 300 feet before Gordon stopped.

"Well, professor," Peter said, "how do you suggest we proceed?"

"For starters, I don't see any need to wade right now. Fishing from the bank should be fine, but we want to keep a low profile. Squat or kneel when you cast so the fish don't see you."

"And what fly?"

Gordon paused and looked upstream and down before answering. "We passed several good weed beds, and there were no fish below them waiting for nymphs to float downstream. Cold as it is, it's probably too early in the day. And we're not getting any sort of an insect hatch on the surface. My guess is that the fish are hiding by the banks, waiting for something to start, insect-wise."

"So we just freeze while we wait along with them?"

"Not at all. We try to start some action ourselves." Peter shot him a quizzical look. "I suggest we start by casting an attractor fly to the edge of the bank and see if that doesn't wake up a trout or two."

"What's an attractor fly?"

"A bigger dry fly that doesn't really imitate any known insect but looks buggy and like a meal worth coming up for. If it was midsummer or later, I'd try a grasshopper, but for now let's start with one of us working a Royal Wulff and one of us a Yellow Humpy. You have either of those in a size 12?"

"Both."

"Pick the one you want, and I'll try the other. We'll see which of them, if either, works, then adjust as we go along."

"I'll take the Royal Wulff," Peter said. "Easier for these aging eyes to see."

"Then I'll work a Yellow Humpy."

"Any particular protocol?"

"Try to put it about a foot off the bank in the current on the other side. Get the fish to make a quick decision on something that's coming by fast. Cast to a stretch of water three to five times, and if nobody's interested, move downstream and try the next good stretch you see. One of us starts here and works down to that clump of sagebrush; the other goes back upstream and works down to here. After we do that, we compare notes"

"Then we have a plan. I picked the fly, so you decide who starts here and who goes back upstream."

"I'll go back up. There are a couple of good-looking spots we passed."

"Tight lines, Gordon."

Gordon walked upstream 200 feet, then moved back from the bank about 30 feet. He lay his rod down on a relatively dry stretch of meadow and began to tie on his fly. Only then did he realize how cold and unresponsive his exposed hands were. Ordinarily, he could tie on a fly in less than a minute, but it took three or four, and the brief rain shower that broke out halfway through the task made it no more pleasant. Ready, finally, he held the rod in his right hand, bent over so his torso was parallel to the ground, and approached the stream bank. When he got there, he dropped to his knees.

A slight narrowing of the stream channel created a moderately fast current against the opposite bank. Stripping out some line, he cast about ten feet upstream, but the stiff breeze blew the fly back toward the middle of the creek. Adjusting quickly, he cast again, this time placing the fly at the edge of the current by the bank. It drifted cleanly for about 15 feet, but nothing happened. He tried again with the same result. On the third pass over the same water, a fish suddenly smacked the fly. It resisted valiantly, but Gordon finally got it to net. It was a 12-inch rainbow trout, and even on this dark gray day, its colors gleamed as he held it in his hand, the pink stripe down its side standing out against the silvery scales. He removed the hook from its lower lip, and lowered it gently into the water, where it swam back from whence it came, then put his hand in the frigid water to get the fish slime off, and stood to share the news with Peter.

"Fish on!" Peter shouted, and his rod arced from playing it. Gordon smiled, forgetting the cold and gloom entirely.

Throughout the morning, it rained intermittently, and a bitterly cold wind gusted from time to time. The dense cloud cover, blotting out the sun, remained much the same all day — if anything, growing darker as the day wore on. Gordon and Peter worked their way downstream. The fishing was sporadic, and the fish were smaller on average than those in Eden River, running 11 to 13 inches for the most part. They were all beautifully colored native trout, however; most were rainbows, several were brown trout; and Gordon even caught a 13-inch brook trout, large for that species in a creek this size. When they reached the parking area a bit after noon, each man had had about 15 fish rise to his fly, but Peter, lacking Gordon's athletic reflexes, had hooked and landed fewer of his fish. All in all, it was a good morning, and they were both pleased and cold when they decided to break for lunch.

4

SITTING IN THE CHEROKEE, they ate box lunches of ham sandwiches, potato salad, coleslaw and an apple. Under the circumstances, the simple fare was a better meal than any five-star restaurant could have served, and they washed it down with hot coffee from a thermos Gordon had thought to fill at the lodge before leaving. When they had finished, they sat contentedly for a moment before Peter reached into the back seat and produced a half-pint bottle of Jack Daniels from underneath a sweater of his.

"Could I interest you in a little something to take the chill off?"

"No thanks," Gordon said. "Too early, and I want to get back on stream."

He had no sooner spoken than a torrential downpour, the heaviest rain of the day so far, began to fall. A gusting wind blew it straight into the windshield, and the large drops landed heavily on the car roof, bouncing off it with loud metallic clangs.

"Almost sounds like hail," Peter said taking a swallow of the whiskey.

"Almost." Gordon looked at his friend. "What the hell, I'll have a sip if you don't mind. I don't have to drive for a few more hours." Peter passed the bottle over and Gordon took a moderate swallow, enjoying the warmth and smoothness of the alcohol. The rain kept falling relentlessly, hammering the vehicle's roof with a steady staccato and cascading down the windshield. The flat stretch of creek in front of them, to the extent they could see it, was whipped into a frenzy by the pounding of the heavy drops.

"I guess the Van Hollands are leaving tomorrow," Peter said. "I'm going to miss them — well, her at least. She's managed to bring a frisson of tension into what otherwise would have been just a fishing trip with bad weather."

"Don't give up on the weather yet, Peter. It's seldom bad for more than a couple of days."

Peter took another swig of the whiskey. "My keen scientific mind has hypothesized that you don't want to talk about our Wendy. Am I correct?"

Gordon shrugged. "She's a disruptor, and I don't come to the mountains for disruption. So far, she hasn't provoked anything too bad, but she likes to stir things up if you will. That can have unintended consequences."

"True words. Some day I'm going to write a book about the top ten gunshot wounds I've treated involving men who couldn't resist the allure of some woman's charms."

"Is it only the men who get shot?"

"No. Sometimes it's the lady. Sometimes both of them. Never turns out well in any event. Now me, I figure we have attorneys and divorce laws to take care of that sort of thing. It's a pain, but not nearly as much of a pain as sitting in state prison for years."

"Better to choose wisely in the first place."

"Ah, the romantic weighs in. But then, you've never been married. When you've had my experience, you begin to realize that your judgment isn't as good as you think it is when you're in love or lust or whatever you want to call it. It's amazing, absolutely amazing, what you don't find out about a woman until after the ink is dry on the marriage certificate."

"And of course she would never discover anything shocking about you."

"Certainly she does. And I wouldn't have it any other way. What kind of a fight would it be if I was the only one who had any ammunition?"

"I guess I never thought of it that way."

"Take my advice and get married, Gordon. You don't have to do it right the first time, and I'm guessing you could afford to get out if it wound up being the thing to do. But it would probably teach you some humility, not to mention a lot about human nature. It would broaden your horizons. My third wife certainly did."

"That's not quite how my mother makes the case for marriage, but I'll keep it in mind. And I think the rain's stopped."

They climbed out of the Cherokee. The air felt colder than before, but after the heavy shower, it had an astonishing freshness and purity, even by the standards of mountain air. Breathing it in deeply was like drinking an invigorating tonic that sent a tingle to the toes and fingertips. The cloud cover seemed to have moved lower, and a slight breeze was wafting clouds of mist across the meadow.

"Gordon!"

"What?"

"I think I just felt a snowflake hit my cheek."

Gordon laughed. "Let it go, Peter. I hope you brought swim trunks because by the end of the week it'll probably be so hot you'll be wanting a dip in Eden River to cool off."

They moved downstream, fishing likely spots for the next few hours. Gordon spotted a couple of pods of fish feeding below the surface behind weed beds and caught several by drifting a nymph to them in perfect fashion. One was an 18-inch brown trout that proved to be the biggest fish of the day. Peter did well, too, catching several fine fish. All in all, they got enough action to make it worth enduring the cold and damp. Several showers came and went during the afternoon, but none as fierce as the one when they were having lunch.

At 4:30, Peter proposed calling it quits.

"It's been a good day," he said, "but it's getting really damn cold. I think it's time to call it a win and get back to the warmth of the lodge."

Gordon would happily have stayed another three hours until sunset, but agreed with Peter, if only to keep the peace. He had learned over the years that, on a fishing trip, he couldn't expect his friends to keep up with his passion and stamina, and that it was better to yield to them when they said they were done.

Back at the parking area, they took apart their rods and removed their waders. Gordon realized that his socks and pant legs were soaking wet, something he had put out of mind while fishing. Tired, hungry, cold, and in good spirits, they climbed back into the Cherokee and took a last, long look at the meadow before leaving.

"This is a special place, Gordon. I'm glad you found it and grateful that you invited me to join you here. I'll remember it fondly for a long time. Now let's get the hell out."

Gordon laughed. "Maybe I should bring you back in August, Peter. When it's 95 degrees in the shade, only there's no shade. I'll bet that would make you appreciate today."

"Shut up and drive."

5

AFTER TAKING HOT SHOWERS and changing into dry clothes back at Harry's, they began to feel the comfortable lassitude of fatigue, as the warmth and dryness of their cabin drove away the memory and the physical sensations of the cold and wet weather in which they had spent their day.

Walking to the lodge, they caught another break. It didn't rain, and they arrived dry. It was not yet seven, and they repaired to the Fireside Lounge for a drink before settling in for dinner. Rachel and Stuart were there, sitting on the couch facing the fire, and they motioned the two men over to the chairs on either side of them. Peter came with his martini glass, Gordon with his wine glass. Rachel was drinking white wine, and Stuart a single-malt scotch with no ice.

"Tell me all about your day," said Rachel. "I hear you went some place exotic."

"Not really exotic," Gordon said, "but new and interesting. We were at Hubbard Meadows, a section of private stream. Peter and I had the whole meadow to ourselves."

"No fish?" she asked, arching an eyebrow.

"Of course, fish. Beautiful little creek full of native browns, rainbows, and even a few brookies. We did pretty well."

"Sounds delightful. You seem to have a knack for finding these places, Gordon. How do you do it?"

"I'd like to tell you," he said, "that it took a lot of detective work, but the fact is that when the catalog from The Fisherman's Friend came a few months ago, Hubbard Meadows was listed as a new destination they were handling. It sounded good to me, so I picked up the phone and booked two rods for today." Rachel laughed, and listening to the warm sibilance of the laugh, Gordon realized it hadn't changed at all since he had known her in college. "How did you do today?"

"Pretty good," she said. "I went up to Saddle Creek and caught a half-dozen nice fish."

"A lot of people there? It can get crowded."

"A few, but not too bad. None of them were Drew and Alan so I didn't have to listen to their bickering."

Gordon smiled and turned to Stuart. "And were you along for the ride?"

"Afraid not," he said. "I stayed here with a good book. Appropriately enough, it was called *The Rainmaker*."

"The new Grisham?" Gordon asked, and Stuart nodded.

"Just out. I bought it right before we left."

"Any good?"

"It passed the time." He downed the last of his single-malt. "Ready for dinner, darling?"

"I'm starved," said Rachel, standing up. "See you guys in the dining room."

Gordon and Peter looked contentedly into the fire for several minutes without saying a word. April remained behind the bar, polishing glasses, waiting for an order.

"Can I ask you a question?" Peter said.

"You can always ask."

"This Jennifer of yours," Gordon winced but said nothing. "Is there any reason you didn't invite her on this trip instead of me?"

"Come on, Peter. We'd just had our first date when Sam had to cancel. And even though it went well, it would have been premature to suggest going off together for a week."

"But as a general proposition, it wouldn't bother you to bring a woman you were seeing to a place like Harry's?"

Gordon took a sip of wine as he considered his reply. "I guess it would depend on the woman and the condition of the relationship. Why?"

"So you *would* have a bit of a reservation about that. I was thinking as I thawed out in the shower that we're seeing three couples here exhibiting some distinct tension because one of them wants to fish all day and the other isn't too crazy about it."

"Three? Where do you get three?"

"The Van Hollands, Rachel and Stuart, and Drew and Alan."

"I don't think Drew and Alan are a couple, Peter."

"Not in *that* sense, but they're starting to bicker like a couple. Alan is more obsessed with fishing than anyone I've ever seen, even you. But I have a feeling our friend Drew has had enough after three hours. After that, he'd probably be happier having a piña colada by the side of the pool and enjoying a long nooner with a frisky and willing lady."

"I'll concede the second part of the argument."

"So have you ever stopped to consider what the lesson of these couples means for your matrimonial prospects? If you're limited to women who'd want to come to Harry's for a week, you're fishing in a pretty small pond."

"But you're making a bad assumption. I don't have to marry a woman who loves fly fishing and wants to go to

Harry's. I just need to find someone who's all right with my coming here for a week, as long as I go to Paris with her, or whatever. That's why computer dating doesn't work most of the time. The computer looks for the quick fix and tries to set me up with a woman who loves basketball and fly fishing, when what I really need is someone with an agreeable temperament and a sympathetic understanding."

Peter raised his empty martini glass. "Happy hunting."

Gordon raised his half-full wineglass. "Tight lines."

Drew and Alan came in the front door of the lodge, voices raised.

"I told you you were quitting too early," Alan said. "The fishing really picked up in the afternoon."

"I believe you, Alan . But a day and a half of feeling like a popsicle is enough for me. Call me again when the sun comes out.

"But when it's really bright, the fish go down. A day like today is when they're feeding."

Drew threw his hands in the air and looked at the ceiling. He stopped at the bar across from April and flashed her his best roguish smile.

"Hello, gorgeous. You're a sight for sore eyes on this chilly night."

"Wow," said April. "You must have gone to Harvard to learn to talk like that."

"Nope. Just the school of hard knocks. And you can cushion the blows by getting me a nice Jack on the rocks."

"Lady feel-good. That's me. And you'll be wanting another martini?" she said to Peter, who was approaching. He nodded. "And you?" she asked Alan . He had taken a small rusty spinner from his shirt pocket and was looking at it intently.

"Oh," he said, startled. "Just a beer."

"Any particular brand?"

"Whatever you got."

She poured a generous whisky for Drew, then took out a pilsner glass and drew a Samuel Adams on draft for Alan. He carried it to the couch in one hand, holding the fly in his other hand.

"I think the Sam Adams is wasted on Alan," Peter murmured.

"Boss's orders. If the customer doesn't say, give 'em the best."

By the time Peter returned to the fireside, Alan had found out about Hubbard Meadows from Gordon and was pressing him for details. Three times, Gordon said without effect that Alan could probably get on the meadows later in the week by calling The Fisherman's Friend the next day and making a reservation.

"What do you say, Drew? Should we give it a try?"

"How cold is it supposed to be the rest of the week?"

"Who cares? It's a place almost nobody has fished!"

"So you came back early today?" Peter said to Drew .

He nodded. "Spent most of the afternoon in the cabin. Actually took a nap for a couple of hours. It felt pretty good. I was working mighty hard to finish everything at work before taking the week off."

"All alone in the cabin," said Peter, and a hint of a smile flickered across Drew's face. "But I guess if you were sleeping, it didn't matter."

Drew nodded, and flashed a quick smile again.

The Van Hollands entered and went straight to the bar, but on the walk across the room, Wendy blew a kiss toward the group at the fire.

"Hi, Drew. Hi, Gordon. Good to see you guys again."

"The usual scotch and soda?" April said to Charles. He nodded. "And you, ma'am?"

"I'll have a Zombie," she said, giving April a hard look. "And don't tell me you can't make it."

April stiffened, and Charles glanced at Wendy with a look of a man who feels he's walked into the middle of a conversation he doesn't understand."

"Coming right up," April said softly.

"It's our last night here," Wendy said to the group at the fireside. "I wanted to celebrate this great trip with a special drink."

The Van Hollands went straight to the dining room after getting their drinks, and Drew and Alan followed shortly afterward. When Peter and Gordon were alone again, Peter leaned forward and spoke softly.

"Well, I don't think our friend Drew was alone in his cabin this afternoon, and whoever he was with, I doubt you could describe what they were doing as sleeping." He downed the last of his martini.

"Let's eat."

6

LATER, GORDON WOULD THINK back on what happened in the dining area, wondering what he had missed. Like everyone else who was there that night, he saw and heard plenty, but what did it mean?

As he and Peter walked into the dining room, trailing April, it was obvious that something was different. The window tables were taken by Stuart and Rachel in the far back corner, Drew and Alan next, and the Van Hollands after that. The fourth window table, closest to the door, was occupied by a man and woman in their sixties, who were working on their soup and not speaking. Gordon figured them for locals who had been married too long. In the row next to the window tables, three smaller tables had been pushed together to create seating for eight, with two of the places occupied by high chairs for infants or toddlers. April led Gordon and Peter to the table beyond the large one, which put them across from Drew and Alan and at a diagonal from the Van Hollands and Adderly-Bingham.

"This all right, guys?" April asked.

Gordon nodded, and they sat down. Peter cast a doubtful glance at the high chairs.

"Big party coming in?" he asked.

"Wedding anniversary. They should be here any minute, but all I know is they have two little ones."

"On second thought," Peter said, "I *will* have another martini."

She made a note and looked at Gordon. "You?"

"Still working on this," he said, holding up his wine glass.

April disappeared, and in what seemed like seconds, Sharon was between their table and the one occupied by Drew and Alan.

"Can I run through the specials for both of you?" she said, looking back and forth between the two tables. The four men nodded, and she continued, "We have beef in burgundy sauce, served over saffron rice; chicken kebabs with pepper and mushrooms and new potatoes; and salmon in a dill cream sauce, with wild rice on the side. They're all really good. How was the fishing today?"

Alan began to speak, but Peter talked right over him. "Pretty good. That meadow was a real find. My friend, Gordon, knows these things. We caught a lot of fish, but it was hard, cold work."

"And I told my friend here he was leaving too early," Alan said. "The fishing really picked up in the afternoon," He looked at Drew. "You should have been there."

"I was fine in the cabin, Alan."

"That doesn't sound like you, Drew." Out of the corner of his eye, Gordon saw Wendy hesitate ever so slightly as she lifted her glass to her lips. It was a slight enough gesture that even though he thought he noticed it, he couldn't have sworn to it.

The front door opened, and a little girl, between two and three years old, ran through it, shrieking at the top of her lungs, and turned into the dining area. A woman of medium build and disheveled hair, who looked barely 21, came right behind her and shouted into the dining area:

"Carrie Ann! Stop that racket and come back here right now!" The woman who was shouting was clearly pregnant.

"Where the hell is that martini?" Peter muttered.

The little girl came up to their table and looked up at Gordon. She stopped screaming, and when he smiled at her, she smiled back. He stood up.

"You must be Carrie Ann," he said calmly. "I'm Gordon."

She turned to her mother, then looked up at Gordon and pointed.

"Tall man!" she said. With the exception of the older couple, everyone else in the room chucked. Don appeared from the back.

"Good evening, good evening," he said in a hearty voice. "Am I right in guessing that you're the Peterson party?"

By this time they had all come into the entryway. The group consisted of a sandy-haired man in his mid to late forties; his wife of similar vintage, wearing a black cocktail dress with spaghetti straps; and two younger couples in their early twenties. The younger woman who wasn't Carrie Ann's mother was holding a toddler with a pacifier in his mouth, and the men with them had longish hair and looked ill at ease and younger than they probably were. The sandy-haired man stepped forward.

"That's us," he said.

"Welcome to Harry's," said Don. "Is this your first time here?"

"First time since the new owners took over," Peterson said. "We used to come here a lot when I was a kid. When Harry was still here."

"Harry was quite a guy," said Don, "and we're doing our best to carry on his tradition. Is there a special occasion tonight?"

"Wedding anniversary," said Mrs. Peterson. "Twenty-five years. We had the reception here. Carl," nodding to her husband, "was on leave from the Army. He had six months to go, but we just couldn't wait."

"Bet she had a bun in the oven," Peter said in a low voice.

"Mommy!" Carrie Ann shouted. "What's a bun in the oven?"

Rachel gagged on the water she was drinking, and began coughing and laughing at the same time. Mrs. Peterson thankfully didn't pick up on the question. Wendy looked annoyed by the newcomers. Drew and Alan looked distractedly out the window at the rain that had started again and was illuminated by the porch lights as it fell in a steady, heavy shower.

"I love kids when they're this age," Don said. "They want to find out about everything. Anyway, here's your table. If there's anything we can do to make this a night to remember, just say the word. Can I bring you a complimentary bottle of champagne?"

Peterson shook his head vigorously. "We don't touch it." The two younger men looked as if they would very much like to touch some alcohol, but fidgeted and said nothing.

"Not a problem," said Don, without missing a beat. "Then the first round of non-alcoholic drinks are on us. Our way of wishing you many more good years to come. Miss Flowers will be here right away to get you started."

April came in with Peter's martini and set it in front of him. She looked back at the Petersons just as the little boy spit out his pacifier and began wailing with an incredible display of lung power. She looked back at Peter and his drink.

"Hope it helps," she murmured.

She took orders for soft drinks and iced tea at the Peterson table then moved over to Drew and Alan's table.

"Hello, trouble," said Drew with a wink and a smile.

"It takes two to make trouble."

"Is that an offer or an observation?"

"Just pointing out you're one short. Are you going to have another drink or just keep me here asking questions?"

"That's hardly any way to respond to a friendly question. But sure, I'll have another. Alan?"

"No thanks."

"Be right back," she said.

Gordon had been watching the exchange for want of anything better to focus on, and he had a direct view of Wendy at the table behind Drew. He thought her countenance clouded over a bit as Drew flirted with April, but, again, it was hard to tell for sure.

"April Flowers," Peter said, shaking his head as she left the room. "Can you believe it? You know, Gordon, I don't generally approve of capital punishment, but I think if I was on a jury, I could send a parent to The Chair for giving a kid a name like that. She must have been teased like hell when she was little. So unnecessary."

Gordon lowered his voice. "Remember the name of the guy you're talking to. And speaking of unnecessary, you need to watch what you say when there are small children around. Bun in the oven. Really!"

"Perfectly good English euphemism for 'knocked up.' And be grateful Carrie Ann didn't learn that one tonight. They lose their innocence too fast these days as it is."

Johnny came through the front door with a large box in his arms and set it down on top of the reception desk. Don emerged from the kitchen area to get it and motioned Johnny to the dining room. Gordon waved him over.

"Thank you, Mr. Gordon," Johnny said as he sat down. "My dinner's on the house tonight. Don needed the liquor cabinet resupplied, and I was done for the day so I fetched it for him."

"Good for you," Gordon said.

"He has a room I can use, too, and I might take him up on it tonight. It's really raining. Indeed it is."

"How's it look for tomorrow?" Peter asked.

Johnny shrugged. "Looks like we'll go out one way or another. I'm hoping this storm blows through overnight."

"I think we're all hoping that," Gordon said.

April returned with the Petersons' beverages and Drew's drink. She served him first, and he said something to her in a low voice. It was apparently intended to be provocative, as she responded with an overdramatic arching of her eyebrows.

"Really, Mr. Evans! What would your wife say?"

"Don't have one, sugar. Footloose and fancy free, as they say."

"Maybe you should do something about that," she said. He laughed, and with a quick pivot she moved to Gordon's table.

"Hi, Johnny. The usual?" He nodded. "How about the rest of you?"

"I think I'll switch to wine when I finish this," Peter said. "What am I having for dinner again?"

"You haven't ordered yet."

"Right. I knew that. Well, when I do, bring me a white or red, whichever works best."

"I'll wait until I order, too," Gordon said.

April turned back toward the bar. Wendy raised an arm in a weak gesture, and April either didn't see it or chose not to. As she walked past the table, Wendy shouted, "Hey!"

All heads turned in her direction. "What's a girl have to do to get served here?" she asked.

"I'm sorry, ma'am," April said in a voice so even she had to be strictly controlling it. "What can I do for you?"

"How about a glass of your best Merlot?"

"Maybe you should slow down a bit, dear," her husband said.

"Don't worry, Charles. I'm fine. And besides, it just makes me more affectionate."

"Coming right up," April said.

The evening proceeded slowly. The Peterson grandchildren periodically brought all conversation to a halt with their own versions of shrieking, grating wails. Whenever April walked past his table, Drew made a suggestive comment and laughed at her retort. Johnny opined that he had rarely seen such a long streak of bad weather this time of year. Wendy had two more glasses of wine and seemed generally in an ill humor. Peter, sedated with alcohol, had become less voluble. Rachel appeared to be trying to engage Stuart in conversation with only sporadic success. Alan made periodic attempts to talk about fishing details, but neither Drew nor anyone else was interested.

The older couple had just left, and most of the other guests were finishing dinner when April came in to take dessert orders. She started with the Van Hollands.

"Tonight we have cherry cheesecake, chocolate death cake, and strawberry or vanilla ice cream handmade by Ruben's in Red Gulch. Can I tempt either of you."

"I'll have the chocolate death cake," Wendy said, "and a double Courvoisier to go with it."

April looked uneasily toward Charles for confirmation. He shifted nervously in his chair.

"Maybe you should skip the brandy tonight, darling."

That tore it. "What the hell's going on here?" Wendy shouted, then turning to April: "Listen, honey. I'm the customer. Your job is to serve me. And my husband isn't a doctor, so you don't ask him for a second opinion."

April stood fixed and speechless. From the tension at the corners of her mouth, it was clear she was struggling to hold herself back.

"I've had it up to here with your attitude," Wendy continued. "You've been dissing me all week, and don't think I don't know why. You can't stand it that the men here aren't just looking at you. Well, maybe they would if you took better care of yourself." She heaved an overly dramatic sigh. "Dumb slut."

In one swift and fluid move, April slammed her tray on the table, grabbed Wendy by the arm and jerked her to her feet. Wendy responded with surprising quickness and agility, giving April a hard shove in the chest that sent her flying backward on to the middle of the Peterson table. It fell over under her weight and impact, sending dishes and glasses clattering to the floor.

April was instantly on her feet again and lunged at Wendy, who was coming toward her. They threw their arms around each other, and, grappling like Holmes and Moriarty at the waterfall, crashed into Drew and Alan's table, knocking over all the glasses and spilling the contents on the men's laps. After bouncing off that table, they went down on the edge of Stuart and Rachel's table, taking it and its crockery to the floor with them.

"That's enough," Gordon said. In two quick steps he was over to where the women were struggling on the floor, Wendy on top, trying to grab April's throat, and April pushing up on Wendy's chin. He slid his long right arm between the two of them, pulled Wendy to him in a bear hug, and lifted her upright. Taken by surprise, she let go of April, who scrambled to her feet. Rachel immediately leaped forward and restrained her.

"Calm down, sister," Rachel said. "This isn't doing anybody any good."

As the two combatants stood glaring at each other and breathing heavily, Carl Peterson turned to his wife.

"Just like your cousin Ronnie and my friend Ben at our wedding? Remember?"

She smiled and nodded.

Hearing the noise, Don and Sharon had come back to the dining room.

"Is everything all right?" he said.

"It will be when you fire this bitch," Wendy snarled. "She assaulted me. Everybody in this room saw it."

From behind her, Van Holland made a "hold it" gesture in Don's direction, and when Don didn't immediately reply, her bile rose again.

"What the hell is wrong with this place?" she snapped. "All sorts of things have been going on around here, and I could tell some good stories. Maybe I will."

Gordon had loosened his grip on her by now, and she threw off his arm. "I'm going back to the cabin," she said. "Thank God, it's the last night. And don't bother following me, Charles. I need to be alone."

With that, she stomped across the room and left through the front door of the lodge, slamming it violently on the way out. Van Holland had the sick look of a man who has been gut-punched on a full stomach.

"Please don't blame April," he said softly to Don. "She was provoked. And add the damages for this to my bill."

"I appreciate that," Don said, "but let's sort it out later. If you'd like, I can put you up in one of the rooms in the lodge at no extra charge."

Van Holland nodded. "Thank you. I probably should let her calm down."

Drew and Alan quickly excused themselves. Rachel and Stuart stayed a few minutes longer to be polite, then headed back to their respective cabins. The Petersons called for their check, but Don told them that under the circumstances the evening was on the house, and they left smiling. Gordon offered to stay and help clean up, and Peter followed his lead. Don came back with two brooms and dustpans, giving one of the brooms to Gordon. Sharon came in with a mop and bucket.

"Look at this mess," she said, shaking her head.

"Cost of doing business, honey," Don replied.

"This is one thing I'll never get used to. And what did Mrs. Van Holland mean about all sorts of things going on here?"

"I think there's been a little tension among the guests," Gordon said. "And maybe some flirting. Nothing serious, but with the bad weather and people cooped up inside, maybe some of us are getting on each other's nerves."

They quickly restored the room to order, and Don offered Gordon and Peter drinks on the house to thank them for their help. Gordon asked for a small brandy; Peter, a large one. They stood at the bar looking at the dying embers of the fire.

"So you've been in the business for 20 years," Peter finally said. "What's the worst fight you ever saw?"

"Funny you should ask," Don said. "I was just thinking about it, actually. It was at Le Chat Blanc, a high-end restaurant in Sacramento. I was assistant manager and working Monday, which is usually a slow night. It was about 9:30 and there were a handful of people in the bar, including this lobbyist and his girlfriend. They were having a quiet drink, when his other girlfriend walked in on them. Before anybody knew what was happening, those two women were in a catfight, and it was a lot worse than what happened tonight. It went on for five minutes before anybody could separate them. Ten thousand dollars in damage."

"Wow," Gordon said.

"Still, it could have been worse."

"How?" asked Peter.

"His wife could have walked in, too."

They finished their drinks and prepared to leave. Peter got to the front door first, while Gordon was still getting into his jacket, and when he threw the door open, he did a double take.

"Gordon! I thought you said it doesn't snow here in May."

"It doesn't."

"Then what the hell is this white stuff falling outside and sticking to the ground? Sure looks like snow to me."

And so it was.

Wednesday May 10

1

HARRY'S LOOKED LIKE A SCENE from a Christmas card that morning. The snow had stopped falling in the middle of the night, but there were several inches of it on the ground, and the lawn leading up to the lodge was covered in white. Snow also covered the sloping roofs of the lodge, and smoke curled from the chimney of the Fireside Lounge.

The sun remained hidden behind a dense overcast. Gordon was losing faith in his optimism and wondering if there would be any decent weather at all this trip.

Peter, on the other hand, could scarcely conceal his glee at having been vindicated in predicting snow. "Do you think Johnny will take us out today?" he said as Gordon finished buttoning his shirt.

"Of course," Gordon said irritably. "Why wouldn't he?"

"Well, there's the matter of the snow, which I've been told numerous times is an impossibility here in May."

"Freak occurrence. You could live to be a hundred and never see this again. Besides, the fish are in the water, not the snow, and this kind of weather could make them start feeding aggressively."

Peter shook his head. "I'm beginning to worry about you, Gordon. You're starting to sound like our friend Alan. Have you ever actually caught fish when snow was falling?"

"Sure thing. Just three years ago, in late October, I was fishing the Henrys Fork of the Snake River in Idaho, and it snowed for four hours. I probably caught 20 fish."

"There has to be an easier way."

When they stepped outside, the air, while cold, was not as biting as they had expected. They could see their breath as they exhaled, but there was no wind and it seemed milder than yesterday.

"Looks like our diva hasn't come out yet," Peter said, gesturing with his head to the Van Holland cabin.

"How do you know?"

"Elementary, my dear Gordon. There aren't any footprints in the snow between her cabin and here. And I don't think she's witch enough to fly to the lodge. Let's go. If we're lucky, we can be on the river before we have to say goodbye to her."

Sharon, looking distracted, greeted them at the entrance to the dining room and took them to a window table. Charles Van Holland sat at the corner window table alone, poking listlessly at a plate of eggs and potatoes. As she poured coffee, Peter said:

"I guess it's none of my business, but is April ...?"

"Don's meeting with her at ten o'clock, and he told her to stay out of sight until then. I'm so upset about what happened last night."

"Sooner or later it'll happen anywhere," Gordon said. "Don't worry about it."

They went to the buffet and loaded up their plates. Johnny came in and joined them. As they sat down again, Van Holland came over.

"I wanted to apologize for last night," he said. "That whole thing should never have happened. It was a mistake to bring Wendy here."

"That's not necessary," Gordon said.

"Nothing you could have done," said Peter. "It all happened so fast."

"Very generous of you," Van Holland said. "But I'd hate for that to be what you remember about the trip."

"Let it go," Gordon said. "Everybody else has."

"I'd like to believe that. But Wendy should be here by now. I'll head over and rouse her so we can check out and go home. It's been a pleasure knowing both of you."

They all shook hands.

"Go, Bears!" Gordon said, and Van Holland smiled.

At the front door he met Drew and Allen coming in, and repeated his apology to them. Drew made a noncommittal reply, and Alan tried to help.

"Looks to me like your wife needs something to do," he said. "You should try teaching her to fish."

Van Holland thanked him and began walking out to the cabin. Gordon watched him out of the corner of his eye as he ate breakfast and looked at the river, running between snow-covered banks. When he reached the cabin door, Van Holland knocked normally, then more forcefully. Finally he shouted, "Wendy!" loud enough that they could hear it faintly in the dining room. He shook his head violently and started back to the lodge. He encountered Sharon as he walked in.

"Something's wrong," he said. "She's not answering the door."

"I'll get Don," she said.

He was out in less than half a minute. "Is there a problem?"

"Wendy didn't answer the door."

"Did you try opening it with your key?"

"No. Left it on the nightstand here."

"Let me run over. Maybe we need a neutral party."

And he was out the door, walking briskly toward the cabins. When he got to Pale Morning Dun, he knocked on the door, normally at first, followed by a heavy pounding. He shouted something they couldn't hear in the lodge, then took a key out of his pocket and put it in the lock. As he leaned into the door, it opened a few inches, and stopped. Gordon could see Don turning his head to get a better look through the small opening.

What happened next was unexpected. Don lifted his right leg and gave the door a hard kick. He did it again, then a third time, at which point the door flew open and he staggered inside.

"Peter!" Gordon said sharply.

Peter and Johnny had been sitting with their backs to the scene and hadn't seen any of it. They turned around and looked where Gordon was pointing.

Less than a minute later, Don came out the door and closed it behind him. Even from a distance, they could tell from his body language that he had experienced a shock. Rather than walking back purposefully, as he had gone out, he half stumbled back. Gordon, Peter and Johnny rose and went to the front door, followed shortly by Van Holland.

"She's dead," Don said, his voice sounding dry and parched as the words came out.

"Oh, my God," Van Holland said, burying his face in his hands.

"Not so fast," Peter said. "I'm having a look. Gordon, you come with me."

"I'll call the sheriff and an ambulance," Don said.

Peter and Gordon ran down the snow-covered slope to the parking area, where Gordon unlocked the Cherokee. Peter took a medical bag and a portable CPR kit from the back, handing the latter to Gordon.

"Fast!" he barked. "Every second counts."

They started for the cabin at a trot, and Rachel and Stuart came out of their lodging as the men passed by.

"Is something wrong?" she said.

"Nothing you can do," Gordon said. "Get back to the lodge." Still in condition, he beat Peter to the front door and waited a few seconds for his friend to arrive.

"Stand by the front door and watch me, but don't come in unless I tell you to," Peter gasped.

After pulling on plastic gloves, he opened the door, and they could feel the warm air from inside the cabin. As Peter went in, Gordon could see the legs and torso of a woman, presumably Wendy, lying on the floor, but the head was out of sight behind the bed. With three long strides, Peter was next to it and squatting. In less than half a minute, he stood up again.

"She's been dead a while," he said. "Looks like she was strangled with this bungee cord, though I'd want to hear what the medical examiner has to say. He looked around the room, taking in the details, and walked over to one of the two windows. He looked at it for a minute and shook his head, then moved over to the next window and looked at it. Lifting his bag from the floor, he walked to the front door, stepped out and pulled it closed.

"This is bad," he said. "Really bad. We now have a contaminated crime scene, in a case where the detectives could use a good one. In fact, they'll need every break they can get. The two windows are locked from the inside. The chain lock was secured from the inside; you can see where Don broke it off. When we left our cabin this morning, there were no footprints going in and out of here. So you tell me: How did someone get into a totally locked cabin, murder her, and get away without leaving a mark in the snow and the cabin locked from the inside?"

Gordon had no answer, so Peter continued:
"I hope they send a good detective out on this case."

2

HARRY ROGERS liked to think that he was a good detective — emphasis on *was*, in the past tense. Right now, he was a short-timer who felt no need to make an impression on anyone. After 30 years in law enforcement, everybody knew what he had done and could do, and he was looking forward to two milestones coming up in the next three months. On Friday June 30 he would be retiring from the Lava County Sheriff's Office, and on August 2 he would be celebrating, if that was the word, his 54th birthday, most likely alone. Six weeks ago his wife told him she wanted a divorce because she'd had enough of being ignored, and she didn't think the marriage could handle the strain of making it up after he retired.

Confused and grappling with the impending changes in his life, he was assuming the mode he adopted for two years in the Army: Keep your nose down, do what you're told, don't volunteer for anything, and don't be a hero. Every morning since the beginning of April, he had begun his work day by looking at the wall calendar in his cramped but tidy office and counting the days until retirement. Looking at today as day one, he had 37 days to go, assuming nothing came up that would require him to work over Memorial Day weekend.

Lava County was not a high-crime area. It was geographically large, sprawling from the Sacramento Valley to the mountains to the east, but its population was relatively small. Red Gulch, the county seat, had a population of 60,000 people, and another 60,000 or so were scattered around small towns and the countryside elsewhere. Murder was a once-a-year occurrence, if that, and most of the work done by the small detective bureau was in the realm of property crimes and drug production. Rogers was killing his final days on the force trying to find a pattern to outbreaks of burglaries in two of the small mountain towns and came to work that Wednesday expecting to be reviewing reports, making phone calls, and perhaps taking a drive to one of the towns to see the crime scenes for himself. Nothing strenuous, nothing urgent, and that was the way he wanted it. He was hoping to fade away in a long succession of eight-hour days.

Unfortunately for him, Eden Mills was just inside the eastern boundary of Lava County. At 8:40 a.m., he had reviewed the logs from the preceding day and had set out a dozen burglary reports on his desk for further review. He was thinking about how to approach the reports when Linda Barnes, the secretary, appeared at his cubicle.

"LaDow wants to see you now," she said.

John LaDow was the only captain in the sheriff's department. He was second-in-command to the sheriff and responsible for overseeing the patrol, detention and detective divisions. Rogers tolerated, rather than liked him, and knew better than to keep him waiting too long. He sauntered over to LaDow's office, stopping to fill a paper cup with water along the way.

"You still working on those burglaries?" LaDow said, as Rogers walked in.

Pausing to consider the meaning of "still," Rogers nodded his head, and added, "Just started yesterday."

"They'll have to wait. We have a homicide."

Rogers felt his stomach tighten. LaDow continued:

"The call just came in a few minutes ago. A young woman on vacation with her husband was strangled near Eden Mills. Patrol's on the way over, and I'm getting the forensics team together to go out." In a sheriff's department of 75 men and two women, the Lava County forensics team consisted of a jailer and a patrol deputy who had each taken a couple of classes and were minimally trained. "It happened at a place called Harry's Riverside Lodge."

"Oh, my God. Don't tell me that joint is still there?"

"Brings back memories, does it?"

"It used to be the place to go in East County 30 years ago. I just assumed it had gone under by now."

"Well, the vic was a customer, so I guess not."

"Who's going with me? Perkins?"

LaDow shook his head. "You're forgetting Sutton's on vacation, so I need Perkins here. "You'll have to take this one yourself."

"Isn't that kind of irregular?"

"Come on, detective. You know what the budgets have been like the past few years. We'll be lucky to afford the mileage to get *you* out there."

"If that's the way it is. But I don't like it."

"All right. Let's play 'Complete the Sentence.' When a married woman is murdered ..."

"It's usually the husband."

"Now you're talking. Chances are it's an open and shut case, and you'll have a confession out of him in 48 hours. Plus the deputy working out there day shift doesn't have much to do. Pull him in as your assistant, and maybe he'll learn a few things from the master. With any luck at all, you'll be home for the weekend, and our ace forensics team won't even have to testify."

"Anything else? If not, I'll pick up a change of clothes and hotfoot it over there."

"Nothing else. You know as much as I know. Get out there and work your magic. You can do it."

Rogers went back to his cubicle feeling depressed. Five years ago, he would have leaped at the case, but now all he wanted was 37 days of regular routine. Apparently that was too much to ask.

"Magic!" he snorted under his breath. "Magic!"

3

CYNTHIA HENLEY was dreading the prospect of another routine day. She had slept in a bit, knowing that she would be up late that night covering a water board meeting for the Lava County *Beacon-Journal*. When she woke up that morning, she began to think, as she had been wont to do lately, about how it had all gone wrong. She'd gone to Cal, been managing editor of the *Daily Californian,* and had acquired a master's degree in journalism. In a sluggish job market after graduation, the best offer she got was to be the East County reporter for the *Beacon-Journal.* That meant living in Muirfield, a town of two thousand about 15 miles northwest of Eden Mills, and spending her days writing formulaic paragraphs about minor crimes and her nights covering school boards, water boards and fire boards — meetings where it was sometimes hard to tell who was more ignorant: the board members themselves or the people in the audience who were criticizing them.

"Still," she said, dragging herself out of bed, "it could be worse. At least I'm working for a daily newspaper. A lot of people in my class are stuck on weeklies."

In the bathroom, she took a good look at herself in the mirror. She was 28 years old, not trim, not fat, with pleasant features, a mop of curly chestnut-colored hair, and a winning smile when she bothered to flash it, usually when she wanted information from a source. Once dressed, she would put on a pair of designer glasses, her one luxury purchase in the past two years. She had been willing to spend the money because she felt the glasses both complemented her appearance and made her seem more trustworthy when she did interviews.

Before getting into the shower, she flipped on the police scanner on the kitchen counter. Her apartment, in a 12-unit complex at the edge of town, was small enough that she could hear the scanner even with the water running. She was rinsing the shampoo out of her hair when the chatter picked up. There was a report of a dead body near Eden Mills, then a second report that death had been confirmed by a doctor on the scene, then two minutes later an announcement that the deceased had been strangled and the case should be treated as a possible homicide.

Hair rinsed, she jumped out of the shower and toweled herself off briskly. Looking outside, she could see that there was still snow on the ground; it had begun falling just as she was leaving a recreation district meeting the night before. But the road to Eden Mills should be open and she would drive carefully. After all, no other reporter would get there before her. As she dressed quickly, putting on a pair of brown slacks, a rust-colored blouse and a patterned sweater in various earth tones, she wondered briefly who the murder victim might be and felt a slight twinge of conscience about not feeling worse than she did that a fellow human being had left the world violently and prematurely. But the twinge passed. If what she'd heard on the scanner panned out, it would be her first big story in a year and a half with the paper.

4

ELDON LILLY had Zones 3 and 4 all to himself. That meant that on this particular morning, he was the only sheriff's deputy covering the easternmost part of Lava County, more than 200 square miles. On a day like today, he thought, that was probably one more deputy than the area needed.

All through the winter he had been working swing and graveyard shifts. Even in a sparsely populated, low-crime rural environment, there was some action at night — drunk driving arrests, crashes involving the drivers who hadn't been arrested, barroom brawls and domestic disputes. The common denominator was alcohol, and his brief experience on the job confirmed in his mind that he had made the right call in being a Christian teetotaler. As he drove by a church with a large parking lot, fronting on the state highway and surrounded by forest, he reflected that the isolation and harsh weather in the mountains tended to make people gravitate toward either alcohol or religion, and sometimes both.

Lilly was 24 years old, five-eleven, and of stocky but muscular build. His thick, wiry red hair was cut to a length of a half-inch or less, and his glasses with heavy black frames made him look more like a young high school chemistry teacher than an officer of the law.

He knew the area he was patrolling well, and realized that on a cold, overcast weekday like today, his primary job would be to show the flag — to drive around the vast territory on the busiest roads, such as they were, and remind people that the law was present. When he checked in at the substation, there was nothing to follow up on from the previous night, and he figured the most exciting thing that could happen this day was an auto accident. He hoped it didn't. He had no great appetite for carnage, and would much rather be helping schoolchildren cross the street at the end of the day.

When the dispatcher radioed with the news from Harry's, Lilly was momentarily taken aback. Still, he went through the checklist as he learned it in training and confirmed that he was on his way over. He knew the area by heart, so he not only knew exactly where Harry's was (20 miles away, at this point) but also what county road would offer the best shortcut to it. He turned on his flashing lights, made a U-turn on the deserted highway, and hit the accelerator.

A minute later, it began to rain.

5

WHEN GORDON AND PETER returned from the cabin, the mood at Harry's, already tense, grew more somber. The previous night's catfight had already strained relations between the guests, leaving them wondering what to say this morning. Now, with one of their party dead, shock had set in, and there was no social road map for how to behave. A sullen silence therefore prevailed.

They congregated in the Fireside Lounge and sat in separate clusters, looking from time to time into the fire, which Don brought to a roaring blaze by adding three large, dry logs. Everyone was seated but Peter, who paced nervously and fidgeted, walking to the dining room and back several times. Gordon knew that his friend's experience in emergency rooms probably gave him the best understanding of anyone present as to what the sheriff's office might do or need, and what Peter had said as they were leaving the cabin indicated a high level of concern.

Don and Sharon tried to put everyone at ease as much as possible, but it was an impossible task. Their own strain came through clearly; the murder aside, the publicity the case would bring could hardly be helpful as they tried to get Harry's back to its former luster. Alan was disappointed at not being able to head out fishing, but understood that this was more important. Drew was uncommonly low key and unsocial, as though something was weighing heavily on his mind. Rachel made an effort to facilitate a conversation, but no one was responding and she quickly gave up. Stuart sat holding her hand, looking wordlessly into the fire. Johnny shook his head and said, "Bad business," when Gordon and Peter came back, and was now on his third cup of coffee. Charles sat in the corner, hands in his face, emitting a choking sob from time to time. No one knew what to say to him.

"Holy hell!" Peter said from the dining room, as he looked out the window. "I can't believe this. Everything's going wrong."

Gordon moved over and saw that Peter was looking at the rain that had begun falling outside. Just as he reached his friend, Peter walked past him as if he wasn't there and opened the front door. Gordon joined him, and Peter motioned outside. They closed the door and stood under the wooden overhang.

"Look at this," Peter said, tapping the thermometer by the door with his hand. "Fifty two degrees. It was 37 when we came in for breakfast. Between the warming and the rain, the snow will be gone in an hour or two, and so will any evidence it might have offered. Whoever killed Wendy should buy a lottery ticket, because it's definitely his lucky day."

"How do you know it was a he?"

"Point taken. With that bungee cord, any reasonably strong woman could have done it. I feel sorry for the poor bastard in the sheriff's office who draws this case."

They stood watching the rain, which seemed to be coming down harder. Already there were a few spots on the lawn where the snow had melted, leaving small circles of grass visible amid the whiteness. Gordon could almost see the circles growing in diameter as the rain kept falling. Ten minutes later, they heard a car engine and saw a Lava County sheriff's patrol car — white with green striping and the county seal on the driver's door — fishtail down the drive into Harry's and come to a stop. The lone occupant hopped out, pulled on a waterproof jacket and headed for the front door.

"Deputy Lilly of the Lava County Sheriff's Department. I'm going to have to ask you to ..." he stopped in midsentence.

"Hello, Eldon," said Gordon. "I'm glad to see you took that law enforcement class."

"Mr. Gordon. I wasn't expecting to see you here. Are you involved in this?"

"Only as a witness after the fact. This is my friend, Dr. Peter Delaney. He confirmed that the victim was dead."

Lilly nodded. "Where is she?"

"Last cabin by the river," Peter said. "The door's unlocked."

"I'll have to ask you to get inside, please. I need to make sure nobody leaves until the detectives arrive. How many people have been to that cabin?"

"The owner, Don Potter, was out there first and found her," Peter said. "I went out to see if there was anything medicine could do, but she was beyond that. Gordon was with me as a witness."

"You forgot Charles," Gordon said. "Her husband went out there first and knocked on the door to try to rouse her but he couldn't get in. Then the owner went out afterward."

"Am I missing something?" said Lilly. "How come her husband wasn't with her to begin with?"

Gordon and Peter exchanged glances.

"It's a long story," Peter said.

"Might as well have had the whole town out there," Lilly said. "I'll stabilize the people inside and at least make sure nobody else gets near the scene."

He followed them inside and approached Don. After making sure that all guests and staff were in the building and accounted for, he told everyone to stay put and not to discuss the case with each other, not that he expected the second direction to be obeyed. Gordon and Peter followed him to the door to help orient him. As he opened it, they could see the figure of a woman in brown slacks and a sweater walking across the diminishing snow toward the cabins.

"Hey! You!" Lilly shouted at the top of his lungs, and set off after her at a run.

Intercepted halfway to the murder cabin, Cynthia Henley was ordered back to her car, where she sat, fuming. Her editors had made it clear to her that she was to cooperate with the police and follow orders from them at a crime scene, but she chafed at being put out of the way. There was no telling when other reporters might arrive, and her edge in getting to Harry's first was beginning to erode. From the parking area, she could see Lilly, in a yellow rain slicker and rubber boots, protecting the cabin area. She found herself wishing it would rain even harder to soak him for his efforts, and for several minutes it did.

6

A LESS CONVIVIAL PLACE than Harry's that morning would have been hard to imagine. With Van Holland present, no one felt like talking about what had happened, but it colored everyone's thinking to such an extent that no one could talk about anything else. Alan and Drew asked an occasional question about what might happen next, but no one seemed to have any answers. At one point, Don disappeared for half an hour, and at the end of that time April came into the lounge with a pot of fresh coffee, filling cups for those who wanted it. Gordon and Peter wanted it.

"Good to see you again," Peter said.

April looked around, and, seeing that the others were not paying attention or were carrying on quiet conversations between themselves, replied:

"I caught a break. Don read me the riot act but said I could stay on under probation and that he'd deduct ten percent of my pay to cover the damages. That's tough, but I guess it's fair."

"He must have realized you were provoked," Gordon said.

"I still shouldn't have lost my temper. I don't know what it was, but she really pushed my buttons like nobody else."

"You still have a job."

"Yeah, and when the cops get here, I'll be a prime suspect. I mean, when they ask if she had any enemies, everybody in this room saw what happened last night."

"Look, April. I don't think anybody in this room believes you had anything to do with it."

"Then who did? Everybody else here is respectable and well off. I mean, look around you. Does anybody here look like a killer?"

Gordon had to admit no one did. But then he had had some experience in that regard and knew it could be hard to tell. He took his coffee cup into the dining room and went through the sliding glass door onto the deck. It had stopped raining for the moment, but wisps of mist floated overhead in the sky, which remained as dark and dense as ever. As Peter had predicted, the snow had mostly melted by now. Gordon looked toward the cabins, where Lilly was standing watch, and tried to recall as much specific detail as possible about what he had seen that morning. When the detectives arrived, he wanted to give good answers.

The sliding door opened behind him, and Charles Van Holland came out on to the deck.

Gordon's immediate reaction was that he didn't want to talk to the man, and his second thought was to castigate himself for being a coward about it. He was trying to sort through those feelings and think of the appropriate thing to say when Van Holland spoke first.

"All right if I join you? Maybe some fresh air will help. Nothing else has."

"It can't hurt. This has to be very hard on you. I'm sorry for your loss." The instant the last sentence was out, he turned away and winced. It sounded like a formula condolence from a cop movie. Van Holland showed no indication he noticed.

"Thank you. That's kind." They stared silently at the river for a moment. "Actually, I'm not sure what I've lost. Last night I felt as if the bottom had dropped out of my marriage. I was up most of the night trying to figure out if anything could be saved. I came to breakfast terrified about what the drive home was going to be like. Guess I was worrying about the wrong thing."

"So you didn't see Wendy again after she went to the cabin last night?"

He shook his head vigorously. "I wouldn't have gone if she'd called me. And she didn't. What I saw in the dining room wasn't the woman I thought I'd married." Gordon made a vague noise in reply. "You married or been married?" Gordon shook his head. "Maybe in your generation it's not such a big deal. Leave if it's a bother. That's not how I was brought up to think about it. You've probably guessed that I was married before. After almost 30 years, it had run out of gas. My wife didn't understand me, and with the kids gone, we had nothing to talk about any more. I could see myself spending another 20 or 30 years feeling trapped."

"And then Wendy came along?"

"Wendy came along. She actually laughed the first time we went out to dinner. I couldn't remember the last time my wife laughed when we went out. Wendy was interested in what I was doing and seemed to understand what I needed. I couldn't believe it. I thought God was giving me a second chance when I was giving up on life, but it still took everything I had emotionally to walk away from that first marriage. It never occurred to me that two years later, the second marriage might come undone."

"You never saw it coming?"

"Not at all. I mean there were a couple of times Wendy had too much to drink, but she just got silly and affectionate. Not nasty like last night. I thought she was doing a good job of entertaining herself while I was fishing, but I guess being alone was putting more of a strain on her than I realized. I'm kicking myself for not noticing that."

Gordon couldn't help thinking that there was quite a bit Van Holland hadn't noticed, but he knew better than to say anything. He looked to his right and saw a Lava County Sheriff's sedan coming down the driveway.

"And now this. I mean, my God. Who would want to kill Wendy?"

"I don't know," Gordon said, "but it looks as if the people who are supposed to find out just arrived."

7

AFTER HAVING a long conversation with Lilly and taking a careful look around the Van Holland cabin, Rogers went to the main lodge, leaving the murder site to the attention of the forensic specialists — such as they were — who had arrived 20 minutes after he did. A severe downpour broke out as he was walking across the open lawn, and when he arrived at the front door of

Harry's, he was soaked and in a mood as foul as the weather. It was 11 a.m., about three hours after Wendy's body had been discovered.

Don was at the front desk when Rogers entered.

"You in charge here?" Rogers asked.

Don introduced himself and asked how he could help.

"Three things," Rogers replied. I need a room where I can talk to people one or two at a time ..."

"We have a couple of vacant rooms on the ground floor. I can open one up for you."

"Do that. Second, I've got a deputy who's been freezing in the rain out there for an hour. Forensics will be sending him over pretty soon. Can you have a cup of hot coffee ready for him?"

"Coffee and sweet rolls, too, if he wants them."

"Good. And finally, who are the two idiots who went out to the crime scene after you found the body?"

"That would be Mr. Gordon and Dr. Delaney, sir, but I don't think they're idiots."

"I'll be the judge of that. Set me up in that room and send them over right away."

The two of them disappeared down the hall behind the front desk. Gordon and Peter, who had overheard most of the exchange, looked at each other.

"I think we're about to be given a hard time," Gordon said.

"Leave it to me. I'm used to handling cops right after a crime. I'll deal with the detective tactfully."

Don returned a moment later. "I don't know if you heard ..." he began.

"We heard enough," Peter said. "Let's get it over with."

They followed Don down the hallway, past the restrooms and a service closet with an open door. It came to a T-intersection, with the lodge office on the left and a hallway to the right. There were four doors in the hallway, one of them open, and Don took them to that one.

"Good luck," he whispered.

Rogers was seated on a chair by a small writing table in a corner. He stood up when they entered and fixed his harshest glare at the two of them, saying nothing for 30

112

seconds. Gordon was beginning to feel uncomfortable, but Peter was impassive.

"What in God's name were you two jackasses doing, going out to the crime scene after the body was discovered?" Rogers said. "Don't you watch television? Didn't you realize you were disturbing a crime scene and tainting evidence that could convict a killer? What were you thinking?"

The tone of his voice indicated he wasn't expecting an answer, but Peter stepped forward and extended his right hand.

"I don't believe we've been introduced," he said. "I'm Dr. Peter Delaney and this is my friend Quill Gordon."

"Rogers," he snapped, not taking the hand. "and I repeat, what the hell were you doing out there?"

Peter sat down on the double bed and crossed his legs before delivering the "tactful" response he had promised Gordon.

"Let me tell you something, detective," he said, almost spitting out the last word. "I'm a surgeon, and I spent several years working emergency rooms in San Francisco and Oakland. Work the ER and you see a lot of things, and one thing I saw several times was somebody being brought in clinically dead, but we managed to bring them back. So when somebody who was young and healthy-looking last night is reported dead, I have to ask myself: Am I going to take the word of an innkeeper for that, or should she be looked at by someone with the best medical training, someone who might be able to do something for her, if it's not too late? If you think about it that way for a minute, instead of working overtime at being a dickhead, maybe you'd see the point."

Rogers was speechless.

"And by the way," Peter continued, "my friends don't call me jackass. They call me asshole."

Gordon stifled a laugh, and even Rogers smiled briefly before quickly retracting the expression.

"All right," Rogers said. "Let's start over. Have a seat. Since you went over to the cabin together — and we won't debate the wisdom of that right now — were you in each others' sight at all times while you were there?"

They both nodded. Rogers looked at Gordon.

"Tell me what you saw the doctor do."

"We went to my car and he got his bag and CPR kit. Then we jogged to the cabin ..."

"Did you see anyone?"

"Stuart and Rachel came out of Cabin Three, Rusty Spinner, on their way to breakfast."

"Did they say anything?"

"They asked what was going on, and I told them to get to the lodge."

"That was all?"

"That was all. Then when we got to the cabin door, Peter put on his latex gloves and told me to stand at the door watching."

"Were you watching him or looking around the outside, too?"

"Totally watching him."

"And what did he do?"

"He went over to the body, which was partly behind the bed, and kneeled beside it."

"Was he holding the equipment?"

"No. He put it all on the floor first. Then he reached out to the body, but I couldn't see exactly what he was doing. After 15 to 20 seconds, he said there was nothing he could do and stood up. Then he walked around the edges of the cabin looking at the windows, and everything else, I guess, but not touching anything. Then he picked up his bag and the CPR kit and came out."

"About how long was he inside?"

"Minute, minute and a half, max."

Rogers turned to Peter. "You agree with that?"

"Yep."

"Anything to add to it?"

"No. My friend is a good observer."

"Were the windows locked from the inside when you looked at them."

"They were. I commented to Gordon about that."

"And there were signs the door had been broken in because it was chained from inside?"

"You could see the hole in the wall. Plus, Gordon saw the owner kick the door in just before we went over."

Rogers sighed. "Well, it's not as bad as it could have been, but it's still not good. Too many people on the scene after the fact."

"I realized that when we went over, but if there was any chance she was still alive ..."

"But we're agreed she's not. And now the real work begins. OK, we know how bad the crime scene is, so I'll be talking to everybody here one at a time. Doctor, let's start with you. Gordon, you can go back to the lounge for the time being. I'll call you back later."

Gordon left. When he got back to the entry, Lilly was coming through the front door, dripping water on to the wooden floor. Sharon was at the front desk and told him to just drop his rain gear onto the floor.

"You must be freezing and tired," Gordon said. "They ordered up some coffee and rolls for you."

"I could really go for that," he said.

"In there," Sharon gestured toward the lounge. Gordon accompanied him in. April was behind the bar, where a coffee pot with a warmer had been placed.

"Hey, April," Gordon said, "can you get the deputy here a cup of coffee?"

"Ooh," she said. "Is he going to handcuff me if I don't? That would be exciting."

Lilly blushed, and Gordon just shook his head.

8

HALF AN HOUR LATER, Rogers and Peter walked out together, clearly on more cordial terms than when they first met, though with a bit of mutual wariness showing through. Rogers stopped at the entrance to the Fireside Lounge.

"All right, Gordon. Let's talk to you next. And deputy, you come along and take notes."

"Yes, sir," said Lilly, standing up, as Rogers turned to go back to the room. "But, sir?"

"What is it?"

"Shouldn't we do something about the reporter?"

Rogers stopped in his tracks. "What reporter? We're supposed to have someone up at the main road now keeping people out."

"Miss Henley of the *Beacon-Journal*, sir. She covers the east county and lives in Muirfield. I've talked to her a few times before. She got here right after I did. I intercepted her on her way to the cabin and ordered her back to her car."

"And how long ago was that?"

"About an hour and a half, sir."

"Mother of God. You mean to tell me she's been stewing in her car for an hour and a half? I don't want to see the story she writes after that."

"I'm sorry, sir. I didn't want to send her to the lodge because she could start talking to people before we did. And I didn't want to order her off the property before we had a chance to talk to her. Sending her back to her car was all I could think of at the time."

Rogers said nothing for 30 seconds, then replied softly:

"Probably not a bad decision, deputy. And at least you thought it through." He sighed. "I guess I'd better deal with her before we talk to Mr. Gordon."

"Excuse me, but could I use the bathroom?"

They turned to see that Cynthia had come in the front door and was standing behind them. Rogers looked at Sharon, who was at the front desk and jerked his head slightly."

"Right this way, ma'am. Just follow me."

As soon as they were out of sight, Rogers said:

"Go down the hall, turn right at the end, and take Mr. Gordon to the third room on the left. I'll be along as soon as I feed her some bullshit."

Rogers came into the room ten minutes later. He sat down and began reviewing his writing on a yellow legal pad, then looked up.

"The doctor tells me you're Judge Gordon's son."

"Afraid so."

"I should have made the connection. Is he doing well? I haven't seen him here in a few years."

"He retired last year, but he's keeping himself available for assignments in the mountains. You might see him again."

"I hope not, since I'm retiring myself in a few weeks. But I always liked it when he was working a trial. Didn't

116

take any nonsense. I remember about ten years ago he was handling a marijuana-for-sale trial, and I was testifying about what we'd found on the perp's ranch. The defense attorney was practically making me describe every breath I took during the raid, and the deputy DA almost had steam coming out of her ears. After about five minutes of that, the judge leaned forward and said, 'Is there a line of questioning here, counsel? Because I'm not seeing one.' Everybody laughed, and the attorney got back to the facts."

"Sounds like Dad," Gordon said.

"Yeah, well anyway, let's get down to business here. Starting with last night. When was the last time you saw Mrs. Van Holland?"

"When she stomped out of here after the fight. I take it you heard about that? It was probably around nine o'clock."

"Did you see her reach her cabin safely?"

"It was dark and raining by then, and we were still digesting what happened. So no."

"Did you see her when you went back to your cabin later?"

"No, but the light was on in hers, so I assumed she was there."

"But you didn't actually see her?"

"No."

"Shadow moving behind the blinds, anything like that?"

"No."

"When you and the doctor got back to your cabin, did either of you leave afterwards?"

"Not until we came out for breakfast this morning."

"Are you sure of that? Are you a pretty light sleeper?"

"It depends on the night, but I take your point. I was pretty beat from slogging through a muddy meadow all day yesterday, so I slept like a brick."

"Could the doctor have slipped out while you were asleep without your knowing?"

"I suppose so, but I'm sure he didn't."

"Stick to the facts. Do you admit it was possible?"

"Possible. Yes."

"For whatever it's worth, he says he slept poorly and is sure that you never left."

"Glad to hear it."

"He said something else. He said he got up to pee at 1:45 and looked out the window. It had stopped snowing, but the light was still on in the Van Holland cabin. Then a minute later, when he came back from doing his business, it was off. You see that?"

"Like I said, I was sound asleep."

"Did he tell you the next morning?"

"This is the first I heard about it."

Rogers paused and looked at his legal pad. He tapped it with his pencil several times.

"This morning, when you left your cabin, did you notice anything about the Van Holland cabin?"

"Not really. Well, actually, there were no footprints in the snow by it, so we assumed she was still inside."

"Did you notice that by yourself?"

"Peter pointed it out first. But I saw it, too."

"Did you think it was unusual that he would point out something like that?"

"No. He's pretty observant."

"That's not the sort of thing most people would notice."

"What can I tell you? He did."

"And now the snow's gone, so we have just your word for it."

Gordon shrugged. "I suppose so."

"Do you own a bungee cord?"

"Quite a few. There should be three in my car right now."

"We'll want to look at them."

"Be my guest, but I think it's a waste of your time."

"And why would that be?"

"Because," Gordon leaned forward, "there's a supply closet between the dining room and the restrooms, and the door's been open most of the time the past few days. There were a couple of dozen bungee cords on the floor. Anybody who's been here could have seen them and pinched one. You probably passed it yourself on the way to this room."

Rogers stared at him for a minute. "All right. Let's go back to the events of last night. I understand that Mrs. Van Holland got into an argument with one of the staff last night. Would that be accurate?"

"Argument would be an understatement. More like a catfight. It didn't last long. Rachel and I stepped in and separated them."

"Rachel?"

"Rachel Adderly. She and her husband are staying in Rusty Spinner."

"Is there some reason she got involved instead of Mr. Adderly?"

"She's taller and more athletic than he is. And his name's Bingham. Stuart Bingham."

"I see. Kept his name, did he?"

"She got elected to the Oakland City Council before she married him, so I guess she kept hers, too."

"A politician, eh? There used to be a lot of them coming to Harry's, but they were all men back then. So tell me how the fight started. Who threw the first punch?"

"Verbally, Wendy. Physically it was April, but it only happened after Wendy called her a dumb slut."

"And is she? A dumb slut, I mean?"

"Nah, she's pretty bright. Young and a bit confused, but basically a good kid. And she reads people pretty well. She read Wendy well enough."

Lilly coughed. "If I could say something, sir. She has a bit of a mouth, but she comes across as trying to get attention, not mean."

"Point taken, deputy. So let me ask you, Gordon. Did this fight last night come out of nowhere, or were there indications they didn't like each other?"

"I'd say there were indications, yes. Wendy was pretty high-maintenance and could be a bit haughty. April got sort of passive-aggressive with her, and I think Wendy picked up on that. But I'd say it was simple irritation on both sides — hardly enough to lead to murder."

"I'll be the judge of that, and so will the jury, if it gets that far. When somebody ends up dead right after having a fight with someone else, I have to give that someone else a good look."

"Of course you do. But I don't think you'll find anything there."

"How about the rest of the people here? Mrs. Van Holland get into it with any of them?"

Gordon took a deep breath and looked at the ceiling.

"It did look to me as if she was flirting with one of the men here."

"Which one?"

"Drew Evans."

"Any indication it was mutual?"

"He seemed to be flirting back. I don't know if there was any more to it than that."

"Was she flirting with anyone else?"

"Not that I can remember."

Rogers tapped the legal pad with his pencil three times.

"Is that your story? Because I heard she was coming on to you pretty good the night before last."

Gordon blushed. Damn Peter, he thought.

"Sorry. Yeah, she did come on to me a bit in the Fireside Lounge, but there was nothing to it. I think she was just killing time until her husband got there."

"Funny way to kill time, don't you think? But then I never did understand San Francisco lifestyles."

"I'm sure no married woman in Lava County would do such a thing. But as my father would say, detective, is there a line of questioning here?"

"Don't be a smartass. When a married woman has been murdered after flirting with two men other than her husband, I have to give the two men and the husband a good look. How would you say her husband took this 'flirting' as you call it?"

"He was oblivious. She was pretty careful to do it behind his back."

"So it may have been more than flirting?"

"Not with me."

"How about Evans?"

"You'll have to ask him."

"How about the doctor?"

"Nothing that I saw."

"Sakamoto?"

"You've got to be kidding me. If he was looking at a trout fly, she could take off her clothes and sit in his lap and he wouldn't notice."

"Back to her husband, then. Are you sure he didn't know what she was doing?"

"As sure as you can be by observing. He just married her at the end of last year, and I think he was still on a pink cloud."

"He'll be off it pretty fast. This'll all come out now, and who knows what else. That's the hell of a murder investigation. All right. You can go now."

Gordon stood up. "Do you want me to stay at Harry's?"

"I've talked to you and the doctor already. If you want to leave the property for a couple of hours, that's OK. But don't go back to your cabin until we've covered that whole area, don't talk to any reporters, and don't discuss the case between yourselves. Got that?"

Gordon nodded. "Understood."

9

THEIR FISHING RODS were in the cabin they couldn't go back to, so Gordon and Peter were at loose ends. They offered to pay Johnny for the lost day, but he flatly refused. Finally, they decided to drive to town and have lunch at Casa Rosita. It began to rain halfway there, and they had to run 60 feet through a downpour to get into the restaurant.

It was a weekday, so the girl who had served them on Sunday was probably in school. A pleasant-looking woman who may have been her mother served them. There was hardly anyone else in the place, and it wasn't long before Gordon and Peter began discussing the murder, in defiance of Rogers' orders. After going around on it a few minutes, Peter said:

"I don't think this is going to turn out to be a roving serial killer. It has to be somebody at Harry's. The dinners are going to be a lot more awkward from this point on."

"Never mind *our* discomfort. I just hope Detective Rogers sorts it out fast. I didn't like the way he was questioning me."

"He can't be sure you didn't do it, Gordon. He has to look at everybody. He was grilling me about why I noticed the absence of footprints this morning and about whether I was sure the light went out in her cabin at 1:45 in the morning."

"Which you didn't tell me about, by the way."

"Sorry about that. But once we were back in the lodge, everybody else was there. If I mentioned that in front of the killer, it would give him an edge, knowing that."

"Or her."

"I guess that's possible, but somehow I don't think so."

"Me, too. So did you rat out Drew, too, or did you just tell him she was flirting with me."

"I told him about Drew. But I just remembered something. The day we arrived, you saw someone coming out of Wendy's cabin when we were standing on the pier. We assumed it was her husband, but Johnny said it couldn't have been."

"God, I forgot all about that." He stared at his chips and 7-Up for a minute. "I don't like this, Peter. There's only one person it could have been."

The bell on the front door jangled, and they looked up. A very wet Cynthia Henley was standing in the doorway, and she immediately made a beeline for their table.

"I thought you might be here," she said. "Mind if I join you? Cynthia Henley from the *Beacon-Journal*."

Gordon and Peter looked at each other. There was no polite way to refuse.

"Please do," Gordon said. He picked up a chair from the next table and set it perpendicular to his and Peter's. "But we can't discuss what happened at Harry's."

"That's OK. But I had to run over here without breakfast, so I'm starving." The waitress showed up with another bowl of chips. "Number Two with a chicken taco, please, and a Dr. Pepper."

"So did you just stumble across us, or were you looking for us?" Peter asked.

"I was looking."

"And how did you find us?"

"I figured you were going to have lunch, and there are only so many places here. You picked the best one. I saw the silver Cherokee out front and recognized the license plate."

"You knew that?" Gordon said.

"I was in the parking lot at Harry's staring at it for an hour. I know every car that was at Harry's by make and license plate."

"All right," Gordon said. "But this lunch is off the record, or whatever you call it when you don't quote anything we say. And since we can't talk about what you want to talk about, tell us a bit about yourself."

"I'm not that interesting. Just another frustrated journalist."

"Are there a lot of those?" said Peter. "I wouldn't know."

"Oh, yeah. A lot of us got into it because we thought it would be a way to make a difference. So we ran up a debt getting a graduate degree, then we wind up in a place like this, covering water board meetings and school bake sales."

"The road to the *New York Times* has to start somewhere, I guess," Gordon said.

"*New York Times*, hell. I'd be thrilled to death with an offer from the *Sacramento Bee*."

"Is there much of a future? Seems as if cable TV is siphoning off some of the advertising, and the Internet, if it turns into what people are predicting, could affect it, too."

"People have been writing obituaries for the newspaper industry for 75 years. It's not as big as it used to be, but it still keeps going and makes good money. Not that the reporters see much of it."

"I hear you. My college roommate works for the *Chronicle* and he says the same thing."

"About the Internet or the money?"

"The money."

The three of them laughed.

"That snow didn't last long," she said.

"Not surprising, considering it's May," Gordon said.

"Actually," said Peter, "I was told by several reliable sources that snow at this time of year in this place is an impossibility."

"It's unusual," she said, "but not impossible. The weather in the mountains can be totally screwy. I've been told that five years ago, Cavalry Mountain got a dusting of snow in the third week of August. But this snow melted so fast when the rain came, it probably washed away all the footprints around the murder cabin."

"It would have if there'd been any," Peter said.

"Peter!" Gordon snapped.

Cynthia looked back and forth at the two men.

"You mean somebody was killed in a cabin surrounded by snow and there weren't any footprints?"

"Maybe we should change the subject," Gordon said.

"How could that happen?"

"Probably a lot of ways, and you should probably get the information from Detective Rogers."

"Sorry. I said we weren't going to talk about the crime."

"That's all right," Peter said. "You're just doing your job."

Their plates arrived, and they stopped talking for a few minutes to eat. The rain picked up its intensity, and they could hear it landing hard on the roof of the restaurant and the pavement outside. Cynthia resumed the conversation, staring at her plate as she spoke.

"Rogers said the victim was a younger woman here with her older husband. She must have been popular — a pretty young woman at a place like this, with a lot of men around."

She looked up in time to see Gordon and Peter exchanging glances of disbelief.

"You mean she wasn't popular? Why not?"

"For someone who wasn't going to talk about the crime, you certainly keep coming back to it," Gordon said.

"It's what she does," Peter muttered.

"It's what I do," she said. "I can't help it. There's going to be a lot of interest in this story, and I want to be sure I get it right."

"Is that because of the reputation of Harry's?" Gordon asked.

"I didn't know it had one."

"Oh, yes. Quite a history." Gordon looked at Peter. "Let me tell you about it."

With that, he launched into the tale he had told Peter at the same restaurant three days earlier. He kept it going until they finished the meal and the waitress brought the check, which he paid after saying goodbye and good luck to Cynthia Henley.

10

THE RAIN HAD LET UP by the time they returned to Harry's, and the driveway to it was sealed off by a sheriff's car and a Highway Patrol vehicle. Two TV crews from the small stations in Red Gulch were also at the entrance, mostly huddled in their vans for as much warmth and dryness as the vehicles could provide. Gordon gave his name to the deputy standing sentinel, who waved him through.

"You have to report to the main lodge," he said, but they should be opening up the cabins a bit later."

Inside the lodge, the scene looked superficially cheery at first, with a good fire going in the lounge and people in small groups reading, talking in low voices, or playing board games. But the way everyone quickly and nervously looked up when Gordon and Peter entered, betrayed the tension they all felt.

"Can I get you anything to drink?" asked April from behind the bar.

"Any coffee left?" Gordon replied.

She poured him a cup and looked at Peter.

"What the hell," he said. "I'm supposed to be on vacation. Let me have a beer."

She drew him a pint, and he joined Gordon, who had moved to a table with a chessboard on one side of the room. On the opposite side, Rachel and Stuart were at a similar table, deep in play, saying nothing to each other. Rachel was playing white, and from a quick glance it seemed to Gordon that she had more pieces on the board than her husband and that several of them were on his side, in an attack position. Drew and Johnny were sitting in the chairs near the fire, alternating silences with bursts of low-voice conversation. Charles Van Holland sat alone at a table in the middle of the room; a whiskey glass was in front of him, and he lifted it in their direction. Gordon raised his coffee cup in reply.

"I don't see Alan," Gordon said. "I guess he's being interrogated now."

"Now that would be a low-percentage proposition," Peter said.

They sat in silence for several minutes until Rogers returned with a bewildered-looking Alan next to him. Alan broke off from the detective and headed for Drew.

"Gordon!" Rogers called. "Could I have a few more minutes of your time?"

They walked back down the hall to the room. Lilly was still in his chair, and his notebook was considerably more filled up than it had been that morning. Gordon took the same seat as before. Rogers stared at him for 30 seconds before speaking.

"I talked with Sheriff Baker this afternoon and told him Judge Gordon's son was on the crime scene. He suggested I talk with Sheriff Baca[1] down in Summit County."

Gordon stiffened slightly. "I hope he's well."

"Pissed off at the world as always. He sent his regards and said you're a man who doesn't miss much."

"Kind of him."

"He wouldn't have said it if he didn't mean it." Rogers took a deep breath and looked at Lilly. "You don't need to be writing this down, deputy. So here's the deal, Gordon. I need something from you." He stopped and looked at the ceiling, collecting his thoughts.

"I can't recall that I've ever handled a case like this before. The crime scene is a hotel, all the suspects are staying here, they're mostly from out of town and can't leave yet, so they're going to be here for a couple of days talking to each other and saying God knows what.

---

[1] See the first Quill Gordon mystery, *The McHenry Inheritance*.

There's a chance that somebody will say something important when I'm not around, and if that happens, I need to know as soon as possible. But I need someone with judgment paying attention to what's being said and reporting to me. In short, I want you to be my eyes and ears when I'm not around."

"You want me to spy on the other guests?"

"I want you to help me catch a killer, dammit. You saw what Mrs. Van Holland looked like in that cabin. Did she deserve that? Does anybody?"

"No, you're right."

"I'm not asking you to take any initiative. I'm not asking you to do something by yourself or search somebody's cabin. All I'm saying is pay attention to what's happening around you, and if anybody says something interesting, tell me about it."

"I guess I can do that."

"Good man. That's all I'm asking. We'll meet before dinner the next night or two, however long I'm here. Don't hesitate to tell me anything at all that you see or hear. This case is a mess, so some little thing you ovehear could make a difference."

"I'll do that, but don't I qualify as a suspect?"

"Of course you do. And if the evidence points to you, I'll have no problem arresting you. I'm keeping an open mind. But I want someone to be paying attention, and you seem like the best bet for now."

"You didn't consider Alan?"

Rogers laughed. "He hardly knew the victim was here. You, on the other hand, sized up the situation pretty well, and nothing you said was contradicted by anyone else."

"Mind if I ask how the case is going?"

"Of course I mind. It's an outhouse full of shit. That give you the picture?"

"I think I get it."

"We have an impossible situation, a disaster of a crime scene, weather wiping out the evidence, a dozen suspects with alibis that aren't alibis, a victim who was begging for trouble and got it, and almost everybody holding back information. Other than that, it's such an open-and-shut case that the captain figured I could handle it without a partner. I should have retired last month."

Gordon smiled. "I'm sure it'll work out. Anything else?" He stood to leave.

"Now that you mention it, there is one more thing." Gordon sat down. "I'm not saying you're deliberately holding anything back, but I'm getting the sense there's something you haven't told me. Maybe something you forgot about and remembered later; maybe something you didn't think was important enough to mention. My gut tells me there's something, and my gut is rarely wrong."

The two men looked into each other's eyes for 15 seconds.

"I thought of something at lunch," Gordon said. "It happened a few days ago, and I didn't remember it right away."

Rogers nodded and let him keep talking.

"Sunday afternoon when Peter and I got here, we saw a man leave the Van Holland cabin and head toward the woods. At the time, I assumed it was her husband. But he was on the river with Johnny, so it couldn't have been him. Don Potter was in town, so it wasn't him. Drew and Alan hadn't arrived yet, so they're out. There's only one man it could have been."

Rogers raised his eyebrows.

"It had to be Stuart Bingham. I don't know what he would have been doing there ..."

"Come on, Gordon. I think we both know what he was doing."

"You're probably right. But I really don't want to hurt his wife."

"Yeah, I know about that, too. But this gives us two more people with a motive now."

"You mean ...?"

"She's big enough and strong enough to have done it. I'm not reaching any conclusion — just stating the evidence."

"Shit," said Gordon.

"That's the hell of a criminal investigation. All the dirt in everybody's life gets stirred up. Just collateral damage."

"Just."

"I'll have a word with both of them after dinner. I'll be as decent as I can, but it's bound to come out. The poor bastard should have kept it in his pants, but easier said than done."

"Are you done with me?"

"For now. Don't tell anyone about our conversation — and that includes the doctor."

"I won't."

"Of course you will. But I have to tell you anyway. Enjoy the dinner. I hear the spaghetti Bolognese is going to be good tonight."

11

THE SPAGHETTI was indeed excellent, but dinner was otherwise a leaden and desultory affair. Sharon made a point of sitting with Van Holland from time to time and trying to cheer him up, but it was a hopeless proposition. Alan forgot to bring his trout flies along and had nothing to talk about; Drew was in no mood for conversation anyway. Rachel's gift for making small talk availed her nothing. Gordon and Peter ate by the window, looking out as passing showers came and went.

Rogers and Lilly dined at a separate table at the far end of the dining hall from the others. Shortly after eight, as most of them were finishing the meal, Rogers got up and walked over to Rachel and Stuart's table.

"Excuse me, Mr. Bingham. Could I ask you to come by the interview room for a few minutes when you're done with dinner. I have a couple more questions for you."

Slightly surprised, Stuart simply nodded in reply.

Gordon and Peter lingered over their coffee as long as they could, and shortly after 8:30 headed back to their cabin through a steady light shower. As soon as they arrived, Peter poured himself several ounces of straight scotch from another bottle in his suitcase and offered some to Gordon, who declined. After taking a big gulp of whisky, Peter looked at his friend.

"So what's going on with Stuart?"

Gordon shrugged.

"Come on, Gordon. Rogers was done with all of us until you went in to see him again, then Stuart gets an encore, too. You had to have said something."

"I'm not supposed to talk about it."

Peter took another sip and kept looking at Gordon without saying anything.

"All right," Gordon said. "I told him about Sunday — when we saw Stuart coming out of Wendy's cabin. It had to be him. Everybody else was gone."

"Poor bastard. He'll break down and admit it right away, and then his wife will find out. I'm glad I'm not in his shoes tonight."

"I feel pretty rotten about this, Peter. She's going to be really hurt."

"It can't be helped, and it would have come out anyway. After we talked about it at lunch, I pretty much made up my mind I'd bring it up if you didn't. You just beat me to it."

"I suppose so."

"Are you still carrying a torch for her?"

"No, it's been a long time."

"Not even a little bit? Are you going to tell me that when you read about her in the paper, your heart doesn't flutter just a teense?"

"Maybe a teense. But it's a fond remembrance, not a call to action. I'm sure you have a woman or two in your past that you recall with pleasure."

"Those would be the ones I didn't marry. But I know what you mean." Another sip of whisky. "Not wanting to be disrespectful or anything, but do you think we're going to get any more fishing done this trip? It's awfully tedious sitting in the lodge all day."

"I hear you. Who knows?" They were silent for a few minutes. "There's something else, Peter. Rogers asked me to keep an eye out on the guests and let him know if I see or hear anything."

"If you're asking for my help, I'm in."

"Thanks. But it bothers me. I feel like I'm spying on people."

Peter finished the whisky in his glass. "Not surprising that he'd turn to the judge's son for help. I wouldn't worry about it. This is a serious business. Let me tell you something about crime victims, since I've operated on quite a few of them. As a general rule, people don't get shot or stabbed for behaving like the Chamber of Commerce man or woman of the year. They probably provoked it in some way, but even so they didn't deserve it. The stabber, the shooter, or in this case the strangler reacted to a provocation in a way society can't allow. Wendy was a piece of work, but what she deserved was a divorce without alimony — not this. I, for one, will happily keep my eyes and ears open and tell Detective Rogers anything at all that might help him catch the person who killed her. And even if it was somebody I liked a bit, I won't feel at all sorry when they're led off in handcuffs. They made a decision and they have to take the consequences."

"You're right. Eyes and ears open. Both of us. And I'll pass along anything you see or hear."

"The Hardy Boys to the rescue." He reached for the scotch bottle. "And now I'll have a little nightcap and turn in."

"Peter! You already had a nightcap."

He poured out a few more ounces of Scotch and looked at Gordon.

"Please," he said. "You're beginning to sound like my fourth wife, and I'd hate to see you pass out of my life like she did."

Thursday May 11

1

GORDON WAS AWAKE for 15 minutes before he realized it had been raining steadily. The rain had been such a constant presence the past few days that he hardly paid conscious attention to it.

Peter was grumpier than usual. "We could be here for months," he said when Gordon emerged after taking a shower. "We're in the middle of an unsolvable murder case with an overwhelmed detective. God knows how long he's going to ask us to stick around while he investigates. Plus the weather's so crappy we can't do anything. We might just end up spending the whole summer at Harry's while we lose our jobs and our friends gradually forget about us."

"I don't have a job," Gordon said, "and I'm hungry. Let's get some breakfast."

"We might have to swim to the lodge. Can we at least wait until the rain lets up?"

"Fifteen minutes," Gordon said. "Then we go to breakfast no matter what."

A quarter-hour later the rain was, if anything, falling even harder, so they donned parkas and sloshed up the path and across the lawn to the lodge.

It was warm when they entered the building, and Sharon was there to greet them.

"Would you like a copy of the local paper?" she asked. "Compliments of the local reporter."

Gordon took one. "How bad is it?"

"The story? Pretty bad. You'll see for yourself."

She took them to a window table and poured their coffee. It was just before eight, and only two other people were in the dining area. Rogers was sitting alone at a table as far back from the window as possible, but with a good view of the dining room and its inhabitants. Stuart was alone at the corner window table, poking distractedly at a plate of food. Gordon set the paper down while he and Peter went to the buffet. By the time they got back to their table, Stuart's plate looked untouched from when they had last seen it a few minutes earlier. Gordon decided not to ask and instead sat down with his food and opened the paper to the front page. The top story said:

BAY AREA WOMAN, 27, STRANGLED AT HISTORIC RIVERSIDE RETREAT

No footprints

Found in snow

By death cabin

Was It Witchcraft?

By CYNTHIA HENLEY
Beacon-Journal Staff Writer

EDEN MILLS — Lava County Sheriff's Detectives are scratching their heads at the murder of a 27-year-old Bay Area housewife found strangled to death at Harry's Riverside Lodge, a historic local landmark.

The reason for their puzzlement: Wendy Van Holland of Hillsborough was alone in a cabin at the bucolic hunting and fishing resort the night she was killed. When she was discovered Wednesday morning, the cabin was locked from the inside including a chain lock in place on the front door, which had to be forcibly broken to gain entry.

Adding to the mystery was the fact that although several inches of snow had fallen the night before, no footprints were found in the vicinity of the cabin prior to the discovery of the body.

Detective Harry Rogers, in charge of the case, was abrupt with reporters, saying only, "We're still talking to people and evaluating the physical evidence."

Asked if there were any suspects, Rogers snapped, "Everybody at Harry's is a person of interest at this point."

Rogers declined to say how many people that would be, but according to the registration log at the front desk, there were eight guests, including Mrs. Van Holland and her husband Charles, an insurance executive, plus an unspecified number of hotel staff on the premises.

It was not immediately clear why the victim's husband, Charles Van Holland, was not in the cabin on the night in question. One of the other guests said he had been every night up to that point.

The almost supernatural aspect of the murder is in some ways in keeping with the history of Harry's, which, according to local lore, has been under a witch's curse for the past 20 years or so.

Harry's was opened in 1947 by Harry Ezekian, a Sacramento restaurateur who acquired the lodge from a logging company that had been using it as an executive retreat. During the 1950s and 60s it was a popular weekend and summer getaway destination, especially with politicians from Sacramento who favored it for extramarital affairs.

After Ezekian's death, his son Bob took over the business. Gossip began to spread among local residents that the son's wife, Ariel, was the head of a coven of witches that met regularly in the dense forests of eastern Lava County, and some locals contend that witchcraft is still practiced in the woods on dark nights to this day.

The son's wife left him and the area in the mid-1970s, but before leaving she reportedly put a curse on the lodge, saying that there would be no love there. The lodge went through a period of declining business after that, culminating in Bob Ezekian's committing suicide in a boat on Eden River one night. Locals say the spot where he killed himself is widely avoided after dark by local residents.

Since then the lodge has been through a succession of owners. The current operators, Don and Sharon Potter, have been praised by many local residents for making improvements to the property and beginning to draw more business to it.

Detective Rogers, who is investigating the case with the assistance of deputy Eldon Lilly, has moved into a room at Harry's and said he will stay at the lodge until the case is solved.

He set the newspaper down on the table, then picked it up and offered it to Peter, who shook his head.

"Summarize," he said.

"Your typical journalistic exaggeration," Gordon said. "Witchcraft, supernatural elements, unsolvable crime."

"They may have the last one right. But there's nothing supernatural about this — just a smart and lucky killer. Too bad the snow didn't last until Rogers got here."

Breakfast was finished in silence. Part way through their meal, Stuart, his plate largely untouched, rose and left without a word. Drew and Alan came in and sat a few tables away. Alan was absorbed by two streamers (larger flies that imitate minnows) he had taken from his box; Drew appeared nervous and kept glancing over at Rogers. Deputy Lilly came in and joined Rogers as Gordon and Peter were wrapping up their meal. April followed him to the table, topped off Rogers' coffee cup and asked if the deputy wanted some.

He hesitated for a couple of seconds. "Maybe just one cup," he said.

"Wouldn't want to get carried away," she said. As she leaned over the table to turn his cup right-side-up on the saucer, her arm brushed against his and he flinched slightly.

"Real strong this morning," she said. "It'll put some hair on your chest." After which she flounced over to Gordon and Peter's table to top off their cups for the last time.

"You have a new person of interest?" Peter asked in a low voice.

She chuckled. "He's so straight I can't help teasing him. He worries more over a cup of coffee than anybody else here does over a drink. Besides, ever since Drew talked to the detective yesterday, he's stopped making advances toward me."

"Is that a problem?" Gordon said.

"Let's face it, they were pretty pathetic advances, but at least they were attention. A girl's gotta feel wanted, after all."

She moved over to Alan and Drew's table, where Drew welcomed her with all the warmth normally shown to a tourist asking for directions. April looked back at Gordon and Peter and shrugged as she headed back to the kitchen.

Johnny came in a few minutes later, waved at Peter and Gordon, and went to Drew and Alan's table. Alan looked up.

"Are we going out today?"

"Well, sir, that depends," Johnny said. "I expect that's up to detective Rogers."

Rogers and Lilly had been conversing in low tones, but Rogers apparently heard the remark and rose, heading over to their table.

"Sorry for any inconvenience," he said, "but this *is* a murder investigation. That said, it looks like I'll be doing some paperwork and reading reports coming in on the fax machine the next few hours. You boys can go out and do a little fishing if you like, as long as you're back by one o'clock." He looked over at Gordon and Peter. "Same for you."

Everyone thanked him. On the way back to the cabin, in rain that had become a light drizzle, Peter said:

"It seems a bit disrespectful to the dead, but Harry's is getting me down. Is there any place nearby where we could fish, or try to, for a couple of hours?"

"I know just the spot."

2

FROM HARRY'S THEY DROVE to Eden Mills and turned west on the state highway. Halfway to the town of Muirfield, Gordon turned right on a narrow, cracked and bumpy paved road. They followed it through chaparral for a mile and a half before stopping at a gate and cattle guard at the entrance to a dirt road.

"You know the drill," Gordon said. Peter got out and opened the gate, closing it again after Gordon had driven through. They drove up a rise and came into a meadow dotted with grazing cattle. At several points in the meadow the road was under a deep puddle of water, but it was always passable. The rain had stopped, the skies were still gray, and the meadow grass, at least a foot high in most places, was swaying in the wind. After three quarters of a mile, the dirt road went down a slight incline and ended at a small parking area by a creek 50 to 60 feet wide, rolling slowly through a grassy meadow. No one else was there. They parked and sat looking at the stream.

"Is this more of gabby Bob's property?" Peter said.

"Nope. This is the Copper Bridge parking area at Saddle Creek. Owned by Fremont Light and Power, with cattle-grazing rights leased to somebody and public access available to all who can find it."

"So where's the bridge?"

"There hasn't been one in at least 40 years, but if you go a couple of hundred feet upstream you can see a few posts. That's all that's left."

"Pretty place, anyway."

Gordon gestured to the left. "If you go downstream about a quarter of a mile, there's a nice meadow section with some good weed beds in the water. Almost always some decent fish there."

"Sounds good to me, but there's a sheer cliff on this side of the stream?"

"With a trail on it. Let's go."

They rigged up their rods and started for the cliff. The path Gordon referred to was carved into the side of the cliff and was no more than two feet wide at any point — sometimes less. The path rose to a point about 40 feet above the water before beginning its descent into the meadow on the other side. At the top they stopped and looked straight down into the clear, pure water. A large bed of weeds was in the middle of the creek, with sand-gravel bottom on either side. On the side closest to the cliff several trout 12 to 18 inches long were hugging the bottom by the weed bed.

"Looks like they're nymphing," Gordon said. "I haven't seen any fish rise yet."

A sharp blast of cold wind made the men temporarily teeter on the narrow trail. "Probably won't if the wind keeps up."

Once in the meadow, the path more or less followed the creek from a distance of ten to 60 feet, depending on the landscape. They fished along the creek, tempting the trout with nymphs several feet under the water. The wind became more persistent and a bit colder as the morning wore on. Gordon caught and released three good trout and Peter landed two.

At 11:30, Gordon announced that they should leave, and they trudged back to the car. On the way back to Eden Mills, they decided that there was no sense in checking out alternatives on a short time frame, so they stopped again at Casa Rosita for lunch.

3

PETER HAD JUST TAKEN the first swig of his beer when the bell over the door jangled and they looked up to see Cynthia come in.

"I was hoping you'd be here," she said as she walked to their table. "I need a doctor."

"I only do surgery," said Peter, "and right now I'm out of anesthetic."

"Very funny. You'd be a big hit at comedy night at Sam's Pizza. Seriously, I was hoping you could answer a couple of questions for me."

"That's what everybody says at parties."

She sat down. "You might be interested in this. Can I join you?"

"Looks like you already have."

"What I really want to know about is establishing time of death."

Gordon leaned forward. "Does this have to do with …"

She waved him off. "I'm just asking a hypothetical question."

Peter, who had been slouching slightly over his beer, sat up straight. "All right, I'll play along. It's not my area of specialty, but it was one of the more interesting lectures in medical school, and I don't think the science has changed much since then."

"Good," she said. "So what's the best way of determining time of death?"

"Well, the best way is to have a witness who sees the crime and looks at a reliable watch he's wearing. But would I be correct in assuming that in this hypothetical case, we don't have a witness."

She smiled and nodded.

"Then you'd look at several other factors. If the death was fairly recent, say within 12 hours, the first thing you'd look at is body temperature. It's easy to measure at the scene, and if you count backwards to 98.6, it can narrow things down to within a couple of hours."

"So, if the hypothetical victim was in a cabin with a temperature of 68 degrees, it would be pretty straightforward."

"It should be. But you raised a good point. If the victim was lying in a snowdrift or next to a blast furnace, that would obviously affect the rate at which the body temperature drops. But if you know that, you could factor it into the calculation and still come up with a reasonably close time. And after a few hours, all you can establish is a range of time."

"What else would you look at besides the body temperature?"

139

"Several things. Have the eyes started to film over? They usually do that after about three hours. Degree of rigor. Again, that varies, but in a reasonably fresh corpse it can give you some idea. Then if you know when the deceased last ate, you can look at the stomach contents during the autopsy and see how far along the digestive process was when it was so rudely interrupted."

"Chile relleno combination?" asked the waitress arriving at the table. Gordon raised his hand, and she set that plate in front of him and the other before Peter. "Anything for you, miss?"

"If you can eat after this conversation, it's on me," Gordon said. She ordered two chicken tacos a la carte and turned back to Peter.

"Go ahead and eat before it gets cold. I'll catch up later. So here's the question I'm kind of getting to. If our hypothetical victim was in a 68-degree cabin when the temperature was taken at 10 a.m., and the body temperature indicated the cause of death was 12 to 15 hours earlier and the last meal had been three to four hours before death, what would that say to you?"

Peter had just put a forkful of enchilada in his mouth, and he chewed it slowly and carefully before swallowing and answering the question.

"I'd say that if the hypothetical victim is the one you've been writing about, that's hardly possible."

Gordon was shaking his head. "I looked at my watch not long after she stomped out of the dining room. That was 9:10, and she'd just finished dinner not more than half an hour ago. But you're telling me the body temperature says she was dead by ten o'clock, when her food would hardly have been digested. That's crazy."

Cynthia looked at the two of them.

"This is more than I expected to hear," she said. "But that's what the medical report says."

"Wait a minute," said Peter. "Is that what Rogers told you? Maybe there was a misunderstanding."

She took a chip from the bowl, dipped it in the salsa and bit off half of it.

"Well, not exactly," she said while chewing.

"Do you remember his exact words?"

She swallowed the chip. "I didn't get it from Rogers. I read the report."

"He let you read the report?" Peter's voice was rising.

"In a manner of speaking. That is, he didn't stop me." Peter and Gordon looked at each other.

"He told me to wait in the lounge while he interviewed somebody, and I had to go to the ladies' room. On the way there, I had to pass that little office, and the fax machine was starting to run. There weren't any signs telling people to stay out, so I ducked in to take a look, and the medical report was starting to come across. I didn't touch it or anything. I just got out my notebook and took notes while it was coming over. Then when the last page was coming across, I heard the door to the interview room open, so I slipped out and went back to the lounge."

"Have you talked to Rogers about this?" Gordon said.

"Not yet. I didn't completely understand the report, so I wanted to see if you guys were around. When they said you'd gone out but would be back by one, I took a chance and came down here.

"So do you have any explanation for the body temperature showing an earlier time of death?"

"None at all," Peter said.

4

"I GUESS YOU HAVE TO give her credit for initiative," Gordon said as they drove back to Harry's.

"Initiative is an overpraised character trait," Peter said. "Half the problems in the world are caused by people jumping forth and doing things they shouldn't be doing."

"At least she agreed not to quote you."

"A cold comfort at best. You realize, don't you, that this situation is getting beyond out-of-hand. Not only do we have an impossible murder inside a locked room, we also have the victim practically being dead before she got into the locked room. Rogers might as well declare the case unsolvable now and go home. Save the taxpayers some money."

"I'm trying to think back on Tuesday night," Gordon said. "Care to join me?"

"Sure. I'll have my secretary cancel my afternoon appointments."

"Here's what I remember about what happened after the catfight. If you think I'm wrong about something, say so."

"Fair enough."

"So you and I stuck around afterward and helped Don clean up, right?"

Peter nodded.

"Then we all went into the lounge and had a drink. Rachel and Stuart had left for their cabins and so had Drew and Alan. Charles had moved into a room in the main lodge. We were near the front door the whole time and nobody came or went, so we have to assume Charles was still in the lodge."

"Unless he went out through a service entrance."

"All right, leave that as a point to be considered later. In any event, it was about ten when we left the lodge. It had just started to snow."

"Which everybody keeps assuring me was an impossibility."

"Let it go, Peter. What I'm getting at is that the snow was just starting and there was hardly any on the ground. We wouldn't have seen any tracks in it at that point." He paused, and hearing no contradiction, proceeded. "I remember seeing that the lights were on in Wendy's cabin, Drew and Alan's cabin, and Rachel's cabin. I remember thinking that would be enough that we wouldn't need a flashlight."

"You said Rachel's cabin. Wasn't it hers and Stuart's?"

"Whatever. My point is this. Everybody's accounted for at that point. Unless you figure that Rachel and Stuart or Drew and Alan went over together and committed the murder, which is a stretch. Nobody would have gotten over there by ten, which is the latest she's supposed to be alive."

"That's based on body temperature. If you go by digestion, she was still alive two to three hours later. Say up to midnight or one. I saw the light go out at 1:45, so I'm going with the gut evidence."

"Then how do you explain the body temperature?"

"I can't. And I'm betting the district attorney can't explain it either if there's ever a trial."

"We crashed pretty soon after we got to the cabin. Did you notice if any of the lights at the other cabins were on when you turned in?" Peter shook his head. "Me neither. But probably everybody was turned in by eleven. And after that, everybody has the same alibi. They were asleep in a room with someone else who was asleep and can't swear that they were there."

"Except Charles."

"Except Charles. So sometime between eleven and 1:30, somebody slipped out of their place and somehow got into Wendy's cabin."

"If it was one of us, she probably let them in."

"That's what I was thinking. Especially if it was someone who'd been there before. So the question is how did someone get over there without being seen or leaving tracks?"

"That's the easy part. If they came over a half hour or more before the snow stopped falling, it probably would have filled in their tracks. The real question is how did someone turn off the lights and go forth at 1:45 without leaving any marks in the snow?"

"Not only that, but lock the door and all the windows from inside before leaving? That's what we've got to figure out."

"What do you mean *we*, Gordon? This is a job for Rogers, and after hearing your concise summary, I'll repeat what I said earlier. He should give up now and save the taxpayers some money."

5

"YOU!" SNAPPED ROGERS, pointing at Peter as he and Gordon came through the door. "In the interview room. Now."

Peter shrugged and followed the detective. Gordon went into the Fireside Lounge, where Stuart was sitting on the couch in front of the fire, staring intently at the flames, and April was counting bottles behind the bar.

"Any coffee left?" he asked.

"Just made a fresh pot." She poured him a cup. After hesitating a minute he decided to sit on one of the chairs by the fire, near Stuart, who didn't acknowledge his presence. Gordon took two sips of his coffee, then said: "You look preoccupied. Would you like to be left alone?"

Stuart jerked, as if coming out of a trance. "Sorry. I didn't mean to be rude. No, that's fine."

"You were supposed to go home yesterday. This must have disrupted your work."

"A little, but that's not the problem. The problem is … " he looked over at April and lowered his voice, "this investigation and what it's turning up."

Gordon looked at April and caught her eye. He gestured slightly with his head.

"If you guys are okay for a few minutes, I need to go back to the kitchen," she said, and hearing no response, left.

"Too bad about that," Gordon said, turning back to Stuart and lowering his voice slightly.

"I'm sure you know what I mean. You must have seen me coming out of the Van Holland cabin on Sunday." Gordon said nothing, and after several seconds, Stuart did what people usually do to cover a silence. He continued talking.

"I still can't believe it happened. My brother-in-law's cheated on my sister several times, at least that she knows of, and I've seen how it hurt her. I told myself when Rachel and I got married that I'd never do that." He let out a sound halfway between a snort and a laugh. "So much for good intentions. Afterward, I said it was a one-time slip and she didn't have to find out. Once she'd had me, Wendy wasn't interested anymore, and I thought I'd get away with it. No such luck."

"Rogers got you to admit it?"

"He didn't have to work too hard. He dropped it on me like he knew what was going on, and I decided to tell the truth. For a minute it just felt good to get it out, but the really awful part was that I didn't get to tell Rachel myself. He took me out after the interview and called her in right away. The only thing I could say before she went in was, 'I love you.' She gave me a funny look, like she knew something was up."

"I'm sorry. For both of you."

"That was after dinner last night. She wouldn't even have breakfast with me this morning. When she came out after talking with him last night, I knew she knew. She didn't say a word all the way back to the cabin. I've never felt so alone in my life as on that walk. When we got there, she slammed the door shut and said, 'How could you? With *her*?' I tried to say something, but she just said, 'Never mind. I don't think I can stand to hear it.' I guess I had that coming."

One of the logs on the fire burned through and broke in half, one end of it tumbling into the hot coals below. Gordon got up and put another piece of wood in its place, then sat down again. Within a minute, the new log was aflame.

"It's none of my business, Stuart, but if it helps you to talk about it … " Stuart nodded slightly. "Have you thought about why it happened and whether it could again?"

"You know what? This may seem crazy, but I think a lot of it is Harry's. There's some kind of cloud over this place. Everything's been a bit off since we got here. Rachel and I have been on fishing trips other places and I was always fine with reading a book or taking a walk while she fished. Not here. There's been tension of a kind I can't put my finger on. But I really believe there's no way Wendy could have gotten anywhere with me back in Oakland."

"The curse of Harry's."

"What?"

Gordon told him the story of Harry's daughter-in-law, and it was clear Stuart had never heard of it.

"I don't believe in that stuff, and I don't think you do either, Gordon. But that's almost what it felt like."

"The really good writers of the supernatural generally take the approach that the unseen spirits are a manifestation of what people were feeling. Was everything all right with you two?"

"Sure. I mean, nothing that couldn't be worked out."

Gordon said nothing and took another swallow of coffee.

"Actually, we'd been having some disagreement lately." Silence. "About Rachel's career." Silence. "It's not easy being married to a politician. She spends a lot of time going to meetings and she's always on call. Seems like we're lucky if we have dinner together two nights a week lately."

"There are rumors she's thinking of running for the State Assembly."

"That would just make it worse. If she won ... "

"She'll win if she runs."

"Then we'd be living in two homes. I know Sacramento is only an hour or hour and a half from Oakland, but she'd have to stay there during the week when the Legislature is in session. We talked about that. She could come down for weekends, and I could go up to Sacramento a night or two a week. Probably it'd work, but it would be disruptive."

Gordon nodded sympathetically.

"And we've been talking about starting a family. She's 34, you know. But she wants to make the political decision first. So yeah, it's been a bit tense. And I guess we brought a bit of that tension here with us."

April returned during the ensuing silence. "Everything all right? Can I get you some coffee?" Gordon held up his cup and she came over to fill it.

"You mentioned other fishing trips," he said, after she left. "But you don't fish. Where do you like to go on vacation?"

"A city with a good cultural life," Stuart said. "London. Rome. Paris. Venice. New York. I could go to Paris for a week and spend every day in the Louvre from opening to closing."

"That'd get you through about half of it."

Stuart laughed for the first time. "About right. Rachel's okay with that, but we haven't done much of it lately. She doesn't want to be too far from Oakland in case something comes up. She's so damn conscientious."

Rogers and Peter came around the corner of the hallway leading to the interview room. It was hard to say which of the two looked more annoyed.

"All right, Gordon," Rogers said. "Your turn."

Gordon got up to follow him. In the time it took to walk across the lounge, Peter had ordered a beer.

6

BACK AT THE INTERVIEW ROOM, Rogers and Lilly assumed the same positions as before. Gordon sat down and waited for them to start the interrogation.

"Your friend seems to have a bit of an attitude," Rogers finally said.

"He always has."

"How long have you known him?"

"A little over a year."

"Is he a straight shooter?"

"I've always thought so. Why?"

Rogers sighed and looked over at Lilly.

"He's telling us something that doesn't add up with the medical evidence."

"I know."

"You *what?*"

"I'm assuming you're talking about the time of death being before Peter saw the light go out."

Rogers and Lilly looked at each other.

"I'm too old for this," Rogers said. "I just told your doctor friend about that, and he didn't have a chance to tell you before you came in. How did you know about that?"

Gordon smiled. "I hate to be the one to tell you, but you have a security problem. The medical report came in on a fax that was in an open office where anybody could walk in."

"And you did."

"Gentlemen don't read each others' mail, detective. I didn't, but someone else did and told me about it."

"Don't be cute, Gordon. Who was it?"

"Let me put it this way. You'll probably be reading about it in tomorrow's paper."

Rogers snapped his pencil in half.

"Shit. This case is turning into God's way of telling me I should have retired sooner."

"Sir," said Lilly, "that was partly my fault. I saw her in the hallway this morning, but it looked like she was just heading back to the bathroom. I should have put two and two together."

"Don't beat yourself up, deputy. I should have made sure that room is secure. Let's do it now. Go find one of the owners and tell them to keep that office locked and only open it up to us."

Lilly left, and after he had closed the door, Rogers turned to Gordon.

"Sharp kid. He'll go a ways in this business. But back to your friend. If he doesn't swear to the light being turned out at 1:45 in the morning, things make a lot more sense. Someone could have gone over when it started snowing, killed Mrs. Van Holland, and walked away, leaving the snow to cover his tracks before morning."

"And instead, you have a killer who waited for the snow to stop and left without leaving a trace of himself ..."

"Or herself. It could have been a woman."

"Right. And whether you believe Peter's evidence about the light going out, you still have a killer getting away from a cabin completely locked from the inside."

"A minor detail. When we find the killer, we'll find the explanation for that. It's probably pretty simple once you know."

"I don't want to tell you your business, but wouldn't it make sense to find the killer by figuring out the locked-room situation?"

"You've been watching too much TV. When I know who has the best motive, I can probably crack it from there. Right now I'm counting five people with decent motives, so I have to do a bit more weeding."

"Well, good luck. But if Peter says he saw the light go off at 1:45, you'd better work that into your story before the defense attorney does. Peter's been a witness before, and he's probably a pretty good one."

"All right. You been paying attention out there? Heard anything interesting?"

"Just the sound of a marriage possibly cracking up."

"That's tough. You know, one thing about this business that I'll never like is dealing with personal information that starts to come out after a crime's been committed. I still remember the first time I had to tell a wife her husband was cheating. He and the other woman were driving back from a rendezvous when a drunk driver crossed the center line and hit them head-on."

"Oh, man."

"Killed the husband and put the other woman in the hospital for a month. And the drunk just got a couple of bruises. Life's not fair. Anyway, I had to notify the wife. She brain-locked and couldn't sort out whether to be crushed because he was dead or pissed because he was fooling around. I could have handled her doing one or the other, but when she just stood there and did nothing, I almost lost it."

Gordon nodded, but said nothing.

"Still, it could have been worse."

"How?"

"I could have been the guy who had to tell the other woman's husband."

Lilly opened the door and came in with a stack of papers nearly an inch thick.

"The office is locked now, but the reports from Syracuse were there when we went to do it. Sorry, sir, but there's no telling who might have seen them."

"We can always hope for a break, deputy. We're due for one." He took the papers from Lilly and held them up. "This should be interesting reading, Gordon. The dutiful wife was apparently quite well known to the police in Syracuse a few years ago. Go along, now, and let me read it. But don't go too far."

7

PETER WASN'T IN THE LOUNGE, so Gordon started for the cabin. The rain had stopped, and the wind had let up somewhat. The sun was still out of sight, but more of its light seemed to be getting through the clouds overhead. The cold air was bracing and sensually pure. Gordon walked slowly and breathed deeply.

Peter was lying on the bed reading *Vanity Fair* when Gordon came in. He set the magazine down and swung his legs over the edge of the bed.

"How did it go with Buck Rogers?"

"Steady questions as usual."

"You know, Gordon, I don't think he likes me."

"He doesn't like anybody, Peter. Don't take it personally. I get the feeling he barely tolerates me."

"Did he ask you about my seeing the light go out?"

"Oh, yeah."

"Same here, only about 35 times and as many different ways. He seems to think that if he just asks the question different, I'll give him the answer he wants to hear."

"I need to ask you something, Peter. He asked if you could be trusted about that, and I told him he could take it to the bank."

"Thanks, but I doubt it impressed him."

"Still, I have to wonder. You did have quite a bit to drink that night ..."

"Not as much as you think."

"All right, let's not have that discussion, but just tell me. Are you sure?"

Peter didn't answer immediately, but when he did, he spoke carefully and deliberately.

"I'll tell you exactly what I told Rogers. I got up to pee and went into the bathroom without noticing much of anything. When I came back into the room, I could see light coming through our blinds from outside, which seemed unusual. I went over to the window and lifted one of the slats. The light was on in that cabin, nice and bright. The blinds were drawn and I couldn't see anything inside, but you couldn't miss the light being on. And I noticed it had stopped snowing.

"I remember thinking it seemed pretty late for Wendy to still be up alone, so I stepped back to the bed and looked at the alarm clock. It said 1:45 exactly. It runs three minutes slower than my watch, but close enough. Then I looked up at our window again and just then the light went out. I got back into the bed, pulled the covers over my head, and was asleep in probably two or three minutes. But I saw what I saw, just the way I told you."

"That has to be right," Gordon said after a slight pause. "The detail is too convincing. There must be something wrong with the medical report."

"Far be it from me to criticize my profession, but there's usually some slop in those reports. It seems like more than usual in this case, but all I can figure is that there's something that hasn't been accounted for yet."

For several moments, each man was lost in his own thoughts. Gordon finally broke the silence.

"So what should we do for the rest of this afternoon?"

"I'm feeling a bit restless. And thirsty. I was thinking of getting a bit of exercise by strolling up to the lodge and having a beer."

"I have a better idea. Let me show you Roaring Spring."

"What's that?"

"The source of Eden River. It's a little over a mile up that path at the end of Harry's property, through the National Forest land. I think you'll be impressed."

"Sure. Why not? Work up a bit of an appetite for dinner and all that."

At the edge of Harry's property, beyond the cabin where the Van Hollands had been staying, there was a fence three feet high and made of crossed timbers. The path from the lodge to the cabins continued along the river through a break in the fence but narrowed to a width of about two feet. On either side of it grew grass, made a lush green from the winter's rains, with here and there a patch of bluish-purple forget-me-nots. The river at this point was flanked by stands of pine trees of varying sizes and states of health. The path wound through the trees, sometimes running just a few feet from the river, sometimes as much as 150 feet away with the river barely visible through the forest.

Gordon and Peter trudged up the path, not going too fast and trying to take in as much as they could. The farther along they got, the deeper and thicker the woods got, with the path becoming increasingly covered with pine needles, and the smell of the trees more pronounced. From time to time a pine cone would drop to the ground, or they would see a squirrel scampering up a tree or a woodpecker butting its beak against a pine trunk. Otherwise they were alone in a deep, quiet forest, the silence disturbed only by an occasional bird call or the sighing of wind through the canopy above them. For more than 15 minutes they walked and looked, saying nothing, leaving the peace undisturbed.

A sound, indistinct at first, seemingly no more than a distant rumble or vibration, became audible at that point. As they moved on, it began to assume the nature of a roar, the sound of water moving rapidly at high pressure.

"We're getting close," Gordon said.

The noise increased for a few minutes. Gordon and Peter came around a bend in the path, following it out of the trees directly up to the river's edge, where it ended at a wooden deck with guard railings.

Stepping onto the deck, they could see the source of the noise 150 feet away. At that point the topography changed, and the ground rose 30 feet in a straight vertical line to another shelf of land beyond. The exposed side of the cliff they were facing was composed of porous volcanic rock, riddled with holes, and from almost every hole shot a white jet of water that landed in a large pool, a bowl scooped out of the earth by countless years of running water. Near the observation platform, the lip of the bowl narrowed to a width of 75 feet and the water began to flow out of it. That was the genesis of Eden River.

They stood, looking at it for several minutes without saying a word.

"All right," said Peter. "I have to admit I'm impressed. It's like a waterfall, only it isn't."

"The snow that falls on The Mountain in the winter goes into the ground," Gordon said, then runs underneath it for about 30 miles. A subterranean river, actually. It gets here, and out it comes. The volume is the same, day in and day out, no matter what the season. And it's always 52 degrees Fahrenheit, clean and pure as any water can be."

They looked in silence for a few more minutes. A gust of wind kicked up and blew the spray from the falling water in their direction, hitting them with a film of vapor.

"The Native Americans considered this a sacred place," Gordon said, "and believed that the rocks here were a portal to the world of the spirits and that the spirits released the water when they were at peace. You can see how they thought that."

"I guess I don't really believe that," Peter said, "but somehow I prefer it to the scientific explanation. It's a better story, anyway."

The rain, which had been absent during their walk to the spring, began to fall again in a slow, steady, soaking shower. They pulled up the hoods on their parkas and started back toward Harry's.

It was later in the afternoon now, and the forest seemed darker and more ominous than it had on the way out. There was no birdsong at all, and the trees were dripping rainwater that was filtering down from the canopy. It was easy to feel that they were the only two people left in the world. Several minutes along, Peter stopped.

"I'm not sure I'm going to make it to the cabin," he said. "Go ahead if you want, but I'm going to look for a special tree to honor with my presence, if you get my drift."

"I get it. I'll wait here."

Peter headed into the woods away from the river, and Gordon moved under a tree with low-hanging branches where he figured there would be more protection from the rain. As he stood waiting, he tried to sort out the details of Wendy's murder but found himself getting nowhere. He had a vague sense that something he had seen or heard in the past few days connected to something else he had seen or heard in a way that might provide a break in the investigation. But for all his thinking, he couldn't come up with it. He also had to admit that in some way he didn't want to. In some way, he realized, he liked all the flawed and quirky people he had met at Harry's, and he didn't want one of them to be a killer. Even though one of them certainly was.

He snapped back to the moment, realizing that he had been thinking about the murder for far longer than Peter should have been away. He turned and looked into the forest in the direction Peter had gone, just in time to see him walk between two trees 50 yards away.

"Come here, Gordon," Peter shouted. "You need to see this."

With a sigh, Gordon started toward him, making an improvisational path through the trees, walking over wet pine needles and rotten pieces of downed wood, skirting occasional growths of low underbrush. When he reached Peter, they walked another 30 yards into the forest and came to a clearing.

It was irregularly shaped, somewhere between a rectangle and an oval, about 60 feet by 90 feet. There was no dead wood on the ground, just a carpet of pine needles, and at one of the long ends of the oval/rectangle stood an immense boulder. It was 15 feet wide and ten feet high, and the side of it facing into the clearing was almost perfectly vertical, as if the rock had been sliced through with a bread knife. Its white surface formed a backdrop like the overhang of an amphitheater. A few feet in front of the boulder a circle, eight feet in diameter, had been constructed and carefully framed with smaller rocks, six inches to a foot thick. Inside the circle was a large bed of sodden ashes and pieces of what appeared to have been parts of large logs that hadn't finished burning.

Without a word, they walked over to the circle. The rain was falling more heavily, and they were exposed to it in the clearing, but they hardly noticed. They looked into the fire circle and around at the clearing.

"Is it my imagination," Gordon said, "or is it colder in here?"

"Probably your imagination, but I wouldn't want to bet on that."

Gordon squatted next to the circle and reached for a nub that was protruding from the ash by no more than half an inch. Grasping the end of it, he withdrew …

A chicken drumstick bone. With no meat or skin remaining.

He and Peter looked at each other.

"Strange place for a barbecue," Gordon muttered.

"Don't be dense," said Peter. "Can't you figure out what this is?"

Gordon shook his head.

"You have a secluded place in the depth of the forest, a fire circle, and animal parts left over. That suggests to me there's been a witches' Sabbath here, and not all that long ago. Maybe there really was something to the story about Harry's daughter-in-law."

Gordon looked around the clearing and then at his watch, which showed five minutes to four, though with the overcast and rain cutting off the sun, it seemed darker, almost twilight. Involuntarily, he shivered.

"It's none of my business, Peter, but do you mind if I ask how you know about these things?"

"I used to date a physical therapist who turned out to be a Wiccan. That's a sort of modern, New Age variety of witchcraft. She said they had ceremonies in remote parts of the Santa Cruz Mountains south of the City. Since nobody lives on a farm anymore, they'd sacrifice a bucket of Kentucky Fried Chicken instead of using a live animal."

"The march of progress, I guess. So did you break up with her because she was a witch?"

"Of course not. I'm a man of the world and would never allow religion to interfere with romance. She just figured me out faster than they usually do and broke it off herself."

"Well, I have to hand it to you. Your bladder has already turned up more clues than Detective Rogers has."

"You think this is a clue?"

"I don't know, but it's a strange case, so anything strange may have a bearing on it. I think we need to tell Rogers."

"It couldn't hurt," Peter said. "But my next question would be how people get here. Somehow, I can't imagine a coven of witches pulling into Harry's parking lot and tromping past the cabins to walk out to this place."

"Let's look around the perimeter a bit."

"Should we split up and cover more ground?"

Gordon shook his head. "I don't want to get stuck here alone. Let's stay within sight of each other and keep moving away from the river."

They separated slightly and began slowly walking through the woods. The rain had been falling for long enough that it had percolated through the trees and was dripping on them wherever they went. Gordon looked around carefully and thought he saw a small break in the forest to his right. He headed toward it and came to what appeared to be the end of a rough road, more of a cart track really.

"Over here, Peter."

When Peter joined him, they followed the track for about 150 feet, where it gradually widened and took on a more traveled feel. There, they came to an area where there were no trees by the road and ample room for a vehicle to pull off it. Judging from several sets of fairly fresh tire ruts, several vehicles had.

"I think we've found the witches' parking lot," Peter said.

From the direction that the road was heading they heard the faint rumble of a pickup truck in the distance.

"This probably leads to County Road A22," Gordon said. "The road that goes past the entrance to Harry's. I'm guessing that's how the witches got here." He paused. "If that's who they were."

"I'm pretty sure it wasn't the Lions Club," said Peter. "Look what I just found next to one of the tire tracks."

He held up a pink, cylindrical object several inches long. It took Gordon several seconds to recognize it as a vibrator of the type readily available at discreet women's boutiques in the City.

"Don't they say," he finally said, "that a Black Mass usually ends with a sexual orgy of some kind?"

"That's what they say," replied Peter. "And as an eligible bachelor in San Francisco, I'm sure you realize how hard it is for a hostess to come up with a spare man on short notice." Peter fiddled with the base of the device and nothing happened.

"Hmm," he said. "The battery's used up. Must have been one hell of a party."

8

IT WAS AFTER FIVE when they got back to Harry's, and Peter headed straight for the bar while Gordon tried to find Rogers. Don said Rogers and Lilly were in the interview room and had asked not to be disturbed, but he went to knock on the door when Gordon insisted it was urgent. A minute later, Gordon was ushered in.

"Well now, that's very interesting," Rogers said when Gordon finished his story. "But I'm afraid it's out of my jurisdiction. I'm not a ghost hunter, you see. My job is to catch flesh-and-blood criminals."

"You're not going to look into this?"

"Not unless there's something that ties into this murder."

Gordon looked at the two men. Rogers seemed annoyed, as he always did, but Gordon thought he noticed a hint of nervousness in Lilly and decided to gently press on.

"You're the expert, not me," he said, looking at Rogers again, "but is it really a good idea to rule something out without at least looking into it first?"

"Ninety percent of detective work is ruling things out. Some take a while and some are easy. This one seems easy. You found something in the woods a half mile or so from the murder scene that doesn't connect with anything that's come up in the investigation so far." He sighed. "But I'll hear you out. Do you really believe in this supernatural hocus pocus? Tell me why you think this might matter."

Gordon put the fingers of his hands together and looked up at the ceiling. He wasn't altogether sure why he felt as he did or that he could explain it, but he had to try.

"For starters, I don't believe in witches or vampires — at least not as supernatural agents. But there are people who play at it, and ... " Rogers looked at him intently without saying a word. "All right, let me put it this way. You asked me to keep my eyes open, and I've already been more or less doing that since I got here, more than 48 hours before the murder. I can't put my finger on it, but something isn't right at Harry's. And I know that in the past, when I've had a feeling that something wasn't right, it usually turned out that somebody, or several somebodies, had something to hide. That caused them to act a bit off, which was probably what I was picking up on. If Peter and I were right about what we saw in that clearing this afternoon, it's something somebody is almost surely trying to hide. That's all I'm saying."

Rogers nodded his head almost imperceptibly.

"When I was a rookie deputy, like Lilly here, I got called out to a place like what you're describing, only about 20 miles the other way from here. Some hikers came across it and were pretty visibly shaken. I took a short report and went back to the office with it, thinking I really had something.

"Well, guess what. It was the sixties. People were experimenting with all kinds of stuff. Witchcraft. Druid circles. Just getting together in large numbers to smoke, swallow or inject something that would change the way they felt. Some of them were coming to Lava County to do it because there's a lot of lonesome out here. My find was about the fifth one that summer, and later on I learned that people had been coming across that sort of thing in the woods here since at least the turn of the century. In short, it's not that unusual."

Gordon looked at Lilly and thought he was seeing more of the nervousness he'd seen earlier.

"How about you, deputy. Anything to add to this discussion?"

Rogers looked at Lilly and picked up on his unease as well.

"Come on," he said. "Spit it out."

Lilly poured a glass of water from a pitcher on the table in the room and took two large swallows before setting down the glass.

"I've never told anybody about this," he said. "It happened several months ago. On Halloween, actually. I was on patrol and my partner was sick, so I was alone, and it was after dark. I was on Benson Road where it joins A22, and there was a car coming from the right, heading toward Harry's. I decided to let it go instead of pulling in front of it.

"When it passed in front of my headlights, I got a quick look inside the car. There were two women wearing black outfits. That's all I can swear to, but I had a feeling there was something strange about it. I turned left to head up to follow it and was behind the car for a couple of miles. I remember we passed the entrance to Harry's, and maybe a half mile beyond that, the brake lights came on and it made a sharp turn into a dirt road. It would have been right around where Mr. Gordon and his friend found the clearing."

"They were probably just going to somebody's house," Rogers said.

"No, sir. There was no mailbox where it turned in, and as often as I'd driven by it, I hadn't even realized there was a road or driveway there."

He looked at Gordon and Rogers.

"There's one more thing. I recognized the car. It was a Toyota Camry, and I noted the license plate number, but I didn't need to run the plates to make an identification. It had a bumper sticker that said 'One Earth, One People.' There's only one car I've ever seen in eastern Lava County that had a bumper sticker like that."

He took another swallow of water.

"It belongs to the principal of Paradise Valley High School."

Rogers shifted in his chair.

"So you think it was the principal's wife driving the car?"

"No, sir. I think it was the principal, Mrs. Maurillo."

"All right," said Rogers softly.

"You may already know this, sir, but last summer, a couple of months before this happened, her husband died in a fall from their roof. It was officially ruled an accident, but it was pretty well known they hadn't been getting along."

Lilly finished the glass of water.

"There was talk. Some people were suspicious."

9

PETER AND JOHNNY WERE WAITING in the lounge for Gordon when he got out of the meeting. Drew and Alan were there as well, and Charles Van Holland was sitting in one of the large chairs by the fire, staring into it and holding a full wine glass in his hand. Rogers called Van Holland to the interview room, and he shuffled slowly after the detective. Gordon couldn't help thinking how much his movement had changed. He was doing everything more slowly, and he stooped when he walked.

Sharon showed them to a window table, told them the specials, and left. The sun, though unseen, had not set, and they could see raindrops splashing on the deck outside. They looked at the rain falling through the overcast twilight for several minutes without speaking.

Finally, Johnny cleared his throat. "I wouldn't want to pressure you gentlemen, and I know there are more important things than fishing to think about now. But I was wondering if you might have any idea what your plans would be for tomorrow?"

"Shoot," Gordon said. "I almost forgot. We're booked with you, aren't we?"

Johnny nodded. "Under the circumstances, I doubt the Fisherman's Friend would impose a cancellation charge. Still, I'd like to know for myself, if it wouldn't be too much trouble."

Gordon looked at Peter, who nodded almost imperceptibly.

"I can't say for sure, Johnny. You see, Peter and I found something this afternoon that might be important. In fact, Rogers just asked us to take him out to see it tomorrow morning."

"So he took it seriously?" said Peter.

"After some advocacy on my part." Gordon leaned over the table and lowered his voice. "I'll let you in on it, Johnny, but don't tell anybody else."

"You know me, Mr. Gordon. Soul of discretion."

"This afternoon, Peter and I took a little walk up to Roaring Springs. On the way back we went off the trail a bit and found a clearing with a fire circle. We think it had recently been used for a witches' Sabbath. You've lived around here all your life. Does that seem possible?"

"Well, now, I can't say it altogether surprises me. No, not at all. There have been stories about such things, going back to when I was a boy. How much is rumor, I can't say, but at times it got specific enough that certain women in town were mentioned by name as being of that persuasion."

"It's a good thing," Peter said, "that civilization has advanced to a point where at least they wouldn't be burned."

"Nothing like that, no. But in a couple of cases I know of, the talk got to a point where the woman left town. And sometimes it just died down. Of course it was hardly an everyday thing — just something that came up once in a while. I don't recall hearing of that for a few years now."

"I take it one of those women was Harry's daughter-in-law."

"Indeed. A lot of talk there. I was quite a bit younger then, and she was close to my age. She was a wild one, she was, and there was something — I don't know, strange or different about her. She frightened me a bit."

Sharon came back to take their order, but as they hadn't looked at the menu yet, they deferred. Gordon ordered a glass of wine, Peter another drink, and Johnny stuck with the one he was working on.

"There's a saying around here," Johnny continued, "that what happens in the woods, stays in the woods. The mountains are a hard and lonely place, gentlemen, and they have an appeal for people who want to live differently. That's all I can tell you."

Charles Van Holland emerged from the hallway leading to the interview room. Gordon had the best look at him and saw that, if anything, he looked more beaten down than he had when he went in a quarter of an hour ago. April came up to him from behind and put a hand on his right arm. He nodded his head, and she went to get him a drink.

"Guys," Gordon said, "Let's make this a party of four."

He rose, and with several long strides was at Van Holland's side. In a matter of seconds, Gordon was leading him to their table.

"Thank you for asking," Van Holland said as he sat down. "I apologize if I'm not the best of company, but I have a lot on my mind."

"Did Rogers just put you through the wringer?" Peter asked.

Van Holland let out a dismissive laugh. "I guess you could call it that. I'm the husband, so I'm obviously going to be the prime suspect. It's just how it is. What I wasn't expecting was to be told what a fool I was. I lost Wendy once when she was killed, and now I just lost her a second time. I found out what she really was."

No one had an answer for that, so they sat silently until he continued. April brought Van Holland's drink, but he didn't touch it.

"Rogers heard back from the police in Syracuse about Wendy Vitello, which was her maiden name. Their story was a little different from the one she told me. She said she grew up in a traditional Catholic family, went to college for a year but dropped out because she was bored by it, then did clerical work for some nonprofit groups for a few years before coming out to California after her parents were killed in an auto accident. That's pretty much what she had on her resume when I hired her to work in my office. And no, I didn't check her references. She was such a live wire, I knew I wanted to have her around.

"The real story is that she got her first drug arrest when she was 15 and had a few more over the years, along with a couple for petty theft and one for solicitation. The detective in Syracuse said he didn't think she was a real working girl, but just needed some quick money to make a buy and got unlucky. As if that makes it a whole lot better. Three years ago, she went into rehab and cleaned up enough to get off probation. Then, when her parents, who are still very much alive, wouldn't take her in, she stole a thousand dollars from them and came to California. Do you know what her father said when the police told him his daughter had been murdered?"

Gordon, Johnny and Peter looked at him and at each other.

"Her father said, 'I'm surprised it took so long.' "

Sharon headed toward the table to take their order, but Gordon waved her off.

"But the worst thing of all is that when we celebrated her 27th birthday last month, she was really 30. She lied about her age, goddamit! I can understand lying about all the other stuff, but she had no reason to lie about her age. I would have loved her just as much if she was 30. It wouldn't have mattered. But she lied about it anyway. That really hurts."

Van Holland suddenly seemed to become aware of the drink in front of him and he downed half of it in one gulp.

"If only I'd checked her references."

"Don't be too hard on yourself," Peter said after a moment of silence. "My fifth wife hired a private detective to look into me, and she married me anyway. Six months later, she called our marriage the worst mistake of her life. Doing the research doesn't always give you the right answer."

10

SITTING ON THE SEPARATE BEDS in their cabin, while Peter had his customary two large nightcaps, they went over the events of the day.

"I would have liked to have asked Charles if he ever saw any indication that Wendy might have been into the occult," Gordon said. "It may not have had anything to do with her death, but I'd like to know."

"This probably wasn't the time to bring it up," Peter said. "And I doubt he'd have noticed. He was smitten by her."

"Bewitched, bothered and bewildered," Gordon said. "The song could have been written just for him."

"Did Johnny Mercer do that one?"

"Rodgers and Hart."

"Whatever. I think you're going down a blind alley with that line of thought."

"Why?"

Peter took a moment to frame his response.

"What Charles told us tonight added to the story but I wasn't surprised. I didn't have to know exactly what Wendy did in Syracuse to know she was bad news and that she was taking him for a ride. Trust me, I'm developing a radar for that sort of thing. And while there may be some faux witches in these parts, I don't think Wendy was one herself."

"Because?"

"Because she wasn't spiritual enough."

Friday May 12

1

PETER DREW THE BLINDS just after 6 a.m. and looked outside. Between the lingering darkness and the low mist clinging to the ground, it was hard to tell whether or not it was raining softly.

"Just another sunny day in paradise," he said. "Rise and shine, Gordon."

They took turns shaving and showering and left for the lodge shortly before seven. The light was better by then, and the fine rain that was falling could easily be seen through the cabin windows before they left. A damp chill hung in the air, but there was no wind.

Don greeted them from the lounge.

"Breakfast won't be ready for a few minutes, but there's a pot of coffee in here if you'd like to get started on that."

They each took a cup. The fire in the fireplace was beginning to take off, its hiss and crackle filling the room like audible smoke. So early in the morning, with the dreary weather outside, the lounge gave off a sense of comfort and security.

"So how's it going, Don?" Gordon finally asked.

"As well as you can expect, given that one of my guests was murdered and the police have taken over the place. We have two parties coming in tonight, three more tomorrow, and two on Sunday. If they don't hear about this situation and cancel, I'm not sure where I'm going to put them."

"Bad for business, is it?" Peter said.

"You bet it is. I mean, I know the deputies have to do their job. Don't get me wrong. It just seems they could be making more progress."

Gordon said, "Has Rogers said anything about how long he'll be here?"

"As long as it takes is all I can get out of him. That's not much help if you have to tell a caller whether or not you can get him a room on Wednesday."

Gordon decided to change the subject. "Could I ask you a question, Don? Have you ever heard anything about witches in these parts?"

Don put down the wine glass he was wiping off.

"It comes up from time to time," he said deliberately. "Some of the people I know in town think there's a gathering of them active in the area. Me, I figure it's just a subject to keep the conversation going on long winter days."

"You've never heard anything but idle talk?"

"If you mean who's involved and where they meet — no. I mean, really. It's not the thirteenth century any more. Even if it's happening, could anybody really be afraid of it? It would just be some women fooling around harmlessly in the woods."

"Sort of like a bridge club, but outdoors," Peter murmured.

"You could say that. But that reminds me. There actually was a witch disclosure when we bought this place. Sharon did a double-take when the real estate agent told us about it. The agent said there was rumored to be a witch's curse on the property and the owner was required by law to disclose it."

"She also told us," said Sharon, walking into the room with a fresh pot of coffee, "that the ghost of Harry Ezekian's son might put in an appearance. We're still waiting for the first sighting. What's this all about?"

"They asked about witches," Don said.

"Just curious," Gordon said. "We've been picking up on some of the local lore. Have you heard anything about a group of witches active in the area?"

"No, and I wouldn't pay any attention if I did. Wait! Now that you mention it, there was one thing, but it was over a year ago. I was at the grocery store, and the checker tried to tell me that she thought Mrs. Maurillo was a witch. I considered the source and figured it was just someone trying to put down a powerful woman."

"That's been the case with witch-hunting through the ages," Peter said. "Who's Mrs. Maurillo?"

"De Ann Maurillo is the principal of the high school, and a very nice lady from what I can tell. I think it was mean to say such a thing about her. And cruel, too, considering what happened to her husband."

2

AT THE BREAKFAST TABLE, before Johnny arrived, Gordon filled Peter in on what had happened to the late Mr. Maurillo.

"I don't know what to make of that," Peter said, "but I'm beginning to feel better about the breakup with the Wiccan physical therapist."

When Johnny arrived, they told him they still hadn't heard from Rogers and didn't know what to expect for the day. Gordon tried to pump Johnny about the discovery of the previous afternoon, but Johnny had not much to add.

"A lot happens in these woods," he said. "Yes, it does. There's probably not much that would surprise me in that regard."

Drew and Alan drifted in a few minutes later and were seated at the next table.

"So what do you hear?" Drew asked. "Are we going to be allowed to leave — ever?"

"Eventually, I'm sure," Gordon said.

"How long do you think this investigation is going to take?"

"As long as it takes. Your guess is as good as mine."

Alan was looking through his fly box. "I'm thinking of working with two nymphs," he said. "One six inches under the other. Anybody had any luck with that?"

The discussion momentarily paused, then Johnny stepped in.

"It can be a good way of seeing what's working," he said. "Indeed it can. But I'd be sure one of the two is a Pheasant Tail nymph. Size 16 or 18. You can't go wrong on this river with a P.T."

"Or anywhere else, for that matter," Gordon added.

Rogers came in, poured a cup of coffee, and walked over to the others.

"You two," addressing Drew and Alan, "are welcome to go out this morning, but be back by one. Doctor, I want you to take me out to this site you found yesterday."

"What about me?" Gordon said.

"I've heard your story; I want to hear it from your friend now. Cool your heels until we get back, then you can fish a while if you want. Ready, doc?"

Peter shrugged and stood up. "At your service."

"Say, anybody seen Charles?" Gordon said.

"He's probably not up yet," Peter said. "Last night he said he'd been having trouble sleeping, so I got him a mild sedative from my bag."

After Lilly arrived a few minutes later, the two lawmen and Peter started for the Sabbath clearing in the woods. Johnny said that since he had a little time, he'd run into town and pick up a spare part for his boat. Gordon stayed behind, drinking coffee. Rachel and Stuart came in, acknowledged his wave, and sat down to a breakfast marked by tense silence. Charles, looking a bit better than the past two days, came in, took a table, read the newspaper, and ate quietly. The silence began to wear Gordon down so he took his coffee into the lounge, where April was cleaning up behind the bar. He sat on the couch in front of the fire and watched its flames curling around the logs. There was a copy of the *Beacon-Journal* on the table next to the couch, and Gordon read Cynthia's article about the murder. It included a fairly accurate summary of the riddles raised by the medical evidence. If Rogers had read the story, Gordon was glad he wasn't dealing with the detective right now.

"A penny for your thoughts. Can I touch up your coffee?"

"Thank you," he said to April. She filled his cup, then set the coffee pot on a coaster and sat next to him.

"Could I ask you something?"

"You can always ask."

"I saw you reading the paper. Is it true that they think she died almost before she got back to the cabin?"

"That's what one indicator seems to say, but I don't think they're taking it as absolute. Why? Are you concerned?"

"Sure, I am. I was in a fight with her just before she left, and then she died. The detective was really pressing me about that."

"Don't take it personally. He presses everybody."

167

"I don't know. He was asking a lot of questions about the fight. Then after he talked to Drew yesterday, he had me back in and started asking if I'd been flirting with Drew and was jealous of Wendy."

"That's not how I saw it."

"Drew's pretty worried. You know that, right?"

"I didn't know, but I had a sense he was bothered over something."

"He's engaged to be married next month." Gordon raised his eyebrows. "I know. He isn't acting like it. Anyway, she's from a really good family in Palo Alto, and I guess she wouldn't take it too well if she found out he had a little fling with Wendy. He's having kittens over that."

Gordon looked over his shoulder to make sure they were alone.

"If she doesn't find out about this, I'm sure she'll have other chances. To find out about him, I mean."

April laughed. "I think you're right." Brief silence. "You're a nice guy, Gordon. Is there a Mrs. Gordon somewhere? I don't think she'd have to worry about you."

"Not yet."

"Was there a close call?"

"One."

"Rachel?"

"Not her. We weren't ready for marriage then. Too young. How about you?"

"Me?"

"That's what I said."

"You're sweet. I don't think any customer has asked about me before." Pause. "I'm too young."

"Eighteen's the legal age."

"There's a difference between legal and good idea. From what I've seen so far, I'm not sure marriage is a good idea any time."

"Uh-oh. You're sounding like Peter."

"I can only go by what I've seen and it hasn't been pretty. My father was an abusive drunk. He left us for another woman when I was five. Mom should have been cheering, but instead it broke her heart. Go figure."

"I'm sorry."

"Well, it's hardly your fault. I grew up in Alta Vista, about 40 miles away, and when Dad left, the pickings were pretty slim for Mom. She had a couple of boyfriends, but they were married, so it wasn't going to amount to anything. I mean, do all men cheat on their wives?"

"Only half if you believe the statistics. And a quarter of the wives cheat, or so they say."

"The cheaters all seem to wind up at Harry's, I guess. I don't know. I look at my high school, and half the girls in my class are already married. The other half left. The married ones are going to live around here all their lives. The ones who left aren't coming back unless it's for Thanksgiving or Christmas. "

"Have you thought about going to college?"

"Maybe later. I'm kind of over school now. Harry's isn't a bad gig while I'm figuring it out."

"You'll do fine."

"If I get the chance, maybe. I think Rogers has me figured for the one who killed Wendy."

"It doesn't matter what he thinks, April. He won't arrest somebody without evidence, and if you didn't do it, there's no evidence against you."

"I *didn't* do it. Do you believe that?"

"I believe you."

"You know, I didn't like Wendy, and I've been trying to figure out why she got under my skin. I think it's because I didn't like what she did to Charles. God knows, I don't want to work at Harry's the rest of my life, but I don't want to get out of here by marrying someone I don't love and have no intention of being faithful to."

"Wendy told me she used to wait tables, before she met Charles," Gordon said.

"Maybe I reminded her too much of where she came from. That'd explain the mutual dislike. But there was no need to kill her. Not for me, not for anybody. I'm still really embarrassed that I went after her when she said what she did. If there's one thing I should've learned at Harry's by now, it's not to overreact to people you don't like. They all check out in a week anyway."

3

A FIERCE SQUALL STRUCK as the three returning searchers reached the open area at the boundary of Harry's, and they were thoroughly soaked by the time they had crossed the lawn and reached the lodge. It was hard to tell whether Rogers or Peter was more put out by the drenching. Lilly took it with equanimity.

"All right, I've seen your witches' lair," Rogers said to Gordon. "But since we didn't find a wing of bat or tongue of newt at the crime scene, I don't know what it means, aside from some people getting their jollies in a way I wouldn't choose to. I'll make a note of it, but that's all."

Gordon confined himself to saying, "Thanks for looking."

Johnny returned shortly afterward, and the rain stopped. Gordon and Peter went to the cabin to retrieve their gear and joined him at the pier. Although it wasn't raining at the moment, it felt like a possibility at any time, and a light breeze that barely rippled the surface of the river added a pronounced chill to the air.

"Great weather for the fish," Johnny said as they pushed out into the river. "It's perfect where they are."

They drifted downstream for a mile, saying nothing. The only sounds were the whisper of the light wind, the steady burr of the boat's electric motor, and the occasional call of a bird. On the left bank, cattails, yielding to the wind, leaned to and fro. At a couple of points along the way, cattle had come to the water and were drinking. No one could be seen in any of the houses along the way, nor was anyone visibly working the land at any of the farms.

As they moved slowly downstream, Gordon breathed the air deeply, tried to take in all the surroundings, and couldn't help thinking that the sensation of following the river where it went must be like what Huck Finn and Jim had experienced. A light shower began to fall, and he pulled up the collar of his parka. Of course, he thought, the Mississippi was a bigger river, and Huck and Jim had better weather.

They hugged the bottom of the boat as Johnny took them under the low clearance of Indian Hollow bridge. The shower ended as they came out the downstream side of it, and a moment later Johnny cut the boat's motor, dropped the anchor and pointed to the water ahead of them. Several fish were rising to the surface, feeding on insects drifting down the current.

"A couple of nice ones in that pod," Johnny said. "This is a pleasant surprise. I didn't think we'd be dry-fly fishing today. No, I didn't." A small insect fluttered past the boat, and Johnny snaffled it in his right hand, then extended the hand toward Gordon and Peter, opening it up. A small, light tan insect fluttered about in his palm.

"This is what's for breakfast," he said. "Let me get you gentlemen rigged up with a proper fly." He cast his hand upward, and the insect flew away. "Off with you," he said. "Your life's too short as it is."

"True for all of us," Peter said softly.

They each caught two good fish at that spot, then continued downstream. In the next two hours, Johnny put them over three more groups of rising fish, and each time Gordon and Peter were able to catch and release a few. Gordon lost himself in the moment during that time, cleansing his mind entirely of any thoughts relating to the trouble at Harry's. Nothing mattered but the river, his fly, and the dank gray skies overhead.

Around 2:30, the wind picked up, whipping the surface of the river to a choppy froth. The insects and fish disappeared, and Johnny spent the next hour and a half trying various deep-water tactics to get the fish to bite for his clients. Only one fish obliged, and the anglers' effort began to feel more like work than play. At 4:30, after several futile passes through a deep hole, he pulled up the anchor.

"I hate to say this, gentlemen, but I think we're beating a dead horse. We can try a couple of other places if you'd like, but I can't give you any good reason they'd be better than what we've been doing. I'd suggest we head back, and if it looks any better along the way, we can stop and give it a try."

"Your call, of course."

Gordon and Peter looked at each other. Gordon didn't like wearing gloves and his hands were icy and nearly numb. Peter, despite his layers of clothing, was shivering slightly in the bitter wind.

"If Johnny says we're done, we're done. Let's head back," Gordon said.

As the boat moved slowly back upstream, Gordon put his hands in his jacket pocket and pressed his arms against his torso, trying to keep warm. The gray skies seemed, if anything, to be darkening, and the wind was unremitting. They were nearly back to Indian Hollow Bridge when Gordon felt something sting his left cheek.

It was a small hailstone and was shortly followed by a cascade of others. They bounced off the aluminum of the boat with a loud clatter, pelted the hats of the three men, and combined with the wind to make the normally flat surface of the river utter turmoil. Johnny turned the boat to the right and headed toward the spot where the riverbank and the bridge met. The clearance was slightly higher there, and they were able, barely, to remain seated upright as he beached the boat on the river's edge, directly under the bridge.

He cut the motor. "Can't get through here," he said, "but it's our best bet for waiting out the storm."

Hailstones pelted the bridge above them, creating a constant rattling din. The stones were so numerous and close together as they fell from the sky that they blurred the view of the opposite bank of the river and created a darkness almost like approaching nightfall. Gordon was appreciating the show of nature's force when he became aware that Johnny was uncomfortable. Normally relaxed and in his element on the river, he was now fidgeting and looking around nervously.

"Anything wrong, Johnny?" Gordon said.

He shook his head and looked away, but Gordon wasn't convinced.

After ten minutes, the storm ended as abruptly as it had begun, and the wind even let up some. They pushed the boat off the bank and drifted downstream a short distance. Johnny restarted the motor, and they went under the bridge at the middle, just as they had come earlier in the day. When they had got a hundred feet upstream from the bridge, Johnny looked back at it apprehensively.

"Are you sure you're OK?" Gordon said. "You seem really bothered."

Johnny shook his head and took a deep breath. He seemed to be considering whether to say something and finally did.

"Sorry, Mr. Gordon. I don't want to bother you with it, but I don't like to dally around that bridge late in the day."

Gordon and Peter were paying rapt attention.

"I don't know what to make of it, but last fall, another of the guides from the Fisherman's Friend was out on the river with a client. They were coming back right after sunset, but it was still sort of light out, like it is for a half hour or so. Just as they were coming upriver to the bridge, they saw a man in a boat floating downstream on the other side of it. It was all they could make out at first, but they came out from under the bridge upstream just as the other fellow was starting to go under it."

He paused and looked back at the bridge.

"It was then they realized the man in the boat had no head. For a minute or two the guide and his client were so stunned they didn't know what to do. Then they turned to look again. There was no sign of the boat. It just disappeared.

"Ron Belden was the guide's name. A good man, I think, and not given to flights of imagination. Not at all. But ever since that night, he's refused to guide on Eden River again. Can't say I blame him. You asked me about your witches, Mr. Gordon, but there's more than one strange thing that happens in these mountains. More than one. For my part, I'd just as soon not be near that bridge late in the day."

For a few minutes, they moved slowly upstream in silence, broken only by the hum of the motor and the sound of the wind. Even the birds seemed to have disappeared. Finally Peter spoke.

"Quite a story," he said softly. "Wow. Witches' covens, headless boatmen. Paradise Valley must be a supernatural vortex of some kind."

"As far as I'm concerned," Johnny said, "you can add Mrs. Van Holland to the list. What happened to her wasn't natural. I'm not a superstitious man, doctor, but I'm beginning to believe in the curse on Harry's. Something's not right here. Not right in the least."

"But why the headless boatman?" Peter pressed. "What's the story behind that apparition?"

"Well, sir, a pretty obvious one comes to mind. Pretty obvious when you think about it." He looked back at the bridge receding into the distance.

"You see, it was just before sunset at Indian Hollow Bridge that Harry Ezekian's son blew his head off with a shotgun."

4

"AUTO-SUGGESTION would be my guess," Peter said when they were back in the cabin. "If I had to write a scenario for it, I'd say the guide and the client most likely heard the story about Harry's son at the bar a night or two earlier. What with the drinks and all the other tall tales being told that night, they probably forgot it, but it was in the back of their heads somewhere when they hit that bridge at sunset. Makes as much sense as anything else."

"You don't think it could be somebody's idea of a prank?" Gordon said.

"The headless boatman disappeared after he went under the bridge. You know how open that river is, Gordon. How would a prankster pull off a disappearance like that?"

"He could have just stopped under the bridge, up against the pilings. It would be pretty dark under there and hard to see. And I doubt the guide would have gone back for a closer look in any event."

Peter considered the idea. "Well, it *is* a theory," he said. "I'll give it that. But our prankster would have to be pretty ballsy to take that chance. No, I think I'm sticking with my original diagnosis."

He downed the last of the neat whisky he'd poured upon their return.

"Let's get on up to the lodge," he said. "Being out on that river, I've worked up a thirst. A cold beer by a warm fire sounds pretty good right now."

5

IT WAS RAINING AGAIN when they walked to the lodge, but the beers (Gordon had one, too) were cold and the fire was roaring. Some of the people in the lounge were new, and Gordon guessed they had just arrived for a stay or were locals on a night out. The seats by the fire were taken, and Gordon and Peter ended up at a table by a side window, much of it occupied by a chessboard.

They had been seated a few minutes when Rogers came in, ordered a pint, and headed toward them, pulling up a chair from the next table as he arrived.

"I guess this isn't official," Peter said, looking at Rogers' beer.

"Not unless you have some evidence for me. I could use it if you do."

"Afraid not," Gordon said. He took a sip of his Sierra Nevada. "But I still have a feeling about the witches, and something that happened on the river today added to it." He took another small sip. "It does seem as if someone, singular or plural, is trying to make it look as if there's supernatural activity going on here. And now we have someone killed by what seems to be a spirit who floated off without leaving a trace. I can't help thinking there's a connection somewhere."

"Have you ever heard of coincidence, Gordon?"

"Some people say there's no such thing."

"Some people are wrong. I've handled too many cases where we wasted time trying to establish a connection between two things that ended up being random happenings. They seemed as if they *should* have gone together, but they didn't."

"How about the cases where they did go together, but you just couldn't figure it out?"

Rogers looked around the room.

"I don't think this conversation is going anywhere, but for lack of any better leads, let's run with it a bit. Not here, though. Let's go to the interview room."

"Am I invited?" said Peter.

Rogers stood up and gave him a hard look.

"No," he said, and walked off toward the bar. Lilly had just walked in looking for him and the two had a brief whispered conversation before Gordon came up.

"Get yourself a drink, deputy," Rogers said. "It's on me, then come to the interview room."

Lilly stepped up to the bar, where April was temporarily unoccupied.

"Could I have a Coca-Cola please?" he said.

She arched her eyebrows slightly.

"Ooh, going for the hard stuff," she said, leaning slightly toward him. "It has," she paused dramatically, "*caffeine*, you know."

He simply nodded, so she took out a glass, filled it and pushed it across the bar toward him.

"Your funeral," she said.

Back in the interview room, Gordon repeated the story Johnny had told that afternoon and his contention that there might be a connection between the local phenomena and the murder case. Rogers listened patiently and attentively. When Gordon finished, the detective turned to Lilly.

"Well, deputy, you've been working with me on this. What do you think?"

"About what, sir?"

"Let's start with the headless boatman. Was it real?"

Lilly hesitated, then spoke carefully and deliberately.

"I think the person it happened to believes it was. He told the story to enough people in town that it's pretty widely known now. You wouldn't tell a story like that unless it made a strong impression on you."

"Or, to play the devil's advocate," Gordon said, "you were trying to get it planted in the public imagination."

"That's possible," Lilly said, "but in that case I don't see how it would relate to this murder. That story got out seven months ago, and I don't think the Van Hollands were planning to come here at that time."

Rogers looked at Gordon.

"He has a point," Gordon said. "They weren't even married then."

"All right," Rogers said. "Let's put this line of inquiry on hold." He took a large gulp of his beer and set the glass down.

"I'm going to level with you two because I have to talk with somebody before I report to the sheriff." He looked Lilly and Gordon in the eye, one man at a time.

"I'm stumped," he finally said. "Stumped in a way I've never been before. I mean, I haven't solved every case I've handled — no detective does — but usually I felt I had a pretty good idea of who the perp was and why. I just couldn't prove it. But this time," he paused for a swallow of beer, "I have no idea in hell what happened.

"Usually when you follow leads and talk to people several times, you see a connection you hadn't seen before, or somebody's story changes and starts giving them away. It hasn't happened here. We have a case where the crime scene was hopelessly corrupted, the forensic evidence is at odds with eyewitness evidence, several people have a good motive, and everybody has an alibi, but nobody *really* has an alibi. And nothing is coming into focus and nobody is cracking. It's such a mess that even Gordon's supernatural hooey is starting to sound plausible. Which it isn't.

"I hate to say this, gentlemen, but I feel this one slipping away. I'm losing hope that talking to people one more time is going to produce anything, and I can't justify the taxpayers putting me up here much longer. Tomorrow morning, at eleven o'clock, I'm going to turn in my room key, check out, and release everybody to go home.

"Unless you two can help me out." He picked up the beer glass and finished it in two gulps.

"Gordon," he said, "I want you to rack your brains between now and when I leave. You were here three days before this happened, and you know all the suspects. I have to believe you saw or heard something you haven't yet recognized the importance of. Go through it in your mind as carefully as you can, and let me know if you come up with anything. Anything at all."

He turned to Lilly.

"Deputy, you've been really helpful. Maybe some day you'll make detective, but before that happens, you have to learn to think like one. I want you to think like one now. Put yourself in my shoes, and tell me what you'd be doing to solve this case. Show me what you got."

Lilly drank a swallow of his Coke and took a deep breath. As he exhaled, he emitted a soft burp, followed by a blush.

"Excuse me, sir. I'm sorry. I guess if it was me investigating, I'd take another look at the motives. It's possible we just have part of a motive now, and if we had all of it, we could work on that person. Maybe no one's cracked yet because they haven't been made uncomfortable enough."

After a few seconds of silence Gordon said, "I'm not in your profession, but that sounds like a good answer to me."

"It is a good answer," Rogers said, "and one I'd already thought of. But just for the sake of thoroughness, let's see if you two see anything in the suspects that I haven't. We'll start with Charles Van Holland. Motive: He's just found out that he left his first wife to marry a younger woman who's a lying, cheating, grasping slut." He looked at Gordon and Lilly. "There's a reason we usually look at the husband first. Your thoughts, deputy?"

Lilly coughed. "No question he has a good motive, sir. But some things don't fit. He didn't really know about her past until after she was dead and we told him. And watching him when he found out, I'd say that's when he went over the edge. The motive usually comes before the crime, not after."

Rogers looked at Gordon.

"I think Eldon's right," he said. "My sense is he was just beginning to realize his mistake after the scene on Tuesday night. And his temperament's all wrong for this murder. It was calculated and well planned. Charles is a conventional, nice guy, and I don't see any cunning in him at all. The way his mind works, Wendy was headed for a divorce, not a grave."

Rogers nodded. "All right, then. Drew Evans. Motive: He was about to marry into money and society, but our

178

lady from Syracuse compromised him. Which probably didn't take a whole lot of effort on her part. He stood to lose a sweet deal if it came out. Gordon?"

"My question would be how would it come out? The bride-to-be is in the Bay Area, and I don't see Wendy making a point of calling her when she got home to spill the news. She got her thrill by pulling off the seduction; after that, she lost interest. Unless there's something we don't know, the motive seems weak."

He turned to Lilly.

"And like you said about Van Holland, Mr. Gordon. He's not the right type for the crime. First, I don't think he's smart enough, and second, I don't think he'd feel it was necessary. I knew his type in high school — cocky and totally confident he could talk his way out of anything. That's what he'd try to do if his fiancée found out."

Rogers sighed. "Next up, April Flowers. Motive: She didn't like Wendy, and she almost lost her job when Wendy humiliated her in front of everybody and provoked a fight. The fact she responded to the provocation shows an impulsiveness and temper that could figure into this. Who wants to lead off?"

Gordon, after a brief silence, went first. "The temper works in her favor as far as I'm concerned. Maybe I'd look at her if this was a crime of spontaneous passion, and even there I'd almost have to figure it was a mistake. Like she shoved some one and they hit their head falling down. She may be easy to provoke, but she cools off just as fast. I don't see it."

Rogers looked at Lilly.

"Me either, sir. I think she's naughty, not wicked, and this was a wicked crime."

Rogers picked up his beer glass, then realizing it was empty set it down.

"Moving right along," he said, "We come to Rachel Adderly. Future governor of California if this scandal doesn't do her in. Or so I'm told. Motive: One of the oldest in the book. Wendy seduced her husband. Who seems to have given in a little too readily, if you ask me."

"You go first," Gordon said to Lilly.

179

"It'd be a good motive, sir, if she knew it was happening. But we don't have any evidence she did. If it hadn't been for the murder, Mr. Gordon wouldn't have told us about her husband, we wouldn't have broken Mr. Bingham down, and she may never have known. And she was pretty broken up when she found out. Unless she's a great actress, she had no idea until we told her."

Gordon shifted in his chair. "She's a politician, so of course she's a bit of an actress — but not a great one. Watching the two of them before the murder happened, I don't think she knew. And being a politician, especially running a city, her natural impulse is to make things work. She wouldn't go after Wendy. I think it's more likely she'd put her husband in the doghouse for a while … " he took a deep breath, "and trust me, you don't want to be in *her* doghouse, but then she'd stand by her man and give him at least one more chance."

Rogers arched an eyebrow and looked at Lilly.

"What do you think, deputy, does he know what her doghouse is like?"

"Well, sir, they *are* married."

"Actually, I meant Gordon, not Stuart, but we'll let it go. How about Stuart, then? Motive: He'd cheated on his wife, was probably scared shitless she'd find out, and Wendy was a loose cannon who could have blown his cover at any time. Not a bad motive at all. Deputy, what's your take?"

"I agree with you, sir, that it's a good motive. Probably the best one so far. I could see him maybe going over to talk to her, tell her to keep quiet about it, and then things got out of hand. That's plausible. But then we have the question of the snow in front of his cabin and hers the next morning with no footprints. And I don't know that he'd want to take a chance on leaving the cabin without waking up his wife. Actually, when you come to those two, the problem is that each of them is only half a good suspect. He has the motive but not the temperament. She's smart enough and cool enough to do it, but she didn't have a motive until after the crime was committed."

"Gordon?"

"I think Eldon's right all around. Well, almost. I can't see Stuart even going over to talk to Wendy. I had a good talk with him yesterday, and I think he was scared to death of her. She got him to do something he knew was wrong and didn't think he was capable of. If you ask me, he was lying low and hoping he'd get out of Harry's without being found out. Poor bastard. He almost did. And if he's innocent like I think he is — of the murder, anyway — he and his marriage are collateral damage."

Rogers picked up his empty beer glass and tapped it on the table three times.

"You guys aren't much help," he said. "Let's try my last suspect." He looked at Gordon. "Your friend, the doctor." Gordon started to object, but Rogers held up his hand. "Motive: None known, but something might turn up if we keep digging. Reason for suspicion: His fingerprints, metaphorically speaking, are all over this case. We only have his word that the light went out in the victim's cabin at a time that contradicts the medical evidence, and he was pretty eager to get to the crime scene after it was discovered and go in by himself. Maybe he thought he'd forgotten something. Then he was the one who found the witches' shrine and wasted the better part of my morning. Plus, I don't like his attitude very much. He has the arrogant confidence of a cold-blooded killer, and Gordon said he was sleeping like a brick that night, so the doctor had an opportunity to slip out and do it."

He looked at Lilly. "Gordon has a conflict of interest on this one, so you go first, deputy."

"I don't really like him, sir. Not as a person — sorry, Mr. Gordon — or as a suspect. There's not a hint of a motive for him, not even a speck of evidence to build on. He seems to be the only man here that Mrs. Van Holland didn't, well, flirt with, and he was pretty much sitting on the sidelines enjoying the show she was putting on. Unless you can give me a motive, sorry."

Both sets of eyes turned to Gordon.

"All right, I'll concede that Peter can be impossible at times, and he's brilliant enough to plan a complicated crime. Actually, he might enjoy doing that. What I can't see is him caring enough to follow through with it.

Wendy didn't frighten him or anger him. She amused him. Even if you could come up with a circumstantial reason for him to kill her, I'd still argue against it because there wouldn't be an emotional reason."

"What if," Rogers said, "it wasn't emotional? Suppose he's a psychopath with a high IQ who's hidden that side of himself from everybody, including you? People like that exist, you know. If you look at all the ways he's been involved in this case from that perspective — well, you at least have a coherent theory. Plus he's been married five times, so he might, just might, have some issues with women. And hasn't it struck you as odd, Gordon, that every time your friend needs to pee, he comes up with a clue?"

"I'm still not buying it," Gordon said.

"Then just for the record, answer this question yes or no. On the night Wendy Van Holland was killed, could Dr. Delaney have left your cabin for half an hour to an hour without your noticing it?"

Gordon smiled. "I already told you, detective. The way I was sleeping that night, Bigfoot could have broken down the front door and taken the wallet out of my pants and I wouldn't have noticed it. So, yes, Peter could have gone out of the cabin, but I'm telling you, he didn't."

Rogers looked at Gordon and said nothing for 15 seconds.

"That remains to be seen," he finally said. "Anyway, as stimulating as this conversation has been, it hasn't advanced the investigation by even a millimeter. Let's drop it and get something to eat."

He stood up and scooped his beer glass off the table in one motion.

"And by the way, Gordon, I hope you sleep well tonight."

6

CYNTHIA HENLEY WAS WAITING TO POUNCE as they came back to the lounge. Rogers saw her before she saw him, and he muttered under his breath to Gordon.

"Bloody hell. The Fourth Estate. Now I've got to feed her a line about how we're getting closer to a solution.

They don't pay me enough for that, and it's getting old. Like me."

She saw him and rose from her chair, making a beeline for the bar, where he was headed. He got there first and set his drink in front of Don.

"Another?" Don asked.

"Might as well. And allow me to buy one for Miss Henley, as long as it's understood it's my personal treat and not on the county expense account. What will you have?"

"Thank you," she said. "Just a 7-Up. I still have to write my story."

Rogers turned to Lilly. "Did you hear that, deputy? I think we may have found your soul mate."

Lilly blushed. Rogers and Don laughed. Cynthia and Gordon remained deadpan.

"Where's April?" Gordon said.

"Just left on her break. Anything for you, Mr. Gordon?"

"Not right now, thanks."

Don drew the drinks and set them on the bar.

"I have some questions about the medical evidence," she said.

"You have the right to ask questions, and I have the right to remain silent," Rogers said. "But I'll answer what I can. Let's go over to that table by the window, where we can be alone. Thanks for your help, Gordon."

Peter approached. "You were in there a long time," he said. "Fortunately, the establishment maintains a well stocked bar." He was slurring his words slightly.

"I'm starving. Let's eat," Gordon said. "Would you like to join us, Eldon?"

"Thank you, sir, but I need to wait and see if Detective Rogers needs me for anything else."

Peter and Gordon walked across the entryway to the dining room. It was 7:30 on a Friday night and a different scene altogether from what it had been earlier in the week. Several new guests at the lodge, combined with an influx of locals, had filled the dining room nearly to capacity. Compared to the quiet of previous days, the room was now a cacophony of loud and louder voices, clanking plates and silverware. Sharon was waiting tables, along with another waitress Gordon hadn't seen before; both were busy and moving rapidly.

Sharon saw them and came over as soon as she finished the table she was working.

"There you are," she said. "I've been holding the last table in the room for you. Sorry it's where it is, but I couldn't hold a window table any longer."

They sat down, and Peter raised his empty beer glass in a gesture asking for another. Gordon reached across the table and put his hand on Peter's forearm.

"Could you make it a coffee right now, Peter? I need to tell you something."

Peter looked at Gordon, and Sharon looked at Peter, ballpoint pen poised above her order pad.

"I guess my friend knows best. Make it a coffee." She wrote the order down. "But come back a few minutes after you've brought it."

She left them, and an uncomfortable silence ensued. Outside the large windows of the dining hall, the lights were illuminating the deck, and even from their table deeper inside, they could see a hard rain falling. They looked at the rain for a few minutes until Sharon returned with Peter's coffee. He took a sip.

"We didn't really need a window table," he said. "The rain looks the same as it has all week."

Gordon looked at Peter, trying to think of what Rogers had said. Finally, he leaned across the table and, in a lowered voice, said:

"Peter, we need to talk."

"You're starting to sound more and more like my fourth wife, Gordon. And that's not a good thing."

"Can you be serious for a minute? Rogers just gave me a hell of a scare, and it had to do with you."

Peter's eyes narrowed and his body tensed slightly. He put down the coffee cup and leaned across the table to better hear Gordon.

"All right. You have my attention," Peter said. "What's this all about?"

"There's no nice way to say this, Peter. You're on his short list of suspects."

Peter whistled. "You don't say. And does he have a motive for me, or don't they teach detectives to look for that sort of thing any more?"

"No motive, which is why you're merely on the list, instead of being the main person of interest."

"Then why am I even on the list?"

Gordon took a deep breath. "Go on," Peter said. "It can't be anything worse than my ex-wives have said to me."

"It's several things, really. But mainly it's that you've figured in the situations so much. You, we, went to the cabin right away when Wendy was found; you're the one who saw the light go off in her cabin at a time that screws up the medical evidence; you're the one who discovered the scene of the witches' Sabbath. He thinks that's all too much of a coincidence. He's even suspicious about your bladder."

Peter took it in calmly. "There's something else you're not telling me, isn't there?"

"Plus he just doesn't like you. But you probably knew that."

Peter picked up the coffee cup, took a big swallow and set it down on the table, looking at it disapprovingly.

"You should have let me have another beer if we were going to be having this conversation, Gordon. Between you and me, I think Rogers is frustrated because he isn't getting anywhere on this case, and I don't blame him. He's dealing with a killer who has some intelligence, which is unusual to begin with, and who's lucky to boot. I know I've been saying he should give up and go home, but I don't really mean it. A killer who gets away with murder once is an exceptionally dangerous individual because he, or she, I guess, is likely to start thinking that murder might be the answer to the next problem. So I do sincerely hope he catches this killer. If Rogers wants to talk to me about this case instead of going through you, bring him on. I'll tell him what I'm going to tell you now.

"Let's start with going to the cabin that morning. You've probably figured out by now that I don't believe in much, but there is one thing I believe in completely, and that's my professional responsibility. When I was younger and working in the emergency room, I doubted even that. Somebody would come in with gunshot wounds or stab wounds, and I'd wonder why I was bothering to save them. Because there was a pretty good chance most of them would do one of two things: They'd go out and repeat the behavior that got them stabbed or shot in the first place, or they'd be quicker on the draw the next time and be the stabber or the shooter themselves and end up behind bars.

"Somewhere along the way, I stopped worrying about that. I realized I had a gift for surgery and trauma care, and that I couldn't play God with that gift. I had to use it, and at least give the people I was treating a chance, even though only one out of 20 would do anything with it. I have no way of knowing who that one is going to be, so I have to treat everybody as if they could be the one. That ethic is instinctual and automatic now, which is why I immediately rushed out to the cabin when we knew what had happened. If I'd been able to do anything for her, Wendy probably would have joined the Club of Nineteen, but I had a solemn obligation to her anyway. The obligation to at least give her a chance."

He paused for another swallow of coffee.

"Now we skip ahead to the find in the forest. I can see how that looks suspicious because it was dumb luck and coincidence. Some people don't believe in coincidence, but I do."

"So does Rogers."

"Well then he should let up. I mean, listen, Gordon, if I'd stopped to go into the woods a minute earlier or a minute later, I wouldn't have seen that large, cut-off boulder. That's what made me go over for a closer look. I saw it through that slight opening in the trees, and I imagine you did, too once you got off the trail. And once I saw the scene in the clearing, I knew there was something going on. Hell, even Alan would have put down his trout fly and seen that much. After that, I had to call you over and share it. Besides which, does Rogers think I went out there and set up the scene? I've hardly been away from your side since we got here. When would I have the time?"

"Calm down, Peter. I'm not the one you have to convince."

"All right, fine. I'm just saying. Finally, getting up in the middle of the night and seeing the light go off in the next cabin. All I can say is that Rogers is plenty old enough to understand the getting up part, and I know what I saw. I noticed that light on when I rolled out of bed, and I stopped to look at it when I came back. That's when it switched off, and I looked at the clock on the nightstand ten seconds later. That's my story, and I'm sticking to it."

April appeared at the table.

"Ah, the angel of mercy," Peter said. "Could you get me a beer, my love?"

"Sure thing. You boys ready to order yet?"

They hadn't looked at the menu yet, but Peter picked his up and handed it to her.

"I'll have the New York steak with mushrooms, medium rare."

"The same," Gordon said, "but cook mine medium."

"Coming right up," she said, and bounced off. Peter followed her with his eyes.

"Ah, to be 40 again," he said.

Gordon laughed. "I'd hardly say she was your type, Peter."

"I don't know who is, and I've tried five times. But mark my words: April's going to be a good mother."

Gordon shot him a quizzical look.

"She has two of the most important attributes for that job. She's efficient, and she doesn't take crap from anybody. Neither do I. Maybe that's why Rogers doesn't like me, but he's hardly in the minority."

Peter finished his coffee and looked toward the window. The rain was still falling steadily and periodically a gust of wind would blow a sheet of water against the dining room windows. Inside, it was warm and convivial, the room filled with the sounds of laughter, conversation, drinking and eating. It would have been utterly comforting if not for the fact that almost certainly one of the people in the lodge was a cold-blooded killer.

April returned with the beer. Peter picked it up and held it to the light, enjoying its color, then tipped the glass slightly in Gordon's direction.

"Here's to us," he said, taking a swallow. "I'm glad you asked me to come along on this trip, and your friendship means a lot to me. Tomorrow's our last full day here, so let's make the most of it."

Gordon lifted his water glass to return the toast.

"I'll drink to that," he said.

7

IT WAS NINE O'CLOCK when they were finished with dinner, and the crowd in the dining room had thinned out. Rogers, whose meal had been delayed by his meeting with the press, was at a corner table with Lilly, both of them halfway through their dinner. Several people were having after-dinner drinks in the lounge, but Gordon recognized only Stuart and Charles, alone and sullen at different ends of the room. He decided not to join them.

When they opened the front door of Harry's, rain was falling steadily outside, with the wind gusting from time to time. They started down the path to the cabins, but when they reached the point where it forked toward the parking lot, Peter stopped.

"I need to get something from the car," he said. "Go ahead to the cabin if you want."

"I'm wet already," Gordon said. "I may as well come with you."

Gordon's Cherokee was parked near the middle of the lot, and most of the other cars were parked as close to the lodge as possible. When they reached the Cherokee, Peter began fumbling for the spare set of keys Gordon had given him at the beginning of the trip, finally finding them and opening the rear passenger's side door. As he was doing this, Gordon looked to the back corner of the parking lot, where one car stood by itself.

"That's funny." Gordon said. "That looks like Cynthia's car."

"I think you're right, but so what. She's here, isn't she?"

"I'm not so sure. It seems to me she would have left after talking to Rogers, and that was an hour ago."

"She's probably inside writing her story somewhere. And it's pouring rain out here. Let's get back to the cabin."

He started in that direction, and Gordon followed him for a few steps, then stopped.

"No, Peter. This doesn't feel right. Humor me. I'm going to take a quick look.

With a sigh, Peter followed Gordon, who was trudging toward the car at the back of the parking lot. It was dark, and there were no lights in the parking area, just a faint illumination from the distant lodge. But as they got close to the car, Gordon saw something white near the far rear corner of it. He took a small flashlight out of his parka pocket and aimed it in that direction.

A white running shoe with pink markings protruded from behind the right rear tire of the car. Gordon ran the last ten feet to the car and shone his light behind it.

Cynthia Henley lay face-down on the ground, sprawled as if she had dropped suddenly and unguardedly, a sodden reporter's notebook by her side. When Gordon pointed the beam at the back of her head, they could see a large, bloody gash through her soaked hair.

Peter sprang into action, kneeling by the body.

"She still has a pulse, but it's weak," he said. Run back to the lodge and get Rogers."

Gordon turned.

"But call an ambulance first. I'll do everything I can, but she needs to be in a hospital pronto. The bigger and more sophisticated, the better. Go!"

Gordon ran as fast as he could.

8

IT WAS 11:30, and Gordon, Rogers and Lilly were seated in front of the fireplace in the lounge, Rogers in the middle couch with Lilly and Gordon in the chairs at each side. The bar had closed for the evening, but Don allowed them to remain to tend to business. They were wet and weary, but Gordon had carefully added two large logs to the fire, which burned intensely and threw out a reassuring light and warmth. Peter had gone back to the cabin, and Gordon surmised that he was having a generous whisky or brandy from his personal stash. This time, Gordon couldn't hold it against him.

"She's at Muirfield Memorial right now, being treated and stabilized," Rogers said. "As soon as they can, they're going to ship her to Red Gulch Community, which has the best trauma unit in the five-county area."

"Is she … " Gordon's voice trailed off.

"They think she'll live, but she's damn lucky you found her when you did. Another half hour in the cold and rain and she'd have been in a lot worse shape. As it is, it was good she was wearing a heavy coat." Don had poured a generous double of Hennessey for Rogers and Gordon before leaving; Lilly was dipping a bag of Lipton tea in a large, steaming mug. Rogers took an approving sip of his cognac and continued.

"No telling when she'll come around, and of course complications are still possible. Frankly I'm not putting much hope in her being able to help us when she does come to. She was hit from behind in a dark parking area, and with the noise of the wind and rain, I doubt she heard her attacker coming at all. This isn't going to be easy."

"Surely you can trace people's movements," Gordon said.

"Not as much as you might think. A room full of people, with everybody moving around and going in and out all night long is as close to anonymous as you can get. It would have been a lot easier a couple of nights ago when the dining hall was half full. In a big, crowded room, people narrow their environment to what's right in front of them. They hardly notice anything else."

"He's right, Mr. Gordon," said Lilly. "I've talked to most of the guests and called a couple of the locals who were here for dinner. Most of them don't remember if they left the dining room to go to the bar or the bathroom, and they sure don't remember what anyone else was doing."

"Take yourself," Rogers said. "You were at a table with just your friend, the good doctor. Did you leave the dining room at all?"

"No, I was there the whole time. Wait, I did go out to clean up for a minute right after we gave our order."

"See. You almost forgot. How about Dr. Delaney?"

"He got up once, right after they brought dinner, but he was only out a couple of minutes. He wouldn't have had time to go to the parking lot and back."

"Are you sure about that? Most people are lousy judges of time. If you ask ten people about something that took ten minutes, only one will be close on the time. The rest will either say it took two or three minutes or fifteen to twenty minutes."

"I'm pretty sure. Peter isn't in very good shape. He wasn't gone long enough."

"Still, he tried to talk you out of checking her car, didn't he?"

"That's true, but it was cold and wet out there, and there was no real reason to look. If anything, my insisting on checking out her car was more suspicious than Peter being reluctant to do it."

Rogers took another sip of the cognac.

"Don't give me any ideas," he said. "This case is just about the biggest mess I've ever handled. About all I can say for sure is this:

"The three of us got back to the lounge right around 7:30, and she waylaid me on the spot. I talked to her for almost half an hour. She was pressing me about whether or not we were close to an arrest, and she was asking a lot of questions about the medical evidence and the time of death, but I was trying to deflect her, and I'm not sure what she was getting at. We finished the conversation at exactly 7:58 p.m."

"You're sure about the time?" Gordon asked.

"I was on overtime, so I looked at my watch to note when work stopped. After that, it appears she didn't leave right away. April said that after I left, she saw our Lois Lane talking to a few people in the lounge, then at some point in the next half hour, she was gone. April was crazy-busy making drinks and helping with the tables, so I'm surprised we got that much out of her. And until you came running back in the middle of my dinner, that's all we know. We got *bupkes,* Gordon. You know what *bupkes* is?"

191

"It's a lot of nothing."

"Damn right. We got a lot of nothing, And nowhere I can see to start looking for something."

The three men looked silently into the fire for a minute, then Lilly spoke.

"Could I make a suggestion, sir? I'm assuming that we're working on the theory that whoever killed Mrs. Van Holland also attacked Miss Henley." Rogers nodded. "In that case, maybe the question we should be asking is what did she know that the killer was afraid of? She was asking about the medical evidence, so maybe he thought she was on to something. Or getting too close to something. I don't know."

Rogers downed the last of his Hennessey and gave Lilly an approving look.

"Good point, deputy. Let's sleep on it and start down that path tomorrow morning."

9

PETER WAS DOZING IN A CHAIR with a whisky glass on the table next to him. It had an ounce or so left in it. He woke up when Gordon came in.

"Sorry," Peter said. "I was going to wait up for you."

"No problem." Gordon took off his parka and stood by the heater. "Rogers said it looks like she'll pull through."

"That's what I would have said. Dammit, Gordon, I've been too busy for a vacation."

"A regular busman's holiday."

Peter sat up and tried to shake the cobwebs from his head.

"You realize, of course, that this changes everything."

"Meaning?" Gordon said.

"Meaning that up to now we could look at Wendy's murder with a bit of distance. Too bad for her, but we could believe that she brought it on herself, to some extent, through the force of her lovely personality, and that the rest of us weren't in any danger."

"We can't say that now."

"No, we can't. Remember what I said earlier about the danger of a killer who's murdered successfully? That's what we have to worry about now. Our killer thought Cynthia figured something out, and he, maybe she, was willing to kill again to stop her. A better placed blow, another hour in the rain for Cynthia, and this is a double murder case. It's a bad business all around."

"It is. But I can't help feeling that I'm starting to come to some idea about all this. Like there's one connection I need to make and the puzzle will suddenly become a picture."

Peter downed half the whisky in his glass.

"I'd be careful if I were you, Gordon. Everybody here knows you've been spending a lot of time with Rogers and sharing ideas with him. If Cynthia was almost killed for nosing around, you could be next."

Gordon laughed. "Come on, Peter."

"I'm serious. Nobody saw tonight's attack coming, and it may not be the last one. And the next victim may not be so lucky."

He finished the last of the whisky.

"Do me a favor, Gordon. Lock the chain bolt tonight. We'll both sleep better if you do."

Saturday May 13

1

GORDON SLEPT POORLY, his dreams punctuated by vivid and incoherent images involving witches, headless boatmen, and stealthy faceless figures lunging to attack in the dark. He was in the middle of one of those dreams when the alarm clock came on, and it took him a minute to turn it off. He remained groggy after a shave and shower.

"Last full day," Peter said, as they left for breakfast at the lodge. "I've got to hand it to you, Gordon. You gave us a fishing trip to remember."

There was no rain as they walked to the main building, but the cloud cover remained dense, and a chilling breeze cut through their clothes. Even by the standard of the past few days, it was a dismal morning.

"I want you to stick around a while," Rogers said as they arrived. "I may have more questions."

"How is she?" Gordon asked.

"Still unconscious, but better. They're pretty sure she'll pull through."

Rachel and Stuart were sitting at a window table, eating a tense and wordless breakfast. Charles arrived shortly after Gordon and Peter, and they invited him to join them for breakfast. He followed them to the buffet and took a small scoop of scrambled eggs, a single sausage link, and a slice of whole wheat toast to go with his cup of coffee.

"My appetite must be coming back," he said as he sat down at the table. "This is better than the last couple of days."

They ate in silence for two or three minutes, then Charles pushed his plate away, half of everything still on it.

"Sorry," he said. "My stomach is in a knot, and I've hardly slept, though the sedative helped some. Thanks, doc."

Peter nodded, but said nothing.

"I still can't believe this. I've been trying to think about what happened — not just here, but from the very beginning. With Wendy. Did you know I met her when she came to work for me?"

"I think she told me that," Gordon said.

"It was the strangest damn thing. I was looking for a receptionist and had three applications from people I was going to call in for an interview. Scoring the applications, Wendy's was third best out of three, but she was the first interview. Three minutes into it, I *knew*. She was alive, and charming and eager — just what you want in someone who has to deal with customers and the public. At the end of the interview, I offered her the job on the spot, then canceled the other two interviews.

"I think I was half in love with her already. Things hadn't been going well in my marriage. The kids had moved out. Georgia was at loose ends and trying all sorts of things to give herself something to do. But she was doing it alone, and I wasn't part of it. I know it's a cliché, but we were drifting apart. Either of you been married?"

"Nope," Gordon said.

"Five times," Peter said.

"Then you know exactly what I mean. Something goes sour in the marriage, and no matter how hard you try, you can't get the sweetness back. Isn't that right?"

"I don't know," Peter said. "None of my wives was willing to try."

"Then it's the same in the end. Because it ends."

"Well put."

"Right now I'm madder than hell about what a fool I've been, because, like you said before, doc, I should have checked her references. But she didn't deserve to get killed, and part of me is feeling sad. This marriage was bound not to last, but now there will never be a clean ending."

He finished his cup of black coffee.

"I hope to hell they catch the bastard who did this. She deserves at least that." He stood up. "Thank you for listening. I'm pretty raw, and I know it isn't pretty, but it helped to talk. I hope I didn't impose."

"Not at all," Gordon said. They shook hands and he left. Peter and Gordon finished their breakfast and sat at the table, looking out at the river, the gray skies, and the bright green lawn.

"There's a moral in that story," Peter finally said. "You know what it is, Gordon?"

"Don't fool around on your wife."

"Ah, I keep forgetting you're a moralist, and of course that's exactly what a moralist would say. But I'm a pragmatist and a realist, so I take home a different message."

Peter leaned forward and said in a stage whisper, "Don't marry the one you're fooling around with."

2

ON THE WAY BACK TO THE CABIN, Gordon excused himself, saying he wanted to be alone. He turned right toward the pier and walked to the end of it. Johnny had left with two of the new arrivals to Harry's, and looking downstream, Gordon could see their boat disappearing around the bend. Another boat and a kayak were tied to the pier. Gordon pulled his parka up around his neck and looked out at the river. Its current, so slow as to be almost imperceptible, was soothing, and he found himself focusing on a leaf upstream as it slowly drifted along. He stayed with the leaf for three minutes until it was finally too far away to see. Then a trout rose to an insect on the far side of the river, and his brain shifted gears. He looked at the ripples spreading outward from where the fish had surfaced, and tried to calculate whether he could cast that far. He decided he couldn't. He was so utterly absorbed by the river that he didn't hear the other person who had walked up behind him.

"Oh, it's you," he said.

"Who were you expecting?"

"I wasn't expecting anyone. After what's happened at Harry's this week, people have been avoiding conversations."

"You can hardly blame them. It's not the sort of situation that lends itself to small talk."

He nodded.

"Can I ask you something?"

"Ask away."

196

"This isn't easy for me, but I'd like your opinion. I know you'll have one. I just — well, I don't know what to do. I guess you know the story."

"I'm afraid everybody does."

"That's part of the awfulness of it. Anyway, the detective said we can leave tomorrow, so I guess we'll be getting away from the people who know. But then it'll be just the two of us knowing, and I'm afraid that might be even worse."

Gordon cocked his head to the side.

"What would you do if you were me? Would you throw him out?"

"It's not my marriage. I'm afraid I can't answer that one."

"Oh, God, this is awful. I mean the modern woman in me knows it's his fault and he should have been able to control himself. But at the same time I can't help blaming myself for bringing Stuart up here where there's nothing to do. And this filthy weather!"

"The weather's nobody's fault."

"I know, I know. But I'm looking at this and trying to see what I could have done differently. You know, when he and I first met, the sparks didn't begin to fly right away. After the first date, I wasn't sure there would be a second. But I came to see that he was a gentle and decent man, and after a while I could see myself spending my life with him and maybe having his child. I grew into loving him, you see, and because of that I thought I had no illusions and wasn't in the grip of a blind passion. I thought I really knew the man I married.

"And then he jumps into bed with ... with her. I can't believe it, and I don't know if I can ever trust him again. If he cheated once, isn't he likely to do it another time? Or more? How can I stay married to a man if every time he works late, I start to wonder?"

There was a loud splash in the river, and they turned to see an osprey emerging from the water with a handsome trout in its beak. They watched it fly off into the distance.

"It sounds as if you still love him," Gordon said, "and if the question is whether he'll cheat on you again, I do have an opinion. It may not be right, but it's my opinion."

"Let me hear it."

"I think this first came to me when I was working at the brokerage, with a lot of high-energy, high-income men. You couldn't help picking up some of what was going on in their lives, and it could get pretty tangled, especially with romance and marriage. After hearing enough of that, I finally came up with the 80-10-10 rule.

"By that I mean that ten percent of married men are never going to cheat on their wives. They're too moral, too afraid, or both.

"Another ten percent are going to cheat no matter what. It's in their nature and they almost can't help it. They just can't control the impulse. I think our friend Drew might be in that group."

"I think you're right."

"That leaves the broad 80 percent of the rest. They're capable of cheating if the circumstances are right — if they run into an interested woman at a time when the marriage is going through a rough patch, for example. It's a matter of chance, and of course, some succumb easier than others. But my point is that most men *could* do it at some time and place in their lives.

"But here's the other thing. If you figure half do and half don't, there's something I've noticed with the guilty half. It generally puts a hell of a strain on them. It's not easy to make up plausible stories and cover all the eventualities. And most of us — I'm talking about guys now — know at some level that it's wrong. So it usually blows up, and after it does, most of the men in this group are going to tell themselves, 'I'm never going to do that again. It's too much of a strain and there's too much guilt.' In other words, once is enough."

"So you think Stuart ... "

"I think he's in that group. I've talked to him a bit, and he seems genuinely remorseful. Plus, with Wendy, I don't think he knew what hit him. I could be wrong, but my opinion is that he's a long shot to step out on you again. And if that's a fair assessment, I guess the question you have to ask is, can you forgive him for doing it once?"

The wind had been picking up speed for the past few minutes, and a wicked gust hit them with such force they almost lost their balance, and Rachel grabbed Gordon's arm for support. The gust was followed by a large drop of rain, then others. Within seconds, they were utterly exposed to a torrential, drenching downpour. Rachel seemed not to notice. Finally, she let go of Gordon's arm and said:

"So tell me, Gordon. How does your theory apply to you?"

"Oh, I'm an 80 percenter. No doubt about it."

"I doubt it. I think you're a ten percenter."

"Which ten percent?"

She laughed. "I think we both know the answer to that. Thank you so much for talking to me."

"Always."

"Don't take it personally, but I need to get out of this rain and into that nice, toasty cabin. I'll think about what you said."

"Good luck."

She turned and strode purposefully off the pier. When she reached land, she began jogging toward her cabin, and he watched, with a pang, as she ran across the lawn, her long legs moving her forward fluidly and gracefully. When she was inside, he turned and looked out at the river, its calm surface whipped up by the wind and heavy rain. He felt as agitated as the weather. Something he couldn't put his finger on was rattling around inside his head, waiting to fall into the right place, where he could make sense of it. He stared at the river through the hard rain for ten minutes, but couldn't make it come together. Finally, he turned to start back to the cabin, where Peter was no doubt wondering what had happened to him.

Then, as if the tumblers of a lock had fallen into place, allowing it to be opened, he knew.

"Of course," he said aloud. "That has to be how it happened."

Instead of going to his cabin, he walked back to the lodge.

3

IT TOOK TWO CUPS OF COFFEE in the lounge, seated in front of the fire, for him to put it all together in coherent form. When April came by with the pot to offer him a third cup, he waved her off brusquely.

"Jeezo," she said. "Usually it's the coffee that makes a man nervous. You're making the coffee nervous."

Gordon walked to the front desk, where Don was sorting the paperwork for the day's arrivals, and asked if Rogers was around.

"He's with the deputy," Don said. "You want me to tell him something?"

"Just that I'd like to see him when it's convenient." Don nodded and turned to go to the room that was serving as Rogers' office.

For a quarter of an hour he fidgeted and took several walks around the perimeter of the empty dining room. The rain finally let up as Lilly came out.

"Mr. Gordon?"

"Can I have a word?"

"Follow me."

Rogers was hunched over the small table in his room. The table was covered with papers — handwritten notes, medical reports, faxes from the Syracuse police, and much more. The papers were scattered over the top of the table in a state of disarray that matched the state of the investigation. Rogers looked up from them, a hangdog expression on his face.

"Whatever you got," he said, "I hope it's good. This investigation is starting to wear me down."

"Are you getting anywhere with the attack on Cynthia?"

Rogers shook his head. "She's still unconscious, but responding better by the hour. I don't expect much, though, even when she can talk."

"Do you think she was attacked by Wendy's killer?"

"What else makes sense? So have you heard something interesting?"

"Better than that, maybe," Gordon said. He self-consciously paused for effect.

"I think I know how Wendy was killed in a locked room." Rogers, who had been slumping, sat up straight, and Lilly, who was sitting on the bed leaned forward.

"And if I'm right about how, that tells us who."

Seconds passed with only the sound of the three men breathing in the room. Rogers finally broke the silence.

"Bullshit," he said, raising his hand as Gordon tried to object. "Don't interrupt me. Seven years ago, I was investigating the disappearance of a 15-year-old girl. We weren't getting anywhere fast, and all of a sudden this local woman who claimed to be a psychic said she could find the girl. The community was up in arms over her disappearance, and the goddamn *Beacon-Journal* did a story about the psychic. The sheriff was up for re-election in three months, and he ordered me to work with her.

"To make a long story short, she said the girl was dead, but her spirit was calling from the mountains. That woman dragged me and half the news media in Northern California up to a small lake at the end of a dirt road 30 miles outside town. We combed every square inch of that lake — helicopters, boats, scuba divers, you name it. It took two days, we came up with zilch, and you don't want to know how much it cost."

"The day after we finish dragging the lake, the girl's mother calls and says her daughter just walked in the door. Turns out the girl hooked up with the star of the basketball team and on a whim decided to go off to Oregon with him for a few days of adult recreation. I frog-marched that basketball-playing bastard into the courthouse in front of the TV cameras on a statutory rape charge, but the judge let him off with time served.

"And that, Gordon, is when I took a solemn vow that I would resign on the spot rather than letting an amateur tell me they've solved an investigation again. I'm sorry. You're a decent guy and I know you mean well, but you really need to leave this to us."

Gordon was not accustomed to being dismissed out of hand, and for a moment, it rankled. But he quickly recognized that it was the frustration, more than Rogers, that was speaking. He stood up and looked down at the detective. When he spoke, it was coolly and matter-of-fact.

"You're probably right, Rogers. Hubris on my part. I guess I'm getting carried away with my own importance."

Gordon walked to the door and put his hand on the knob.

"Keep doing what you're doing, and good luck catching the killer. If I can help, let me know. But if you change your mind a few days from now, remember I'll be back in San Francisco then. You have my number."

He turned the knob.

"Sir," said Lilly.

"What?"

"Sir, I know Mr. Gordon is probably wrong, but maybe there's something in his idea that could help us. And we *are* stuck. What would it hurt to at least hear him out?"

Gordon's hand remained on the doorknob.

Rogers stared at him with a fixed, surly expression on his face.

"Hell," said Rogers. "It's not like we have another good lead to follow. All right, Gordon. Sorry I snapped at you. That psychic is still pissing me off. Tell me what you got, and like the deputy says, maybe there's something in it that we can use."

Gordon returned to his chair and sat down.

"Thank you." His heart was pounding, and he stared at the ceiling before taking a deep breath and beginning.

Over the next half hour he meticulously laid out the theory he had developed, explaining in considerable detail how the locked-room situation could have been accomplished and why that explanation pointed to one person and one person alone as the killer. Rogers sat with arms crossed as Gordon began, but after several minutes adopted a looser posture and began interjecting a question from time to time.

"Well I'll be damned," Rogers said when Gordon was finished.

"You have to admit, sir," said Lilly, "that it fits the evidence and explains everything."

"And you didn't even drag in those witches of yours, Gordon. I see you've finally given up on that idea."

"I still think they may be relevant," Gordon said, "but there was nothing supernatural about the crime. And if I'm right, it was totally simple."

"So simple it fooled everybody," Rogers said. "Including me. The only thing that bothers me is that your theory is the only thing we have on our suspect. I need to think about how to play this."

"Excuse me, sir," Lilly said. "There may be something more solid. We didn't pay any attention to it at the time because we thought we knew what it meant, but if Mr. Gordon is right, it means something else altogether."

He explained, and Rogers buried his head in his hands.

"If this is right," Rogers finally said, "I've missed so much I should have retired six months ago."

"Where's the medical examiner?" Lilly said. "Couldn't he tell you if Mr. Gordon's idea would hold up?"

Rogers looked at his watch. "He's probably playing golf right now, but I'll get after him." He looked at Gordon. "I may be thanking you later, but right now we have a lot of checking to do on your theory. Leave us to it, and I'll let you know what we find."

4

THE NEXT FEW HOURS were the slowest moving Gordon could recall spending in his fairly young life. He went back to the cabin at first, but Peter kept asking him what was going on, and not wanting to say, Gordon finally went back to the lodge, took a seat in the lounge, and inflicted his surly and nervous presence on April. It was six o'clock before Lilly came into the lounge and asked Gordon to come to the interview room.

"Hard to believe," Rogers said, "but the medical examiner says your theory would account for most of the discrepancies. More importantly, he says he'll testify to that in court. It's not evidence, but it's corroboration."

"And just before she was attacked in the parking lot," Gordon said, "Cynthia came up to you wanting to ask about the medical evidence. She said it pretty loud, and probably a dozen people could have heard her, including our suspect. If we have the method right, our killer would have been really worried about someone figuring it out. A reporter who's nosing around on the issue and who already snatched a medical report off the fax machine could have pointed the way to a solution without even realizing it, just by asking some questions. That would be a pretty good motive for getting her out of the way."

"You don't have to do any more selling, Gordon. Your theory fits like a glove and I even like the suspect. There's only one little problem."

He left a pregnant silence filling the room. Lilly finally broke it.

"No evidence," he said. "Although that test … "

"Right you are, deputy. But we need to ship the test off to an outside lab, and that could take a while."

"There must be something, sir. If Mr. Gordon's idea is right, and our killer's already attacked a second person, well, we're leaving people exposed to danger if we don't make an arrest."

Both men looked at Rogers, who picked up the water glass on the table and took a swallow. He set it down on the table and closed his eyes for half a minute, then opened them again.

"There is one thing I could do," he said. "It's risky and it's not exactly according to Hoyle, but I could try bringing in our person of interest and seeing if I can't get a confession with a bluff. I've actually been thinking about that for a couple of hours, and it might be a blessing of getting older."

"I don't understand, sir," Lilly said.

"Ten years ago, I would have killed this idea the minute I had it. If it went wrong, it could ruin my career. But you know what? I'm retiring in seven weeks, and if I screw up now, there's not much they can do to me. I have the freedom to take a chance, and by God, I'm going to take it. "

He looked at Lilly. "Deputy, go find our suspect, but wait ten minutes before you come back. I need to think it over one more time."

Lilly rose and walked to the door. Rogers spoke again as he reached it.

"And, deputy, one more thing. If you're so inclined, you might want to say a little prayer that this works."

Lilly cracked the barest of smiles.

"Not a good idea to pray for results, sir. But I'll ask for God to guide us."

"Whatever. We'll need all the help we can get."

The deputy left, and Gordon stood up.

"I guess this is where I leave it to the professionals," he said. "Good luck."

"Not so fast, Gordon. I want an independent witness here when I try this, so get your ass back in the chair."

Gordon sat down. "You mean in case it goes badly?"

"Even if it goes well."

The next several minutes passed in silence and at a pace that felt like an hour in a dentist's chair. Exactly on schedule, there was a knock on the door, after which Lilly came in with the suspect, who saw Gordon and did a double-take.

"Gordon. What are you doing here?"

"Don't get excited," Rogers said. "I haven't questioned the two of you together yet, but I want to do it now in the hope of clearing up a couple of points."

The suspect shrugged.

"I'm going to be talking to a few more people tonight, and just to be on the safe side, I'm reading everyone their Miranda rights. I've already done that with Gordon, and I'd like to do it with you. Like I said, just to be on the safe side."

"Sure, but you're wasting your time. I know my rights, and I don't have anything to hide."

Rogers read the warning, and Gordon, trying not to look at the suspect, thought the detective was hamming it up a bit.

"I'll try to make this as succinct as possible," Rogers said. "This case has been a bear from the beginning, and not the least of it is the question of how Wendy Van Holland could have been killed in a cabin locked from the inside, and how there were no footprints in the snow leading in or out. The snow was melted by the time we got here, but three people have told me there were no footprints in it beyond Gordon's cabin. Yet the killer apparently left the Van Holland cabin after the snow had stopped. For a long time the only explanation for that seemed supernatural, but I don't believe in that stuff.

"And then I realized that the answer was right under our nose the whole time."

The suspect remained impassive, but Gordon thought he could read signs of nervousness.

"I now believe the killer didn't walk to the cabin after all. It would have been risky walking across that open lawn, where anyone in the lodge or in the other cabins could see you." The suspect flinched. "I meant you in a general sense, not you particularly. No, I think our killer took the river to the Van Holland cabin. There's a kayak tied up at the pier, and it would have been easy as pie to hop in and quietly paddle a little ways upstream, then come ashore just past that last cabin — the one that Wendy was in by herself that night. That kayak has a stake that can be driven into the bank of a river or lake to anchor it, and our deputy here found a cavity in the dirt of the river bank just the other side of the cabin this afternoon. That seems to support our theory so far.

"Our killer then could have walked along the back side of the cabin, out of sight from Gordon's place, and knocked on the window or the front door. Whoever it was, Wendy knew her killer and let that person in. I expect that person wanted something from her, and when she wouldn't go along, she signed her death warrant."

Rogers paused for a sip of water. The other three people in the room were barely moving or breathing.

"Afterward, the killer decided to wait and see if the snow would let up, and it did. The footprints made on the way in were mostly obliterated by then, and a couple of swipes of the front steps would have gotten rid of all but a trace of them there. The killer could have gone out the window on the back side of the cabin and rolled along the ground for 25 to 30 feet back to the kayak. That would have pretty much wiped out the incoming footprints and ensured there weren't any going out. It was a neat little trick and also very simple when you know how it was done.

"And from a legal point of view, the act of taking the kayak to the cabin could be taken as an indication of premeditation, which could make this a first-degree murder instead of a crime of passion. I'm not sure our killer thought that one all the way through.

"However, this theory doesn't stop there. We still have to account for two more things. There's the medical evidence that suggests an earlier time of death, and there's the fact that in the story I've just told, the killer couldn't have locked the cabin from inside. It's a single-pane window, and there's no way it could be both shut and locked from the outside. Yet it was shut and locked the next morning. There's only one way that could have happened. The killer had to be someone who went into the cabin the next morning.

"And that's why I called you in here, Don.

"You see, I think our killer got a bit too smart for his own good and gave himself away. It probably occurred to him to turn off the heat and leave the window open so the body would cool down faster and cloud the time of death. If he stopped there, he probably would have gotten away with it. But then, on Wednesday morning, it worked out that another opportunity came up, and our killer couldn't leave well enough alone.

"When Charles Van Holland went out to the cabin, you probably figured he'd go around to the side when the door wouldn't open and find the open window. But he was so unnerved, he turned around and came straight back without trying to look in. Then you headed over to the cabin, and that's where you started thinking a bit too much. You kicked in the front door and took off the deadbolt, but the door still closed properly. Once you were inside, it would have taken just seconds to make sure all the windows were closed and locked from the inside and to turn on the heater.

"Your satisfied customers gave you away on that one. Everybody says your electric wall heaters get those small cabins heated up really fast. It was several more minutes before the doctor and Gordon got to the cabin. It might not have warmed up to 70 yet, but it would have been a lot warmer than the outside, and they would have been focusing on the body, not the thermostat. And of course by the time the investigators arrived an hour and a half later, you could have been growing orchids in that place.

"You want to say anything about that?"

207

Don laughed nervously. It looked to Gordon as if Rogers' narrative had shaken him, but Gordon was acutely aware of how thin the actual evidence was.

"That's a tidy explanation, detective. But I guess you don't seem to think you need a motive before you make a serious accusation like that."

"I'm glad you brought that up, Don," Rogers said. "I was going to get to that next. We're still looking into the financials, but it seems there could be a very powerful motive indeed. Because if I'm right, you stood to lose Harry's.

"It took us a while to get somebody to let us into the county recorder's office on a Saturday, but when we ask for something like that, we usually get it. It turns out the deed to this place is in your wife's name, which makes sense when you consider it was her family money that paid for it. Now I've only known Sharon a few days, but she seems like a fairly upright woman who might not take it lying down if she found out that her husband had been sleeping with one of the guests. A younger and more attractive one, at that. You know, Don, in my experience, women don't tend to be very understanding about that. She just might want to throw you out and keep Harry's herself. So when Mrs. Van Holland threatened on Tuesday night to talk about what was really going on here, that had to freeze your heart.

"Everybody but Gordon forgot about it, but that morning, Mrs. Van Holland was complaining about the heat in her cabin, and you went over to fix it. Given the way she was behaving here, I'm guessing she put the moves on you, just because she got a kick out of doing that. I never saw her alive, but she was obviously a looker, and when a woman like that starts coming on to a man, well, most of the time he stops thinking. With his head anyway. No, as a man of the world, I couldn't blame you if you gave in. A lot of us would. But once you did, she owned you.

"I hope it was the best ten seconds of your life, Don, because it's going to cast a long shadow over the rest of it."

Don was even more visibly shaken by now, but he pulled himself together for one last stand.

"Again, a nice theory. But I don't see any proof."

"No, but we know where to look. You may remember that we took the sheets in that cabin as evidence. Back in the sixties, when they were a bit more delicate in the courtroom than they are now, the sheets in that room would have been described as 'soiled,' which is basically shorthand for saying the people in the room were having at each other like deer in season. I didn't order a DNA test on those sheets because Drew Evans had already admitted having a roll with her that afternoon. I figured that accounted for it. But now I've ordered those sheets sent to the lab first thing Monday, and when we finish this discussion, I expect that I'll have an order from one of the judges ordering you to give a sample.

"When that happens, it's over, Don. A competent defense attorney might be able to get the death penalty taken off the table in exchange for a guilty plea, but that's the best you can hope for. You killed her to keep Harry's, but you're going to lose it anyway."

For a minute the room was silent. Gordon saw that Don had his eyes closed and was balling his fists up tight, and Lilly apparently noticed it, too, straightening up and moving a half step closer.

Finally, Don opened his eyes and raised his hands in a gesture of surrender.

"You know what the worst part was? Even worse than killing her? It was knowing I gave in to her. My first wife cheated on me because I was working so hard she said I never paid any attention to her. I swore that if I ever got married again, I'd never cheat and I'd pay more attention to my wife. That was one of the reasons I wanted to buy Harry's. I thought it would give Sharon and me a chance to work together and keep the marriage strong.

"And then, *this* happened anyway. Fuck!"

The air had gone completely out of Don, and Gordon realized that Rogers had been holding his breath; he finally exhaled with Don's expletive.

"Don Potter, you're under arrest for the murder of Wendy Van Holland. Your rights have been previously read to you, but if you have any questions or want a re-reading ..."

Don shook his head.

"Cuff him, deputy, and take him outside into the hall. I'll be along in a minute."

Lilly did as ordered, leaving Rogers and Gordon alone in the room.

"Pretty gutsy, bluffing him like that," Gordon said. "I probably would have waited for the test results."

"I thought about that, too. But once we asked him for a swab, he'd have known we were on to him, and he would have had some time to think about it. And if he was thinking straight, he would have realized it was still a circumstantial case, aside from the DNA evidence, and he might have tried to tough it out. That's why I took a chance and confronted him now."

"Good call."

"It's always a good call when it works. It could just as easily have blown up in my face. But, hey, I'm a short-timer. A few more weeks and it would have been somebody else's problem."

"I don't think you really believe that. It would have been hanging over you."

"Well, now, I guess we'll never know, will we?"

Gordon looked at the door to the room and shook his head.

"Poor bastard," he said. "He deserves what he'll get for killing Wendy, but I do feel a bit sorry for him for getting caught in her snares. He was a hugely unlucky 80 percenter."

"What the hell does that mean?" Rogers said.

5

THE FOUR OF THEM followed the hallway to the front desk. April was at the bar, chatting with Peter, who had a pint in his hand. They were clearly taken aback to see Don being led up in handcuffs.

When they got to the desk, Don turned to Rogers.

"Could I ask you something? I know this is unusual, but could I be the one to break this to Sharon? It's going to devastate her, and it's the least I can do."

Rogers hesitated.

"She's in the office just down the hall. You can watch from here."

Rogers was silent for several seconds.

"All right," he said. "You have five minutes. And don't make me regret it."

He nodded at Lilly to remove the handcuffs. Don walked to the turn in the hallway and knocked on the office door.

"Honey, it's me."

He opened it and went in. Rogers looked at Lilly.

"Something bothering you, deputy?"

"Not by the book, sir. But it's your call."

"He's older and more out of shape than our usual detainee. If he makes a run for it, you and Gordon will have him inside a hundred yards."

Gordon slipped into the bar and gave Peter the short version of what had happened. Peter whistled.

"That's really something. How did Rogers figure it out?"

"He had a little help."

Peter looked at him askance. In the still of the lodge, Gordon could hear the purr of an electric motor in the distance and assumed Johnny was coming back with his client for the day.

"Six minutes, sir," Lilly said.

"Give him one more, then go fetch him," Rogers said.

"Anybody seen Don?"

Sharon asked the question as she walked around the corner from the dining room.

"Is something wrong?" she said, looking at the men staring at her in amazement.

Gordon ran to the window and looked at the river. One of the boats was leaving from the pier, and the clothing identified its operator as Don.

"He's on the river!" Gordon shouted. "Heading downstream."

"Shit," Rogers said, slamming his notebook on the front desk. "Get to your car, deputy, and see if you can get to the bridge before he does. You two," indicating Gordon and Peter, "come with me."

They ran down the lawn to the pier as fast as they could. Don was 200 yards away from the pier by the time they reached it, going five miles an hour with the quiet electric motor. The boat also had a larger, gasoline-powered motor, and Don was fiddling with it as he slowly moved downstream. A kayak and another motorized boat were tied to the pier.

"Whose boat is this?" Rogers asked.

Gordon shrugged.

"It's ours now. You know how to operate it?"

"I think I can," Gordon said.

The three of them piled into the boat, Gordon at the rear by the motor and tiller, Peter in the middle, and Rogers in front. Gordon untied the boat from the pier, started its electric motor and pointed them downstream. They were 300 yards behind Don's boat now.

At the first bend below Harry's, they encountered Johnny and his clients coming back to Harry's. Because of the bend, they didn't see him until he had passed Don's boat, and so were unable to signal him to head it off.

Don was trying to work the more powerful gasoline motor into place to power the boat, but was having difficulty doing that and steering with the electric motor at the same time. The result was some weaving, which allowed Gordon, keeping the following boat moving resolutely forward, to make up part of the distance. They had closed to just over 100 yards as the two boats turned round the bend leading to Indian Hollow Bridge.

The bridge was a quarter mile past the bend, and not long after they turned it, they could see the patrol car roar onto the bridge and stop in the middle. Lilly jumped out, drew his weapon, and pointed it in the direction of Don's oncoming boat.

"We got him now," Rogers said.

"Gordon!" said Peter. "Look!"

"What?"

"The sun's out. First time we've seen it all week."

It was true. The cloud cover had lifted, and they could see the setting sun just above the top of the mountains surrounding the valley. It cast a warm, golden glow on the landscape, showing off Paradise Valley in its best light — not that anyone was noticing at the time. It had even cleared enough that for the first time since their arrival, they could see The Mountain in the distance, the white of its snow-capped sides taking on a golden tinge.

A motor roared in front of them.

"He's got the gas motor going," Peter said.

With a more powerful engine propelling it, the small boat came to life and began plowing through the water at a much higher speed, sending a substantial wake from both its sides. The wind blew a wisp of smoke from the motor to the following boat, and the three men in it could smell the exhausted fuel.

Gordon looked at the electric motor on his boat and shook his head, pointing to an indicator.

"Fast as it'll go," he said. "Can't catch him now."

Meanwhile, Don's boat was almost skipping over the water as it headed toward the bridge. He looked back and forth between Lilly on the bridge and his pursuers falling farther behind him. He was looking back at the pursuers' boat when his reached the bridge.

There was considerable debate later on as to whether Don did it deliberately or simply forgot to duck. The coroner's report said the boat was going nearly 25 mph when it reached the bridge, with Don's head a foot higher than the bottom of the structure. The resulting *thwack* was both emphatic and sickening.

With the collision, the boat veered sharply to its right and ran into the pilings underneath the bridge. It stalled there, its motor trying in vain to propel it against the immovable wooden objects.

As the boat jerked sharply to the right, Don's body toppled out on the left and landed in the water.

His head, cleanly severed by the bottom of the bridge, bounced back ten feet and hit the river with a plop. It floated on the surface temporarily, and Lilly dropped to his knees just in time to see it float directly under him. His body began to heave, and within seconds, he vomited into the river.

Gordon threw the anchor of the second boat into the water and it came to a stop just above the bridge. They could see a dent in the wood where Don's head had hit it at high speed.

Gordon turned to his right, leaned over the edge of the boat, and threw up. Rogers turned to the opposite side of the boat and did likewise. Only Peter, his stomach hardened by years of operating-room gore, was able to hold himself together. When his boat mates were done and had sat upright again, he said:

"Well, detective, I don't think you'll be needing a doctor to pronounce this one dead."

Interlude: Saturday July 15

(From the Lava County Beacon-Journal)

Lawmen Turn Out in Force
To Say Farewell to Veteran
Detective Harry Rogers

By CYNTHIA HENLEY
Beacon-Journal Staff Writer

RED GULCH — If you wanted to commit a crime in Lava County, last night would have been the time to do it. Nearly every law enforcement officer from every agency was packed into the banquet room of the Holiday Inn downtown to send off Detective Harry Rogers, who retired June 30 after three decades with the Lava County Sheriff's Department.

Three hundred fifty people filled the room to capacity, and as tends to happen when law enforcement officers get together, plenty of stories were told, both at the tables and by the many speakers paying tribute.

"We've lost one of our best ones," said sheriff Bud Baker, at the end of the evening. "Good detectives, like good wine, get better with time, and Harry will be hard to replace."

Rogers joined the sheriff's department after leaving the Army, in which he served as a military policeman, in 1965. Lava County was a different place back then.

"The sheriff's department was half the size it is now, and we still didn't have enough to do," he said in an interview before the event. "When I came in as a patrolman, the county hadn't had a murder in five years, The whole drug thing was just getting started and hadn't reached us yet. Nobody had ever heard of a meth lab. It was a simpler, happier time."

Asked about his plans for retirement (he's not yet 54 and in good shape), Rogers said it was still up in the air.

"I'm going to take it easy the rest of the year, and we'll see after that," he said. "I'm kind of looking at several things right now."

Rogers started out patrolling the eastern part of Lava County and made a name for himself before the end of his first year. When the Cascade Bank in Muirfield was robbed at gunpoint, he was 14 miles away but guessed that the holdup men would head east toward Red Gulch.

Driving at high speed on back country roads, he reached the state highway just in time to see the car described by witnesses and radioed ahead. Ten minutes later, a roadblock set up after his radio message stopped the desperados and recovered the loot.

He was promoted to sergeant in 1970 and assigned to the detective bureau in 1975, serving in that capacity for the next 20 years. Numerous speakers talked about the cases he'd handled over that time.

Red Gulch Police Captain Bill Dixon, who worked alongside Rogers at the sheriff's department in the early days, recalled how Rogers had solved a string of burglaries that had been plaguing the town of Dobler.

"Nobody could see the pattern, but Harry figured there had to be one," Dixon said. "Finally he stopped by the offices of the *Clarion,* a weekly paper that used to cover that area. He looked through six months of back issues and compared it with a list of victims. In each case, the house that was burglarized was one where the owner had been in the gossip section of the paper just before, announcing a trip. The next time he saw an item like that, he staked out the house and caught the two men who had been doing the burglaries."

Another tribute came from fellow sheriff's detective Jim Sutton, who told the tale of how Rogers had obtained a confession in less than a minute from a suspect in the rape and murder of a woman.

The woman had apparently been followed home to the Red Gulch suburb of Walton after drinking at the Dew Drop Inn, and all indications were that two men had been involved in her fatal attack. Two men who had been seen together at the bar earlier were brought in for questioning and were in separate rooms.

"Rogers and I were going in to talk to them, when Rogers stopped and took a file folder off a desk in an empty office. I asked him what he was doing, and he said it might come in handy.

"We walk into the first interview room, and Rogers opens up the file folder and looks through it without saying a word. Then he looks up at the suspect.

" 'Well, Clyde,' he says, 'we have a lot of forensic evidence from the crime scene in this file, and your friend is singing like the Vienna Boys' Choir. Anything you want to tell us before it's too late?'

"And the guy loses it. 'It was Jeff's idea,' he says. 'He was the one who wanted to follow her home. She was never supposed to be killed.'

"After we left, Rogers put the file back where he got it, and I slipped over to take a look. It was a bunch of reports about car burglaries on the other end of the county."

The audience roared with laughter.

Sheriff's Captain Jack La Dow brought up Rogers' last big case, the murder of a woman staying at Harry's Riverside Lodge near Eden Mills in May.

"He definitely saved his best work for the end," La Dow said. "I sent him up alone on what I thought was a routine domestic violence killing, and it was a mess. The victim was strangled in a cabin locked from the inside. It was surrounded by snow, with no footprints leading in or out. The crime scene was completely compromised by the people who discovered it, and the medical evidence was at odds with eyewitness testimony. A lot of people would have called it an impossible case.

"And Harry figured it out in just three days. Tell us, Harry, how did you do it?"

Rogers stood up, walked to the microphone, and held up his hands in a "what do I know" gesture, before replying:

"Like Fats Waller says: It's easy when you know how."

Epilogue: Wednesday May 15, 1996

IT WAS A GLORIOUS SPRING DAY in Paradise Valley, and the six people sitting at a table on the deck at Harry's at 5:30 in the afternoon were savoring it. The temperature had topped at 83 two hours earlier, and was now in the high 70s. Not a cloud was in the sky, and a gentle breeze wafted an earthy perfume of fresh-cut lawn and pine needles through the air.

"What a difference a year makes," Peter said, looking quizzically at his club soda with a twist.

"It's what I was expecting last year," Gordon said, twisting the maraschino cherry in his 7-Up by the stem. "Better late than never."

"Well now, the weather gods would be smiling on you, Mr. Gordon," said Johnny. "It's supposed to stay nice all through the weekend." He took a small sip of his bourbon. "And with any luck we might get the morning spinner fall that Eden River's known for."

"I'd have no problem with that," Gordon said.

"What's a spinner fall?" asked Cynthia Henley, holding the stem of a glass of white wine.

"It's a point after an insect hatch where the insects start dying in the air and falling to the water," Gordon said. "It's like laying out a smorgasbord on the surface of the river. The fish go crazy."

"I've been learning a lot more about that," Rogers said, his hand wrapped around a pint of beer. "I was never much of a fisherman before, but now that I'm spending my time up here, I'm starting to get interested. Maybe I'll break down and buy a fly rod. Could I hire you to show me how to use it, Johnny?"

"Perhaps we could work out something in trade. Yes, I'm sure we could."

Rogers finished his beer and set it down on the table.

"So how about the rest of the people who were here a year ago" asked Sharon. "Anybody heard from them?"

They looked at each other, and Gordon led off.

"I saw Charles Van Holland at a restaurant in the City last month. He was with an attractive woman of about 50, and she seemed to be very attentive and interested in what he was saying."

"We always are when we have a prospect," said Cynthia.

"Is that the voice of experience I hear speaking?" Peter said.

Cynthia sighed. "I've been going out for four months with a legislative aide to one of the state senators. I met him a few months after I started working for the *Sacramento Bee.* He's really sweet, but he works long hours, and I'm afraid I've found out more about Central Valley water districts than I ever wanted to know. We'll see if it works out."

"Speaking of seeing if it works out," Peter said, "I ran into Drew Evans in a bar in Danville back in February. That was before I stopped drinking last month. He was with a pretty sultry redhead and neither of them was wearing a ring. Been married less than a year and already looking for greener pastures."

"I'm not surprised," Rogers said. "People change, but not that often and not that much. He'll have a day of reckoning with his rich wife soon enough."

"And land on his feet with another woman who'll think it will be different with her," Gordon said.

"More than likely," Rogers replied, looking at his empty beer glass.

Sharon put her hand on his shoulder. "Would you like one more, darling?"

He looked up at her and smiled. "Thanks, honey, but could you get me a Coke instead?"

She nodded and took his glass. "Anyone else?"

Peter downed the last of his club soda.

"I'll have another," he said. "You know, it's not so bad having a clear head once you get used to it."

Sharon went inside, and Gordon turned to the group.

"I got a postcard from Stuart and Rachel on Monday. They're in Venice, checking out cathedrals and galleries. She's expecting in November, and I guess she isn't going to be running for State Assembly after all."

There was a moment of silence while the group digested the news.

"Wow," said Cynthia. "She really drank the Kool-Aid."

"Maybe not altogether," he said. "There's some talk she might run for Alameda County Board of Supervisors in four years. I don't know how much there is to it."

"And how about our other expecting couple?" Johnny asked.

Rogers shifted in his chair. "Eldon and April are getting married next month. The baby's due in November."

"Eldon!" said Peter. "I didn't think you had it in you."

"He's a good man," Rogers said. "I expect him to make detective in a few years. And be a fine one. He has a feel for law enforcement. And April's already joined his church."

"Give her six years," Peter said. "She'll be the terror of the PTA. Oh, God. It just occurred to me. She'll be changing her name from April Flowers to April Lilly. Can't be helped, I guess."

"And what about you and Sharon?" Cynthia said.

Rogers sighed. "My divorce should be final in July. I don't think it would be right to do anything before then, but once I'm free, I just might ask her if she'll have me."

Gordon swallowed the last of his 7-Up and rose.

"I'm sure she'll be surprised," he said, and everyone laughed. "Excuse me. I think I'll get another one after all. Be right back."

He walked through the sliding glass door and across the empty dining room to the lounge, where Sharon was alone behind the bar. Surveying the empty bar, he realized it was the first time he had seen it without a fire in the fireplace. Sharon looked up.

"You want another drink?" she asked.

"That and maybe something else." She set down the glass she was filling and looked at him. "An explanation," he added.

"I'll do what I can."

"There was one thing that was still bothering me when I left a year ago." He looked over his shoulder to make sure they were still alone. "The witches' coven. I couldn't help thinking it was related to Harry's somehow, but I couldn't figure it out. Then a couple of days after I got home, I was sitting at my desk when it hit me."

"A flash of inspiration," she said. "I've heard of those, but I rarely get one."

"Actually, I was looking at my calendar."

She stopped working and her face became more serious.

"My first night here, you and I were standing out on the deck talking, and you mentioned that Opening Day weekend had been so busy you were barely able to get out for a night with the girls on Sunday. I think that was how you put it. When I was looking at the calendar in my home office, I realized what day Sunday of Opening Day weekend was. It was April 30th."

Sharon swallowed but said nothing.

"As I'm sure you're aware, there are two nights of the year that are supposed to be particularly conducive to calling out the spirits. Halloween, or All Hallows' Eve, is the one everybody knows about. But the other one is exactly six months later, on the eve of May Day. That's Walpurgis Night, April 30th. That had to be when the Sabbath was held in that glen Peter and I found.

"Nothing illegal about it, of course, and depending on your theology, or lack thereof, maybe nothing really wrong with it. But I have to know, and I won't take it any further. Am I right, and were you there?"

"You're right," she said after a pause.

"Thank you. I don't like loose ends."

She filled a glass with 7-Up, added a cherry and handed it to him.

"On the house," she said. "For being smart and discreet."

He thanked her, took the glass, and turned to go, but stopped and faced her again.

"I don't want to push this too far, but given the history of Harry's, with the curse and all that, might I ask if you cast a spell that night? Just between us, of course."

She sighed. "I don't know if you're perceptive or a good guesser, and I don't particularly like your terminology. You call it casting a spell, but it's really not much different from what the Christians call prayer. It's expressing a hope for something and asking The One Who Has All Power to give a sign or some guidance. If that's what you mean, yes, I did.

"When I married Don, I hadn't worked with him, so there was a side of him I hadn't really seen. Watching that come out, I started to have some concerns. Don was a weak man and given to cutting corners. The 'spell' you refer to was nothing more than asking for some guidance or a sign as to what Don's real character was, and whether I should spend the rest of my life with him."

She laughed bitterly. "I guess that was a case of be careful what you ask for."

"Does Rogers know about your ... activities?"

"Don't be silly. Every marriage has its secrets, and we *will* be married. I know that as much as I know anything. But he's not like Don. He's a strong and upright man, the man I deserve, and I'm going to do everything I can to make him happy and keep troubles from him. That's all he needs to know."

Gordon took a sip of his drink as he considered her answer. "I'm not sure I agree with that," he said. "If it was me, just saying, I think I'd want to know something like that by the fourth date."

She frowned.

"All right," he said. "I promised I wouldn't press it any farther. But just one more thing. Mrs. Maurillo, the high school principal?"

"A charter member," Sharon said. "But her husband's death was really an accident. At least I think so. I suppose I don't really know what sort of guidance *she* asked for."

Gordon's face must have registered something, because Sharon immediately became peremptory.

"You're a nice guy, Gordon, but you've been asking too many questions. Better stop now before you get turned into a toad."

"I'm going straight outside."

When he sat down at the table on the deck, Cynthia turned to him.

"We've all been talking about love," she said, "and the doctor here has been telling us about a nurse he's been seeing. She must be a remarkable woman because she's got him to quit drinking. But you haven't shared. Are you in love now? Are you seeing anybody?"

Gordon paused to consider how to reply, and Peter answered the question for him.

"Of course not," he said. "Gordon only does catch and release."

Sharon came to the table as they were laughing at the line, and Gordon decided to let it stand. The breeze picked up again, just enough to make the pine trees whisper. They basked in the perfection of the evening for several minutes without saying a word.

It was Peter who spoke first. Turning to Sharon and Rogers, he said:

"There's one thing I'm wondering about, though. Are you sure you feel all right about running this place together when it has a witch's curse hanging over it." Gordon kicked his leg under the table, but Peter continued. "You know, 'There will be no love at Harry's.'"

"But you left out the second half," said Sharon.

"What second half?" Gordon said. "That's all I ever heard."

"No, no no. The curse was, 'There will be no love at Harry's — until Harry returns.' " She put her arms around Rogers' neck and gave him a hug.

"And Harry's back now."

THE END

Acknowledgements

Thanks are due to a great many people who helped with this book. My wife, Linda, read it as it was being written, offered valuable comments and helped immeasurably with the formatting. Lauren Wilkins did a final edit that caught hundreds of mistakes that would otherwise have made it into print. Deborah Karas produced a cover that captured the feel of the book, and Greg Pio handled the author photos with skill and professionalism.

In the marketing end, I am grateful to John Bakalian for his ongoing research on ebook publication; to Chip Scheuer and Rigo Torkos for creating a dazzling video trailer; to retired Police Chief Terry Medina for playing the detective in that trailer; to Melody Sharp for a complete redesign of the website; and to Karen Kefauver for instructing this analog dinosaur on the intricacies of social media.

Author's Note

This book is dedicated in the spirit of John Dickson Carr (1906-77). Born in America, Carr lived much of his life in England and set most of his mystery novels there. He was a specialist in the locked-room mystery, and in his 1935 classic, *The Three Coffins*, (published in England as *The Hollow Man*) he devotes all of Chapter 17 to a lecture on how a murder can be committed within a locked room, or hermetically sealed area. In several books, most notably *The Burning Court* and *Below Suspicion*, he deals with themes of witchcraft and the supernatural.

Carr wrote dozens of mystery novels under his own name and the nom de plume Carter Dickson. He was a contemporary of most of the Golden Age writers, and Agatha Christie called him one of the few mystery writers whose stories baffled her.

Carr wrote an award-winning biography of Sir Arthur Conan Doyle and was himself the subject of the biography *John Dickson Carr: The Man Who Explained Miracles* by Douglas Greene.

About the Author

Michael Wallace is a former daily newspaper editor and public relations consultant, living in Central California. He is a lifelong fan and student of mystery novels and a longtime fly fisherman.

He publishes a weekly essay blog Wednesdays at outofglendale.blogspot.com and may be contacted through the author page of his website, quillgordonmystery.com

Photo/Greg Pio

Made in the USA
Monee, IL
28 August 2023

41779487R00131